A DRAGON GAMBLES FOR HIS GIRL

A Nocturne Falls Universe Story

Kira Nyte

Shouting out to the wonderful Kristen Painter
for continuing to allow me the opportunity to hang
in Nocturne Falls. A special shout out to Fiona Roarke
and Karen Ann Dell for brainstorming over martinis
to get through the bumps in the road.

And, a huge shout out to all my readers!
Thank you for taking the chance on these fun dragons.

Dear Reader,

Nocturne Falls has become a magical place for so many people, myself included. Over and over I've heard from you that it's a town you'd love to visit and even live in! I can tell you that writing the books is just as much fun for me.

With your enthusiasm for the series in mind—and your many requests for more books—the Nocturne Falls Universe was born. It's a project near and dear to my heart, and one I am very excited about.

I hope these new, guest-authored books will entertain and delight you. And best of all, I hope they allow you to discover some great new authors! (And if you like this book, be sure to check out the rest of the Nocturne Falls Universe offerings.)

For more information about the Nocturne Falls Universe, visit http://kristenpainter.com/sugar-skull-books/

In the meantime, happy reading!
Kristen Painter

A Dragon Gambles for His Girl

Ariah Callahan was raised on tales of dragons and magic and a wonderful hidden realm. The fairytales ended when her father became estranged from her beloved uncle, and cold, hard reality set in. Surviving day to day as her father spirals into addiction and depression is all she can do. When the unthinkable happens, her uncle becomes her only hope.

Alazar Brandvold has made easygoing an art. He's worked hard to ensure no one in the enchanted town of Nocturne Falls sees the tortured, serious soul inside the shameless gambler who is as quick with a laugh as he is to place a bet—which he invariably loses. The Firestorm dragon gets the wakeup call of his life when his Keeper comes out of hiding and shows him a treasure worth more than all the gold in his hoard.

And his race's ancient enemy is hunting her.

He will have to risk everything in the ultimate gamble not only to mm Ariah as his lifemate, but to convince her that fairytales are real and that the damsel can save the dragon.

Website for Kira Nyte: www.kiranyte.com

Kira Nyte on Facebook: www.facebook.com/kiranyte

Kira Nyte on Twitter: @kiranyteauthor

Contact Kira Nyte at: kiranyteauthor@gmail.com

CHAPTER 1

Ariah Callahan stooped behind the dumpster, shoving aside the wave of dizziness induced by her racing heart. Holding her breath starved her brain of desperately needed oxygen. Between the stench of garbage and rampant anxiety, it was hyperventilate until she passed out or get control of her body.

The situation unfolding half a block away? She had *no* control over that.

Disbelief stung her, its poison lancing through her gut. Her entire body shook, straight down to the marrow in her bones.

A new onslaught of sirens and flashing lights joined the first wave of responders. The loud thump of booted feet pounded against the sidewalk. Her stomach roiled. Precariously balanced on the balls of her feet, curled over her knees to make herself as small as possible, she leaned forward and peeked around the corner of the dumpster.

Red and blue lights created blinding beacons in the early evening hour. The stagnant alleyway water glittered beneath the strobe of lights. The events managed to conjure up an impressive crowd in a short five minutes. She still couldn't believe how fast the cops showed up.

A fierce shiver shot down her spine. Goosebumps erupted along her arms.

Terrified, too stunned to cry, the only thing Ariah could think to do after wrestling free of her father's arms was bolt from the auction house and find refuge in the alley. The first swarm of police cars tore down the small, two-lane road moments later. She wasn't sure if anyone saw her flee down the alley, but she sure as heck wasn't going to press her luck for long.

But she needed to know what was happening. What had happened to her father. Glancing away from the main road to the quiet outlet at the opposite end of the alley, she gauged her options. It was only a matter of time before someone spotted her and alerted police. Any hope of saving her father would be dashed.

Sucking in a deep breath of foul-scented air, she stood up and skated along the shadows of the alley until she emerged on a parallel road. The urge to run hit her hard, but she forced herself to keep a steady pace as she looped around half the block, cut down a connecting street, and came up behind the growing crowd of onlookers. Police officers, guns drawn, held positions all around the block.

Ariah pressed her lips together and covered her mouth with the tips of her fingers. She clutched the thick strap of her crossover bag, short nails biting into her palm.

"Ariah, Ariah, Ariah. My sweet little girl. Hear me. Listen to me."

Ariah's breath hitched. Her father's thoughts hit her with such urgency she shuffled back a step. In that small fracture of her mind, a sudden influx of voices and thoughts poured like water into a dry ravine, flooding her with an onslaught of maddening noises. Strangers' thoughts, curious about what was happening.

"Sweetheart, I hope you hear me. Please hear me."

Ariah fought to tune out the noisy cross conversation that tried to claim her mind and focus solely on her father's desperate plea.

"Run. Run from here and never look back. Go to your uncle's home. He will take you in and keep you safe. I stare our threat in the eye and am left no choice. Whatever happens to me, my darling daughter, know I love you from the deepest corners of my heart."

Ariah clenched her teeth behind her taut lips. Tears stung her eyes as she listened to her father's nonsensical instructions. Go to her uncle's? Staring a threat in the eye?

Sadness filled her. *After all these years, he's finally cracked.*

"Ariah, run!"

Ariah backed away from the crowd, instinct demanding she listen to him. Run. The chill that first gripped her in the alley sent icy tendrils into her blood.

An eruption of shouts and commands filled the wild night.

Ariah watched in horror as her father stumbled through the doors of the auction house, hands raised. A gun dangled upside-down on his finger before dropping to the sidewalk.

Officers converged.

Ariah spun on her heel and took off at a quick pace, yet hopefully slow enough not to bring attention to herself. Every muscle in her body was stiff, tight with anxiety. By the time she reached her father's old, rusted-out Toyota in one of the public parking lots, a dull throb stretched up her neck. She clung to the rapidly fraying ends of her composure as she unlocked the car, yanked open the door, fell into the seat behind the wheel, and fumbled to jam the key into the ignition. Adrenaline pumped through her like a double shot of espresso, but somehow, she held herself together.

Guiding the car onto the street, away from the activity surrounding her father's madness, she tried to make sense of this insanity.

Fifteen minutes later, Ariah pulled into the lot of the run-down motel where she and her father rented a room after scrounging up enough money for the week. Endless layoffs on her father's part and her meager wages from the diner left them with little money. Their home had been foreclosed on, medical bills poured in, and her father's outrageous gambling habits only exacerbated their dire situation. Ariah had to wonder if her father's actions tonight were due to a psychotic break brought on by stress.

More than a dozen times in recent months she'd felt

the weight of the world crushing down on her shoulders as she grappled for hope.

Add in her not-such-a-gift gift of hearing the thoughts of strangers and she might very well follow her father down a similar self-destructive path at some point in her life.

Ariah climbed out of the car, pulled the hood of her jacket over her head and beelined for their shambles of a room. She wasted no time gathering up their belongings, packing the car in the matter of a few trips. She returned the key to the clerk and got back behind the wheel.

She just sat there. A frightening calm settled over her. Cold. Hollow. Maybe she was in shock.

Those fearful moments seemed a blur. She remembered screaming. She remembered freezing up as her father yelled at the stunned elite crowd, his words nothing more than a slur of sound in her memory.

The metal. She remembered the metal pressed hard against her temple. A gun. Cold. Ice cold.

Ariah dug into her bag for her phone. When her knuckle scraped against something solid and sharp, her brows cinched. Using the dim yellow glow of the motel's outside lights to see, she opened her bag wider and found an unusual box. Curiosity edged past her shock as she withdrew the intricate box with beautiful gold lacework over dark polished wood. It was no bigger than the box for one of those fancy watches that cost a couple thousand dollars.

A small keyhole had been forged into the front of the box. She looked through her purse, but it seemed no key accompanied the object.

Ariah shook the box. Weight shifted inside, but there was no telltale sound that would help her deduce the contents. Twisting the box around, scrutinizing its intricate craftsmanship, one question haunted her.

Where did it come from?

She'd never laid eyes on it before, and it certainly wasn't in her bag this morning. She knew. She rummaged through it trying to locate a quarter to round off enough money for a vending machine snack.

For a long moment, she sat, the box in her hand, an unseen energy calling to her from within. She tried to recall those hazy moments in the auction house when her father lost it. Had she seen the box among the items up for auction? Did her father snatch it at some point?

"You're going to make yourself believe things happened that may not have happened."

Ariah sighed and pulled out her cell phone, one of those pre-paid flip phones intended just to get her by. She had committed her uncle's home number to memory years ago. His was the only number she cared to know, since her father didn't have a phone of his own. Despite her failed attempts to reach him over the last decade, he was her last hope. Her only hope.

Lifting the phone to her ear after she dialed, she listened to the ring. Once. Twice. Three times. She began to pull the phone away when the call connected.

"Hello?"

The sound of her uncle's strong, gruff voice acted like a hammer against the glass shell holding her together. Her chin began to quiver and moisture coated her eyes. Faint tremors skated along her body.

"Hello?"

"Uncle Mark?"

"Ariah?" Concern pinched his voice. "Oh my gods, Ariah. Honey, are you okay?"

Ariah shook her head. *Keep it together, girl. Come on. You're stronger than this.*

Her tears didn't care. Nor did the ball of emotion swelling at the base of her throat.

"Ariah, what's wrong? Talk to me."

"I...I don't know." She sucked in a breath. When it released, a sob flew out on the exhalation. "Dad...he's...I don't know what happened tonight."

"Honey, calm down. Where are you?"

Ariah sniffled and wiped her eyes with the back of her sleeve. It did little to stave off the pain and fear from gutting her. She couldn't stop the sobs.

"Ariah, where are you?"

The hard edge of command in her uncle's voice fed her a little strength. "At Mountain View Inn."

"Where is that?"

"North Carolina."

"Do you have a car?"

"Yes." Another sniffle. Another flood of tears. "Dad told me...to go to you."

"Are you in danger?"

KIRA NYTE

"I-I don't know."

The commanding tone softened a bit, overpowered by calm control. "I want you to listen to me, okay?"

"Yes." There wasn't much else she could do. Her mind was on a one-way spiral downward.

"I want you to drive straight here, do you understand? Don't stop for anything but gassing up the car. Come straight to me, Ariah."

"I will." Ariah squeezed her eyes shut, wiped at her face again, and let out a sharp breath in an attempt to pull herself together. She jotted down her uncle's address on a crumpled napkin, as well as brief directions once she got off I-95. Her gaze landed on the box when she opened her eyes. "I think Dad stole something tonight. From an auction house."

Uncle Mark said something under his breath.

"I found a strange box in my purse. I-I should bring it to the police."

The line grew unnervingly silent for a long moment.

"A box? What kind of box?"

Ariah tipped the thing in her hand. "A box. Dark wood with pretty gold lacework."

"Is there a key?"

"No, but there's a spot for a key." Ariah tried to pry the corner open. "Something's inside, but the box is shut up pretty good."

"Ariah, you need to get down here immediately."

Ariah's brow creased. "I can't leave my father. He needs help. Regardless what he did, I can't leave him when he needs me."

"I'll handle Mike. I promise, he'll be safe. He told you to come to me. Listen to him. Get your foot on that accelerator and get down here." Uncle Mark's harsh voice set her on edge, but the barked word that followed shot her into motion. "Now!"

Grit scratched her eyes as she pulled into the expansive driveway of the two-story Georgia colonial. At close to two in the morning, she was surprised her eyes remained open at all. Ariah cut the engine and stifled a yawn—and saw a shadowed figure barrel toward her car. Panicked, she reached for the key and started to turn over the engine when the bright glow of the floodlights from the driveway slashed across Uncle Mark's familiar face.

Only, he looked nothing like the uber-composed uncle she remembered from years ago.

Ariah had no time to get her hand on the door handle before he threw the door open, clasped his strong hands on her biceps, and lifted her out of the seat. His dark eyes scoured her from head to toe and back again. He twisted her one way, the other, assessing something Ariah wasn't privy to.

"You're unharmed." Uncle Mark's fierce gaze panned over his expansive yard, scanning the surrounding neighborhood before returning to Ariah. "Go inside. I'll get your things."

"I can—"

"*Go.*"

Ariah shut her mouth, grabbed her purse, and hurried into the safety of the immense home.

"Well, hello, Ariah."

Ariah's shoulders stiffened at the silky sound of her aunt's voice. Slowly, she turned toward the receiving parlor to her left. The willowy brunette sauntered toward her. Bits of silver flashed in the woman's otherwise chocolate brown eyes, enhancing the chill that accompanied everything about the self-proclaimed witch.

"Miriam. I wasn't expecting you to be awake." Ariah narrowed her gaze on the woman. Satin robe and quilted slippers. Waist-length brown hair tumbled in wide waves over slender shoulders. Miriam would be a stunner if she weren't also a devious snake. Ariah hated that her uncle remained married to her after all these years.

After what she did to Dad.

At least there were no pretenses between them.

"It's hard to sleep when my husband is pacing the bedroom for hours, waiting for his misfit niece to arrive." Miriam forced a smile. "I do anticipate that this unexpected visit will conclude quickly, and without event."

"Don't hold your breath," Ariah said, and not a moment too soon.

Uncle Mark came through the front door, his arms full of bags, and kicked the door closed. He rested the bags on the floor beside the curving staircase and brushed his hands on his tailored slacks.

"Miriam, take to bed. I'll be up shortly."

Ariah plastered a grin on her mouth, wiggled her fingers in a "bye-bye" motion, and watched the woman climb the stairs like a disgraced queen trying to hold on to a sliver of dignity. The satisfaction of Miriam's dismissal was short-lived. Uncle Mark waited until his wife was out of sight before draping an arm around Ariah's shoulders and leading her into his office. He pulled the pocket doors closed and dropped the latch lock in place.

"Are you hungry? Thirsty?"

"No." Ariah released an exasperated sigh. "I'm sick with worry. Dad's in jail." She rubbed her hands over her face. "I shouldn't have come down here until I spoke with someone at the police department. Spoke with Dad."

"Ari, I'll handle it. I promise you. Your father will be safe."

"You and Dad don't have a great track record." She cast the door a sharp glance. "Or have you forgotten the reason you two fell out?"

"My brother is still my brother, and I will do everything in my power to help him." A deep crease formed over his brow. He pinched the thin oversized shirt she wore beneath her hooded sweater jacket, followed by her waist. "Geez, honey. You're wasting away." He shook his head. "How bad have things been?"

Ariah shrugged, her anger fizzling beneath the weight of her exhaustion. "We've managed."

"'We' or you?" The sharp edge to his voice made her sigh. Uncle Mark groaned. "I'm sorry, sweetheart. Sit down. Let me get you some water at the very least."

"Thanks."

Her uncle caught her by the shoulders, leaning down to hold her gaze steady. "Ariah, everything will be okay. I'll do everything I can to help him."

Ariah nodded, her shoulders sagging. Uncle Mark nodded and spread his hand toward one of the two leather chairs angled in front of his desk, inviting her to sit. Ariah took the seat and waited patiently for her uncle to pour himself a shot of some super expensive bourbon and take the seat beside her. He held out a textured glass filled with water he'd retrieved from a small bar fridge. She took the glass with another quiet thanks.

"Tell me what happened," Uncle Mark said, his voice deep and calm, a strong and soothing sound after the horrors she experienced only a few hours earlier. Before the debacle with Miriam that split her father and uncle beyond repair, Ariah spent many summers in this house, with this man. She adored him as much as she adored her own father. It was like the ten years that separated them were no more than ten days.

Right now, she needed his reassurance and composure more than anything.

"I honestly don't know. Dad and I had been job-hunting for him all day. We decided to head into town to grab some sandwiches from a cheap deli for dinner when he got all strange and crazy-eyed. I'd never seen him like that and it frightened me. He dragged me into an auction house, disrupting the event, and lost it." Ariah took a long drink of water, avoiding her uncle's penetrating gaze. "It was like he was possessed or something."

She shivered at the potent memory of the muzzle pressed to her temple, closing her eyes against that painful fear that had struck her in the auction house.

"He, um, he turned me into a hostage." Ariah shook her head, waving her empty hand. "I-I was so scared. I know he was shouting something, but I don't know what. I couldn't think about anything except the…"

"What, honey?"

Gosh, she couldn't tell Uncle Mark that his brother, her own father, had threatened to shoot her.

I'm safe here now. He needs to know. Maybe he knows what happened to my dad. He'll have the resources to help him where I can't.

"He held me at gunpoint." Ariah winced as she opened her eyes. Her uncle's eyes were wide. "We struggled before I got free, or he released me, or something. Everything is still a blur. I escaped and hid in the alley until I heard his panicky thoughts telling me to run."

"Did he say why?"

"He mentioned something about staring at a threat and that I needed to come here." Ariah dug into her bag and removed the box. She pressed her lips together

13

and held it up for her uncle to see. The big man's reaction was anything but the incomprehension she expected. A spark flickered in his dark eyes. His tanned face paled before a light flush touched his cheeks. Beneath his neatly trimmed beard and mustache, his jaw worked, but he remained silent. "This is the box I told you about. I found it in my bag, but I'm sure it wasn't there throughout the day. I think he might have slipped it into my bag at the auction house during our struggle."

Uncle Mark stared at the box, unmoving. Unblinking. The tumbler in his hand began to tip at a dangerous angle.

"Uncle?"

Uncle Mark cleared his throat, gave his head a faint shake, and pressed to his feet. Ariah felt the furrow in her brow as she watched her uncle round his desk. He ran a finger across several of his antique leather-bound books, many of which she knew to be first editions a couple of hundred years old. He pulled one book from its designated spot, opened the cover, and tugged at a ribbon poking out from the spine.

Ariah's furrow deepened when a small key dropped into her uncle's hand. "Don't you think we should be calling someone to help Dad? He doesn't need jail. He needs help. Psychiatric help. He'd lost his mind."

"I gave you my word."

She sat in absolute silence as he moved to the far end of the bookcase, ran his finger over the intricately carved wood of one of the shelves.

He fit the small key into an unseen hole and turned it. A thin, narrow compartment popped out from the shelf. Her uncle pulled out an object Ariah could not see before closing the compartment back into the shelf and returning to his seat.

"You remember those summers long ago when I used to teach you about the dragons and the voices?" Uncle Mark asked.

"Why are we wasting time?"

"Do you, sweetheart?"

Ariah nodded, unsure what to make of his question. Her uncle used to fill her summers with stories about a rare breed of dragon—Fire-something—from riding the mythical creatures in a magical parallel realm to devastating wars that nearly wiped out this breed.

Uncle Mark had taught her how to control the voices she heard in her head. He said they were thoughts, a defense mechanism prominent in Keepers. That was the same summer he confided that he had a secret and with that secret came great responsibility, great sacrifice, and great danger.

"We have a gift, my sweet niece. I have not sired a child of my own, but my brother has. A female child, may it be a miracle."

She learned that day she wasn't the only one who heard strangers' thoughts. Uncle Mark did, too. She learned he truly believed in dragons, and that he was a Keeper. That *she* was a Keeper, even though she was not his biological daughter.

She had been seventeen that summer, preparing to

go into her senior year, graduate at the top of her class, and go to an Ivy League school to learn about ancient civilizations. The child inside her held Uncle Mark's stories close to heart—a deep secreted drive to discover myths and legends were actually true.

Fate had other things in store for her.

With reality came a sense of jadedness. Dragons didn't exist. Beautiful worlds outside of this dark and desolate life did not exist. Magic didn't exist.

Miriam might claim to be a witch, but Ariah had never seen her use magic. In Ariah's book, the witch was nothing more than an—itch with the letter b.

As she drew herself from her memories, she saw Uncle Mark's gaze had softened to that of the tender man she once adored. He sipped his bourbon, an expression of ease coming over him.

"Don't fight it, honey. It's not natural," he assured, stretching his arm toward her. He turned his fist to the ceiling and unfurled his fingers. Sitting on his palm was another small, delicate key. "I don't think your father was crazy at all, Ari. A couple years before things went sour between us, a very important object was stolen out of the cabin in Upstate New York. A priceless artifact that, should it land in the wrong hands, could spell disaster for us. *All* of us."

"I don't understand."

Ariah lifted her eyes from the key to her uncle's tender gaze. For the first time since she arrived, he grinned.

"At one point you did. The young woman sitting

with me now has been hardened by life's cruel pitches. Rest assured, that is all about to change." He stretched his hand a little closer to Ariah. "Go ahead."

"How do you know it'll open the box?"

"I can feel the magic inside. It calls to me." Uncle Mark lowered his hand after Ariah took the key from his palm. Doubt plagued her. Her uncle claimed to feel magic? All she felt was a strange hum of electricity, most likely from her tired nerves and her adrenaline crash. "Open it."

"Why don't you?"

"Because."

When Uncle Mark failed to divulge more, Ariah plugged the key into the hole and twisted. The lock clicked open. Ariah chewed her lower lip for a short moment. Uncle Mark leaned closer. The scent of bourbon teased her nostrils. His eyes sparkled.

"After I do this, will you tell me why *you* won't open it?"

Her uncle's smile grew as she lifted the top back on its hinges. Her brows came together as she stared at the contents of the velvet-lined box. Nestled in the center was a smooth, oblong jewel unlike anything she'd seen in her life. Deep, rich amber with slashes and swirls of gold, burnt red, and streaks of black.

The hum of energy intensified the moment the pad of her finger connected with the warm, smooth surface of the jewel. An unseen force rooted deep inside her mind and lured her to an unknown destination.

Was this the call her uncle meant?

The jewel's magical beauty held her so captivated that she didn't noticed her uncle leaning close to her ear until he whispered, "It's time he sees you, at long last."

CHAPTER 2

"It's time he sees you, at long last."

Alazar Brandvold threw off the covers, jumped out of his bed, and tripped over something on the floor. His shoulder smacked into the wall, sending a dull throb down his arm as he rubbed the heels of his palms against his eyes. The disorientation didn't fade when he pulled his hands away and stared straight ahead.

He didn't see his bedroom.

He stared through his dragon's eyes from the curved shape of his dragonstone. Over a decade of that stone lying dormant did nothing to help him orient himself as he fought to make out the strange, contorted vision moving in a hazy blur in front of him.

Well, in front of the stone.

Aww, no. No, no, no.

Oh, yes, buddy boy. Good ol' Mark opened your box.

He frowned. Mark's voice had jerked him from sleep, but the face he stared into as his vision focused and clarified was certainly not Mark's. Not unless his

Keeper lost a good bag of weight and turned female.

"Who will see me? How?"

The quiet female voice rattled him, and not in an unpleasant way, either.

Wouldn't you like to know?

Alazar pressed back against the wall, hands splayed against the cool plaster for support while his dragon perked up at the pretty female's presence. He had no idea what was happening, who this female was, or why Mark thought it was smart to expose *his* dragonstone to the stranger. Cade, the leader of the Firestorm *tatsu* clan on a hunt to locate any other female Keepers, had assured Alazar only a week ago that Mark had sired no children. The female was not his daughter.

"Who is she, Mark? Are you nuts? Letting an outsider see this?"

He rubbed his eyes again. The burnt essence of smoke teased the back of his throat before it curled from the corners of his mouth. His arms prickled, the hairs stiffening before his scales grazed the surface. Oh, man. The dragon's attention on the woman grew steadfast the longer he stared into her obscured smoky gold and red face.

"Will you close that box so I can get my bearings?"

All Firestorm dragons had a dragonstone that allowed their Keeper to communicate with them. After the Baroqueth slayers attacked The Hollow—the Firestorms' magical world separate from the mortal world—and Cade deemed it safest for the Keepers and the dragons to split and go into hiding, contact between them was kept to a minimum.

Like, non-existent minimum. There *was* no communication.

Alazar was aware Mark resided nearby. When he and Zareh—friend and Firestorm comrade—came to the quaint town of Nocturne Falls in Georgia, he sensed his Keeper's nearness. As much as he wanted to search for Mark, he refrained. Contacting his Keeper would bring unwanted attention to him and Mark, placing them both in danger.

Well, his Keeper was about to have him show up on his front stoop if he kept this carelessness up.

"You're making my stomach churn, Mark."

In possession of the dragonstone, Mark could hear his thoughts and answer, if he chose.

Apparently, he chose not to, driving Alazar mad. He began to wonder if Mark realized he was quickly pinning down his Keeper's location.

"Mark!"

The woman's face disappeared behind a sheet of black.

The dragon recoiled in a huff, curling up in the back of his mind. The smoky black tips of his scales retracted into Alazar's skin and the essence of fire from deep within his gut subsided.

Alazar's bedroom reappeared before him. He blinked several times, staring at the rumpled comforter half puddled on the floor. A pillow was wedged between the mattress and bedside table. The fitted sheet had popped off the corner of the mattress. Evidence of restlessness.

"What the heck was that all about?"

Alazar rubbed the back of his neck, gaze drifting to the digital clock on his bedside table. Barely after two in the morning and Mark was entertaining strangers with tales of rare jewels and stones.

"And *I* have issues. Geez."

As he fixed up his bed, he considered heading down the hall and waking Zareh up. Then again, chances were his friend wasn't asleep, and neither was his lifemate, Kaylae. Interrupting *that* would not bode well for him.

With a sigh, Alazar climbed back into bed. Morning wasn't too far off. He'd bring up the issue with Zareh then. He might need to put in a call to Cade so he could investigate the woman.

For now, he reached for the thick gold chain on the bedside table, brought it close to his nose, and sucked in a deep breath of the warm metal. A smile curled his lips and his dragon rumbled sleepily like a child comforted with a teddy bear.

There was nothing like gold to ease him back to sleep.

"Uncle Mark, all due respect, you're frightening me."

Ariah's fingers rested in a painful knot on her knees. Her uncle placed the closed box on his desk, the dainty key beside it, and brushed a hand over his dark hair. The glint in his eyes was something Ariah had never witnessed in her life. She had seen a similar glint right before her father went berserk.

"There's nothing to be frightened of. I'm just…well…I'm anxious."

"Yeah, that makes two of us." Ariah waved a hand toward the box. "What's going on? Who was supposed to see me? *How* were they supposed to see me?" She was so confused and tired, she felt like she might cry again at any moment. "You're starting to act like Dad."

"Sweetheart." Uncle Mark went to his knees at her feet. His big hands closed around hers, tender, gentle, protective. He let out a slow breath. "There was once a time before life dealt you unfair hands that you embraced the history I shared. I still remember the sparkle in your eyes at the mention of dragons and faraway lands. Nothing, Ari, could extinguish that gleam from your spirit until your father and I had our falling out."

Ariah swallowed the small lump that had formed at the base of her throat. "Well, life got real crappy real fast for me after that." She gave the closed doors a pointed look. "After *her*."

"If I had it to do over again, I would've done things differently, Ariah. But I can't change the past. I can only pave a better path for the future." His hands tightened on hers, drawing her attention back to him.

"You have a future. A bright, promising future. One that is as fantastic as the stories I used to share with you."

Ariah groaned, lifting her gaze to the ceiling. "Uncle Mark, don't. I've outgrown that stage of my life. I lost hope of magical lands when reality swept me away. I can barely afford a bag of pretzels from the vending machine let alone a few hours to daydream."

Uncle Mark sat back on his heels, eyes narrowing. Ariah sighed, pulling her hands away from his. She realized her mistake too late. She hadn't meant to share so much information on the extent of their poverty.

"I'm sorry. I'm exhausted. I need some rest. Maybe we can continue this tomorrow after we discuss our plans to help Dad?" Ariah was desperate to escape the fairytales. Her life was not a fairytale. It would *never* be a fairytale. She climbed to her feet, her uncle following her lead. "I can't wrap my head around anything else. I'm burnt out."

"Yes, sweetheart." The concern etched into the fine lines around his eyes and mouth deepened. "Of course. I'll bring your bags upstairs for you."

"Thanks."

Ariah followed her uncle silently as they left the office, paused long enough for him to collect her bags, and climbed the elegant staircase. He brought her to the guestroom she had spent her summers in, leaving her belongings beside the white dresser. Ariah stood just inside the door, watching her uncle assess the space, turn down the bed, and finally step up to her.

He took her by the shoulders and drew her into a loving embrace.

"Oh, Ariah. I have *missed* you. Missed you so."

Then why didn't you ever try to contact me? But pride wouldn't let her say it.

His arms tightened. "Rest up, honey. I'll find out more about your father's predicament in the morning. Leave that to me."

Ariah didn't trust her voice as her throat continued to close up. She nodded against her uncle's shoulder, finding his strength reassuring.

Uncle Mark kissed the top of her head and took his leave, closing the door behind him.

Fatigue swelled, leaving no room for emotions to seep through her shaken spirit. She kicked off her boots, shimmied free of her jacket, and slipped into the welcoming bed.

She never imagined her life could get worse. Lost in a sea of hardships with no lifeline, she'd become intimate with the rocky depths of hopelessness and despair.

Well, life just showed her the rocks she'd been scraping across the last ten years were far from the bottom.

CHAPTER 3

"What's got your tail in a tizzy?"

Alazar plastered on one of his signature happy, carefree smiles and twisted on the counter stool. Zareh stood in the archway, eyes narrowed on Alazar. He tsked once and crossed the kitchen to stand with his hip against the counter.

"Morning to you, fire and sunshine. Sleep well?" Alazar raised his coffee mug in cheers. "Fresh pot on the burner."

"That's not going to work. You've been tapping your talons on the countertop for five minutes." Zareh tugged a chunk of Alazar's hair. "How much have you pulled out fisting and raking?"

Alazar rolled his eyes and swiveled back to the counter. "Kaylae still asleep?"

"For the moment."

Alazar's smile dimmed, but the grin that remained was genuine. His best friend's lifemate was a gem. He loved her like a little sister, right down to the moments when she scolded him for losing a few hundred dollars here and there gambling. Yeah, he had a problem.

Zareh had been pissed when he had to win back Kaylae's new Michael Kors purse after Alazar gambled it away. He put Alazar in his place that night. The keys to his car had been taken away, as well as all of his cash. As if that wasn't enough, his small, portable chest of gold had disappeared. Alazar would have gone all fire-breather if he thought anyone but Zareh had taken it.

Alazar was five hundred and seventy-one years old, and he was grounded.

Indefinitely.

He received his money like a kid received an allowance. Once a week. A hundred bucks.

Zareh lifted the coffee mug from Alazar's hand and took a sip from the opposite side of the rim. "Al, you really need to lay off the sugar."

Alazar patted his flat stomach. "I've got nothing to worry about."

"Seems the uncharacteristic tumble in your room during the night might be something to worry about." Zareh's brow rose when Alazar snorted. "I know it wasn't a woman. Not with the mumblings coming from your mouth. So, want to talk about what happened?"

"I drank too much. Had to go to the bathroom."

"You have a bionic bladder, but nice try." Zareh took another sip of coffee and handed the mug back to Alazar. He rolled off the counter toward the fridge. "If you don't want to talk about it, that's fine." Zareh pulled open the fridge door and cast Alazar a glance over his shoulder. "I'm here if you change your mind."

"Mark showed my jewel to an outsider." The revelation brought Zareh out of the fridge to face him. His friend's expression hardened. Alazar shrugged. "Yep. That's pretty much how I felt being woken up in the middle of the night to stare at some strange, hazy woman."

"Your jewel's been asleep for over a decade. Are you sure it was him?"

"It wasn't Baroqueth, and they're the only ones who can break the magic protecting the jewels without a key." Alazar started to laugh, but cut it short. "Oh, yeah. I know Mark. Big, bad Keeper man. Thinks he needs to swaddle me and sing me to sleep, except for when he's waking me up in the middle of the night with cryptic messages." Alazar scowled, then ticked a finger toward Zareh. "You know, you and Mark would've been a better pairing than we are."

"Don't give me that." Zareh braced his forearms on the countertop and folded his hands together. "You care deeply for your Keeper."

"I care for him, yes. He's my Keeper, but he's a bit of a papa bear when I clearly have a few centuries on him."

"He's a good balance for you. Mark has his head on straight."

Alazar straightened up in his seat. "Last time I checked, mine was on pretty straight. I don't see a scene from The Exorcist happening here." He tapped a finger at his temple. "Straight, Zar."

Zareh kicked the fridge door closed when the alarm began to beep and forewent whatever he hoped to find inside in favor of friend-time. "You know what I'm talking about."

"Painfully. A hundred dollars a week can't buy me a decent meal a day." Alazar let out a long, smoke-free breath. His shoulders sagged. "It's been a month of this nonsense. Can I please have my dignity back?"

"I'll think about it. Tell me more about what Mark said."

"Nothing." When Zareh tipped his head and glared at him, Alazar raised his hands, palms up, and shrugged. "What? He said nothing." Then he remembered. "Oh, there was one thing."

"Ahh. So the silent Keeper did speak."

"Zar, seriously. I was half asleep and it was the only thing he said. He said something about it being time I saw someone."

"The woman?"

"He hasn't made contact with me in over a decade. I doubt he's interested in my love life." Alazar reached for the bag of Vampire Bites he had purchased from the Hallowed Bean earlier—it had become his Thursday morning custom to have Kaylae's favorite donut waiting for when she woke up—and dug into the stash. Kaylae might be out of luck this particular Thursday. His actions obviously amused Zareh, judging by the telling grin teasing the corner of his mouth. "The woman? She's the only one I saw through the jewel, but I have no idea who she is and what Mark's business is with her."

"Um…" Zareh pointed to his chin. Alazar stared for a short moment before he wiped a chip of vanilla glaze from his chin and shoved the rest of the small treat into his mouth. The raspberry filling inside the soft chocolate donut did little to ease his restless dragon. He dug out donut number two as his friend said, "Mark didn't have children."

"I'm aware," Alazar said through a mouthful of goodness. He held up a finger as he finished the second Vampire Bite and washed it down with coffee. "He's close to Nocturne Falls. I can trace the link between the jewel and me and find out what's going on. He wouldn't let a Baroqueth see that jewel. He'd give his life to keep it safe."

"Making contact with him isn't the best idea. Not after the Baroqueth attack on Kaylae."

"That was a couple months ago. Besides, do you really think remaining separated from our Keepers is the best idea?"

Alazar instantly regretted his words when he saw the pain strike through Zareh's eyes. His friend had lost his Keeper, and Kaylae her father, to the Baroqueth slayers a week before Kaylae showed up in Nocturne Falls. Zareh believed he could have prevented Talius's death had they not been separated, and that guilt rode his shoulders like the weight of the universe.

Zareh lowered his head and tapped his thumbs together. "I've thought about that a lot lately."

"What does Cade think?"

Zareh shrugged and pushed off the counter. "I don't know. It's evident after the attack on Kaylae that the Baroqueths' magic has grown stronger over the last three decades. The question is, how strong?"

Which supported his next point. "And while they've grown in power, we've weakened over the last thirty years. We've always been stronger with our Keepers. The magic between dragon and Keeper is at its full strength together. I think the attack was a wake-up call, Zar. The Keepers will not be able to protect themselves against the Baroqueth without us."

"This world strips us of our magic. Leaves us vulnerable, unless we have a Book of Realms."

"I'm not even sure if Mark's family still has one after the Baroqueth destroyed most of them. Regardless, until we know how many more rogue sorcerers there are, then perhaps Cade should call us all back to The Hollow where we can prepare to fight." Alazar took out another donut. "Oh, right. You and Kaylae have that ginormous house you're building."

"If it were only me, I'd go back to The Hollow in a heartbeat. I just think Kaylae needs a place where she can feel she belongs after spending most of her life feeling like an outsider. I'll ask her in a few years how she feels about the idea."

"What idea?"

Alazar watched Zareh's expression go from heavy and grim to light and filled with adoration in an instant. Kaylae snatched the bag of Vampire Bites from

Alazar's loose fingers, pressed a kiss to his temple, then sidled up beside Zareh. Alazar glanced away as the two lovebirds greeted each other with their ritualistic tongue dance, like they hadn't been doing that all night.

He was truly happy for Zareh and Kaylae, but their love didn't dull the empty void in his own chest, or the loneliness he and his dragon suffered together. Firestorm lore provided an inkling of hope that maybe the survivors of the battle thirty years ago would find lifemates. After any devastating blow to the Firestorm population, there seemed to be a strange rise in the number of female Keepers born. Nature's way of trying to preserve their super rare dragon breed, he supposed.

The challenge with finding a lifemate was the female had to be born of a Keeper, or an immediate relative. Mark's brother had been killed in the Baroqueth ambush, according to Cade.

"I'll catch up with you two later," Alazar said after clearing his throat. He climbed to his feet and brought his coffee mug to the sink. He clapped Zareh's shoulder as he rounded the couple, flashed him a smile, wagged his brows, and headed toward the living room. "Oh, can I have my keys? I need to head out of town."

"Al."

"Zar," Alazar retorted in the same stern tone. Zareh turned his head up to the ceiling. Kaylae gave Zareh's stomach a pat and slipped out from under his arm.

"I'll get the keys for you. You got me donuts, even if

you ate half of them. Still, how can I say no?" Kaylae disappeared down the hallway toward the room she shared with Zareh.

Alazar hitched his thumb in Kaylae's direction. "Think some of Delaney's fudge will convince her to, say, quadruple my allowance?"

"All right, all right." Zareh rubbed his hands down his face. "I'll give you your money back." He pulled out his wallet and removed two hundred-dollar bills. "That should hold you over until this afternoon. I have some stops to make. Don't do anything foolish."

Alazar flashed Zareh a full, white-toothed smile and snatched up the money. "Oh, my friend. I'm not the foolish kind."

"One might argue that point."

Kaylae returned a minute later. Alazar thanked her with a kiss on the top of her head, waved the keys, and left the house.

There were times when putting up a façade was as wearing on his spirit as the turmoil that tore him up inside. He was the lighthearted one, the carefree dragon, the funny guy who could lighten the mood no matter how dark. To most, nothing seemed to bother him. He skated through life, happy as can be.

What happened when the funny guy needed a break from the performance, he wondered, when his own situation was as dour as the rest of the clan's?

Alazar jammed the key into the ignition and pumped the accelerator, enjoying the deep rumble of the engine as it roared to life. Where Zareh liked the big luxury SUV types, Alazar loved his sporty black Mustang. Just him, the horses under the hood, and the road.

Right now, open roads and careless speeds would have to wait.

He was overdue for a visit with his Keeper.

Chapter 4

Ariah stared up at the sign and scratched her head beneath the knitted cap.

"Mummy's Diner."

This was the sixth or seventh place in Nocturne Falls that had a Halloweeny name. Uncle Mark had described the quaint town as a hot tourist destination for those obsessed with Halloween who wanted to celebrate it every day of the year outside its October birthday.

Thus far, the town exceeded her expectations.

Nocturne Falls was Halloween in every facet of the word, from the quirky architecture of some of the buildings—those that looked rickety and ready to implode—to the vibrant color schemes. Once upon a time, the bright oranges, pinks, and purples would have made her smile and bounce like a child. Now? She enjoyed morose colors that seemed to paint her life. The black, midnight blues, and darker shades of green suited her palette far better.

Uncle Mark stepped up beside her with a smile, his

dark eyes warm, and motioned to the front door. "Come on, honey."

Her uncle rested a hand between her shoulder blades and urged her forward. He held the door for her and she stepped into the packed diner. The delicious aromas of fresh-cooked meals hit her nostrils, making her jaw ache and her mouth water mercilessly. Her stomach churned and growled. Yes, she could scent the distinct smell of grease, but it didn't smack her in the face like it did at her old jobs. Walking into one of the diners where she worked was like walking into a month-old grease pit with food to match.

"Welcome to Mummy's. How many?" the hostess asked, brushing her bangs from her eyes as she appeared out of the mid-morning melee.

Uncle Mark held up two fingers. "Two, thank you."

The young woman smiled, grabbed up two menus, and led them down an aisle to a two-seater table in the corner of the main dining room. Ariah glanced around, hoping for a booth but coming up short of any empty tables.

Now this is a place where I could actually make a few bucks.

As she sat in the chair her uncle pulled out for her— always the perfect gentleman—she pondered the downward spiral of her life. At seventeen, she had a bright and promising future. At twenty-seven, she was living below the poverty line. She accepted hand-me-downs from coworkers to keep clothes on her body. A coworker who attended cosmetology school did her hair for free. She snagged food from plates when customers were finished with their meals to barely keep her belly satisfied. Never once in a million years would she have believed she'd be reduced to eating off a stranger's plate, but when her boss was a jerk and required money for so much as a breadstick, yeah, she scavenged.

They ordered coffees from the hostess before the woman bounced over to a server with their request.

Ariah lifted the menu and snickered at the tagline.

"'Our food is to die for,' eh?" She shook her head. "Interesting place."

"Some of the best blueberry pancakes you'll sink a fork into." Uncle Mark pushed his menu to the side and folded his hands on the tabletop. He tilted his head, succeeding in catching her eyes. "Are they still your favorite?"

Ariah managed a half-grin. The last time she ate decent blueberry pancakes was almost six years ago. "I guess."

The corner of her uncle's mouth twitched. "You look like you have the weight of the world on your shoulders, Ari. Want to unload some of your burden?"

"No burden, really. It's just been"—how was she to say it without her uncle prodding deeper?—"difficult trying to process what happened yesterday. That's all."

She reinforced her response with a full smile.

"I'll trust your word, Uncle Mark. Blueberry pancakes that are to die for?" She flicked her index finger at him and winked. "You're on."

Her uncle chuckled and shook his head, but concern

didn't disappear from his eyes. "You've got a deal."

Their server came over with their coffees and took their orders before continuing her table hop. Ariah cupped the hot mug, warming her cold fingers, leaned over the steaming black drink and took a deep breath. Ahh, so long since she'd had a good cup of coffee.

She took a sip, earning a quirked brow from her uncle.

"Black?" he asked.

"No reason to dilute a good brew."

"Huh." He poured cream into his coffee and stirred. "You were never one for strong, potent tastes."

"Things change."

His gaze deepened, pinning her. She could almost feel his essence prying back the shutters of her mind, seeking the secrets she buried.

"Yes. They do." After a long moment, he tapped the spoon on the edge of his cup and rested it on his napkin. "I spoke with a contact of mine who has been in touch with an impressive lawyer to take on your father's case."

"You know, he's still your brother."

A sad grin ghosted across his mouth and disappeared. "How could I forget?"

"I should try and call the police station. At least find out where he's being held."

"The less you're involved, the better. If Mike did, in fact, encounter a threat and sent you away to protect you, it's best for you to stay off the radar. Let my contact handle things for the moment."

Silence stretched between them, time ticking by. The server came back with their orders. Ariah inhaled the sweetly delicious aroma of her blueberry pancakes and smiled. A pile of perfectly fluffy steaming goodness.

"Not good table talk. Let's leave the family dynamics for your home office." Ariah picked up her fork and knife, cut a huge chunk off her pile of pancakes, and brought it to her mouth. "Here comes the truth."

The moment the pancakes hit her tongue, she was done for. The diner's tagline certainly earned its reputation in that single bite of sweet, fluffy utopia.

Uncle Mark's spirits seemed to lift as he watched her indulge. "Verdict?"

Ariah nodded, gave him double thumbs up, and dove into another chunk. She couldn't remember the last time she enjoyed such a simple, yet wonderful, meal. She was acutely aware, however, that her uncle continued to watch her in his perplexingly observant way. She sensed sympathy and regret beneath his calm exterior. In her soul, she *felt* the blame he placed on himself for her life's trials. It was like a gray swirling connection that flowed between them, along a link she had sensed since her younger years, but which had dimmed after Miriam came along. Uncle Mark had never explained it, despite her vocal curiosity.

She wondered if he sensed it. If he understood it.

Halfway through her plate of pancakes, her stomach shut down. She couldn't eat another bite, as much as she wanted to polish off the entire plate.

"Done already?"

Ariah washed down her last bite with coffee and dabbed the corners of her mouth with a napkin. "They're awesome and they're definitely coming home with me. I'm full, though."

"You need more meat on your bones. Al will not be happy with me for not taking care of you."

Ariah paused, her hand slowly lowering from her mouth. "Who?"

"Alazar."

Ariah gave a short shake of her head, raising her brows. "Who is that?"

Uncle Mark waved away her question and filled his mouth with steak and eggs.

"Uh-uh. No. You're not sweeping this aside. Who's Alazar? And why would my well-being concern him?" Ariah pushed her plate to the side and leaned against the table. "Uncle Mark. You don't give enough information for me to bite and refuse to share the details. I've lived with that for the last ten years."

"He's a...friend."

"From what I remember, you have contacts and acquaintances. Not necessarily friends."

Another tidbit about her uncle she never understood. The man had a huge heart, but distanced himself from people. His marriage to Miriam was a shock, to say the least. Not that their relationship seemed to be star-worthy.

Uncle Mark chuckled. "How well you know me, honey. Alas, things change."

"I know you can come up with your own passive phrases." Ariah couldn't help the smile that crossed her mouth. She propped her chin on her fist and took in the crowd around them. "Wonder if they're hiring here."

"Ari, the last thing I want you to worry about right now is working."

"I appreciate what you're trying to say, but I need to hold my own."

Uncle Mark finished up his eggs, laid his fork and knife across the plate, and moved it to the corner of the table. Ariah couldn't help but wonder what other people saw when they looked at her polished uncle and the ratty, nearly homeless girl sitting with him. At one time, she was so similar to him. Well-kept and groomed, with some social status. Now, they were in stark contrast to each other. She belonged on the opposite side of the tracks.

"I need to order something for Miriam, drop it off to her, then we'll head toward Main Street and you can do some shopping."

"Uncle—"

He lifted a hand and cut her with a stubborn look. "No excuses. Don't think for a moment I haven't sensed the secrets you're hiding. Your struggles are plain as day, Ariah. I can read them in your eyes, eyes that are far too old and have seen too much. I can read them in your expressions, the exhaustion and the hopelessness. Since your birth, we have had a connection that goes beyond our familial ties. We both know it."

"So you *have* felt it? Why haven't you said anything until now?" Ariah didn't take her eyes off her uncle when the server swung back around, boxed up her pancakes, and cleared the table. Her uncle placed a take-out order and handed the server his credit card. "Uncle Mark?"

"There are things that I have tried to tell you. Things you have stowed away in the face of this harsh reality you've lived. You must remember and embrace the stories, Ari."

"Here we go again," Ariah muttered. She wasn't going to embrace the dragons. She'd seen too much to believe in such nonsense. When Uncle Mark opened his mouth to rebut, Ariah shook her head. Making sure to keep her voice down so nearby diners didn't think she was a loon, she said, "Dragons are myths. Legends. They aren't *real*. And of all people to be obsessed with them, you're the last one I'd expect."

Pain slashed across her uncle's expression. "Oh, Ariah. What has happened to you?"

"Reality. Bitter, cold reality." Ariah shoved back her chair. "Excuse me, I'll be right back. I need to use the restroom."

She couldn't escape the dragon talk fast enough. Losing her belief in dragons had been devastating, a tearing of her heart that ached to this day. It was essentially the death of a previous life before she was led into this current life. In a distorted way, she thought the dragons had let her down, as ridiculous a notion as that was.

She had never seen one, but the stories her uncle shared with her were so vivid she could picture their majestic burnished red scales and giant forms. She imagined their heat, smelled the succulent scent of bonfire and spice.

Uncle Mark made them real. Life took them away.

Ariah slipped into the restroom and stood in front of the counter, staring at her reflection in the mirror. Dark circles ringed her eyes, eyes as dark as her uncle's laced with gold. The fringe of her frame-cut bangs both enhanced the angles of her face while obscuring her sallow cheeks. Thankfully, her clothing was a size or two too big, providing a shield over her too-thin frame.

A faint sting touched the corners of her eyes. She twisted on the cold water and splashed her face. Perhaps returning to her uncle's home wasn't the smartest idea. His persistence in half-heartedly reigniting dragon stories was a brutal blow to her fragile psyche.

"Where would you go? You have nothing. No job, no home, barely a car, and no money."

In her heart, though, she knew this was where she needed to be. She'd suffer the dragon talk and deal with the strange stone until she could convince her uncle to stop bringing them up. She'd get help for her father, then find her bearings on life again and make something out of herself yet.

That meant leaving the dragons in the past with the fairytale-believing Ariah.

By the time she returned to the table, her wicked step-aunt's food had been delivered and the check paid. Uncle Mark led her out to his fancy Jaguar, held the passenger door open for her, then climbed in behind the wheel.

"Where are we going?" Ariah asked, her attention pulled away from the diner and to the upcoming row of stores along Main Street.

"Miriam works at the Nocturne Falls Credit Union. You can wait in the car while I drop off her lunch, if you'd prefer."

Ariah snorted. "Oh, I think it'll be far more interesting if I come in."

Main Street went by in a blur. Either Uncle Mark was trying to hide the authenticity of the town from her until he brought her shopping, or he was in a mad dash to get to his darling little wife.

Both prospects disappointed Ariah. She twisted and turned in her seat to get a better look at the shops while trying to read the signs and people-watch tourists dressed in Halloween costumes. The first whisper of childhood giddiness caressed her battered soul. The smile that played over her mouth was as genuine as it was involuntary.

She couldn't wait to explore this town.

Not even the simple one-story building with Nocturne Falls Credit Union on the front could douse her uplifted mood. She climbed out of the car and rubbed her hands together, ready to play the wicked step-niece in a controlled atmosphere. Her uncle wouldn't let Miriam do a darn thing to her at home, so she knew she was safe to get in some slights and jabs.

The witch deserved so much more than a few measly insults.

Uncle Mark held open the door for her, casting her a silent warning as she moved past and entered the building. She flashed him a smile and earned a good-natured roll of his eyes.

"Mr. Callahan, how nice to see you again."

Ariah arched a brow as a young woman scooted out from a desk to the left and hurried over to them. Her uncle shook the woman's hand. Her eyes lit up. Ariah groaned inwardly, tucking her arms around her body. The small motion drew the woman's attention from her uncle to pin Ariah with a gaze.

"Oh, who is this you've brought with you?"

Uncle Mark wrapped an arm around her shoulders. "Sandra, this is Ariah, my lovely niece. She'll be with me indefinitely."

Ariah laughed. "At least until I can get back on my feet."

"I've so missed her company."

"Well, that's wonderful. Welcome to Nocturne Falls." The woman clasped her hands together and glanced around. A faint crease formed between her perfectly manicured brows. "Miriam is helping a client and should be done in a minute. Why don't you take a seat?"

"Thank you."

Uncle Mark guided her to the upholstered chairs tucked toward the side of the spacious room. Ariah took a seat beside her uncle.

"Fitting place for her to work. Surrounded by money."

"Ariah."

Ariah shrugged. "Just stating a fact."

A door to the side of the room opened, drawing Ariah's attention. A pretty young woman followed a bank teller through the door, but it was the man behind her that made Ariah's back straighten. She watched the couple exchange a few words with the teller, the man's arm around the young woman's shoulders in a bold statement of possession and adoration. They were a beautiful couple.

As they said their goodbyes to the teller, the woman cast a short glance in Ariah's direction. Her smile faded a touch. Ariah tried to look away—it would have been the respectful thing to do—but couldn't. A strange electrical energy hummed beneath her skin the closer the couple came. When she lifted her gaze to the man, she stared into narrowed moss green eyes.

"Mark, my dear."

Miriam's voice was nothing more than a hollow essence of the real thing. Ariah sat, helplessly compelled to stare at the couple as they continued toward the doors. The room around her grew hazy along the edges, the man and woman demanding her sole attention. Time seemed to slow.

Look away, girl. Look. Away.

Her mind was not of her own command. The couple watched her with a mixture of curiosity, scrutiny, and something altogether unnerving. For a split second, she thought fire licked across the man's eyes. When she blinked, the fire was gone. She tried to open her mind, to grasp a thought, an impression, anything that would explain this strange pull.

She received nothing but internal conversations from the other people around her about accounts, budgets, poor decisions, and what to make for dinner.

The man looked away, drawing the woman closer to his side and pressing a kiss to the top of her head. Ariah turned her head down and gasped for breath, trying to brush aside the influx of dizziness that left her head in a spin.

What the heck just happened?

A strong hand rested on her shoulder.

"Ariah, are you okay?"

Ariah rubbed her forehead with the tips of her fingers. A wave of heat, followed by cold, rippled down her body. Her arms and legs trembled.

"Yeah, yeah." She twisted enough to look at the door. The man stood in the open door, the woman with him already outside. There was no mistaking his acute attention on her and her uncle. Uncle Mark's fingers tightened on her shoulder. That shadowy connection between them flared. Tension coursed down her uncle's arm and poured into her shoulder.

The man turned away and left. The weight crushing down around Ariah lifted a little, but breathing was still a chore. She tried to force a convincing smile and looked up at Mark and Miriam. The callous glow behind her aunt's dark eyes and the smirk on her mouth ignited her ire.

Ariah scrunched her face. "You know, Uncle Mark? I was just hit by something terribly...sour. Since you have a stronger stomach than I do, I'm going to"—she hitched her thumb toward the door—"step outside for some fresh air."

Anger flashed in Miriam's eyes and hardened her expression. Ariah wiggled her fingers in parting and headed to the door.

The moment she escaped the building, she looked up and down the sidewalk for the couple. Why, she couldn't be certain. What could she possibly say that wouldn't sound, well, crazy?

Hey there, not sure if you noticed, but there's some weird energy coming off you two. She groaned. *Yup, that's a winner.*

A moment later, a large SUV pulled around the parking lot and drove past her toward the exit. She got a full-face view of the woman seated in the passenger seat, staring back at her.

"...something so familiar about her..."

The soft female voice fluttered through her mind like a breeze. A single thought, nothing more.

As Ariah watched the SUV turn out of the parking lot and disappear down the road, she wondered in return why there was something awfully familiar about the strange woman.

CHAPTER 5

Two and a half hours spent sitting in his car, staring at a beautiful looming Georgia mansion on an impressive chunk of land had Alazar stirring in his seat. There was no mistaking the house for Mark's. His Keeper left a magical fingerprint on everything he touched. The exquisite luxury screamed "Mark", from the shimmering chandelier visible in the second-story window over the front door to the immaculate landscaping.

The beat-up old Toyota in the driveway, however, waylaid Alazar when he first arrived. He caught the tags, noting their North Carolina imprint, and simmered with curiosity.

The shrill ring of his cell phone startled him out of his thoughts. He fumbled for the device on the passenger seat and swiped the screen to unlock the call. The tip of his half-extended dragon talon scratched the glass.

"You've got to be kidding me."

He rubbed at the mark and groaned, answering the call.

"Hey, Zar. What's up?"

"Where are you?"

Alazar dropped his head back on the headrest and rolled his eyes to the mansion. "Picked up a gig. Neighborhood crime watch."

If he stayed parked here much longer, he half expected a cop to come knocking on his window, thanks to some suspicious neighbor.

"Seriously."

"Yup. New side job to keep me busy while I watch our handyman business dwindle into the dark, dank bowels of a lonesome existence, thanks to your lack of participation. I'm keeping little kiddies safe from runaway balls."

"You need to come back to Nocturne Falls."

"Who said I left?"

A grumble crossed the line. "Al, if I were to guess, you tracked your jewel to your Keeper, which I advised against. Regardless, I think you'd like to know that he's in town."

"*What*?" Alazar popped up in his seat and started his car, attention immediately cut from the inactive house. "Are you sure?"

"He's thirty years older, but he's always had a strong essence about him. Eyes haven't changed, neither has his name, but his company has."

"Not sure I'm getting you, Mr. Cryptic."

"He had a young woman with him. Looked to be around Kaylae's age."

Breath rushed out of his lungs. The world around him pulsed at the very insinuation behind Zareh's revelation. He hadn't been able to let go of the feeling that the woman he saw through his jewel was somehow linked to Mark.

He shook his head. He might be carefree and funny, but he wasn't gullible. "That's impossible."

"Two things. First, it's possible. I saw her with my own eyes. Second, I think I might have made a reference similar to that a few months ago."

Hope sparked in Alazar's soul. His dragon coiled. "He has no children and his brother's dead. There's no connection."

"Don't be so quick to discount it. Kaylae recognized something in the woman. More instinctual than anything tangible."

Alazar guided his car around the maze of side roads until he was out of the residential area. He stamped down on the accelerator. The car leaped forward, engine roaring.

"How long ago did you see them?"

"Ten minutes or so. Mark was dropping off food to one of the managers. Kaylae said she caught a thought from the woman about Keepers and dragons when she first arrived in Nocturne Falls. Would make sense if Mark told her about us."

The news made Alazar's head spin. Maybe an exorcism would come in handy. Or a drink. Or a game of eight-ball with a nice gold prize at the end.

A nice, long chitchat with Mark would be best. Find out what my Keeper's been doing all these years. Divulging information, making babies, building fortunes.

"I'm heading back now." A small grin tugged at his lips. "You little devil. You picked up my cash."

"What makes you believe that?"

Alazar chuckled. "You don't bank, have no need to use an institution, but you never closed out Kaylae's safety deposit boxes. That's where you kept my stuff, isn't it? Clever beast."

"I have your stash. It doesn't mean you can hit the games on the rebound."

"Are you going home?" He could use a few bucks. "Or can I meet you somewhere?"

"I'll leave it at the house."

"So, what does the woman look like?"

Zareh chuckled. "That, my friend, is for you to find out. I'd hurry back. I doubt they'll be staying at the credit union for long."

Alazar was already on it. Judging by the needle on his speedometer, the only thing that would delay him would be flashing lights riding up on his tail.

Forty minutes, a verbal police reprimand for going thirty over the speed limit, and a written warning later, Alazar guided his Mustang through the credit union's parking lot. He eyed each of the half-dozen parked cars for a hint that Mark may still be inside. To his displeasure, he saw nothing on wheels that suggested his Keeper lingered — a few older sedans, a pick-up truck, and a bumper-stickered hatchback.

Nope. Mark would pick some fancy new model sport something-or-other, if he hadn't changed too much over the decades. His Keeper had a love of prestige and speed. Clunky SUVs would be out of the question. A nice Ferrari or Bugatti, maybe.

Alazar left the credit union and cruised down Main Street, keeping his eyes peeled for a Ferrari. Then he came upon a sleek Jaguar F-Type coupe that screamed Mark.

Mark straightening out of the driver's side was pretty good confirmation, too.

Alazar pulled into an empty spot a few cars down and stared at the man he hadn't laid eyes on in three decades. Last time he and Mark were partnered up, his Keeper had been in his mid-twenties, young, fierce, and fearless. The older Mark still possessed a fierce edge and wisdom etched into the fine lines around his eyes. He'd grown a neatly trimmed beard and kept his hair a tad longer than most his age.

His gaze shifted as Mark stepped onto the sidewalk, shouldered through a crowd of tourists funneling out of Hallowed Bean, and paused next to a young woman who'd gotten out the passenger side of his car.

The young woman.

Alazar's heart fluttered wildly as his dragon reared. His skin tingled, his scales pressing to come forth, but he reined in his beast, down to his talons. His vision pulsed, his line of sight shifting, changing, taking on an orb-like picture with more clarity, more detail than his human eyes. His dragon fought for freedom, grappled for the unseen connection that sprang to life the moment he spotted the woman. Heat coursed through every inch of his vascular system, infused by the fire stoked low in his belly. He swallowed down the curl of smoke creeping up his throat, choked, and coughed out a thin plume of light gray.

When he looked up, Mark and the woman were gone.

"Oh, no you don't."

Alazar jumped out of his car—actually, stumbled in his disoriented state—and took a few seconds to compose himself. He engaged the car alarm and fell in step with the wave of people crowding the sidewalk, unable to enjoy the costumes and the excitement, especially on the children's faces. He had one goal, one target, one *need*.

His dragon followed the connection, the pull, toward the Hallowed Bean, pausing only to let customers out before he ducked into the packed coffee shop. He silenced his thoughts, cloaking his presence as much as possible. Walking up to Mark like a kid at Christmas wasn't the best idea. Nocturne Falls had been marked by their enemies. He didn't need to wave a surrender flag.

Alazar lifted the collar of his leather jacket around his neck, ducked his head, and moved to an angular alcove near the hallway to the restrooms. His height was a curse when he needed to blend in. Slouching cut about an inch off his six-four stature. Incognito was not in his repertoire.

Behind his sunglasses and jacket collar, he pretended to glance over the crowd while really keeping an eye on Mark and the woman as they moved closer to the order station. Mark rolled out his shoulders a handful of times, scanning the coffee shop every now and again. Even containing his presence, Alazar did not doubt Mark could sense him close by. Part of the Keeper-dragon package.

Ultimately, it was the woman who claimed his focus and held on tight. From his position, he could not get a clear look at her. The layers of clothes and knitted hat didn't help his cause. She hugged herself with one arm while biting her thumbnail, her face close to the pastry case. Heat nudged through his veins. Whispers taunted the back of his mind as the strange connection intensified.

Mark and the woman placed their orders and moved to an empty table tucked in a small alcove across the way. Alazar debated making his presence known until Mark climbed out of his seat to gather their drink orders and settled back down at the table. The woman took a sip of her coffee, clutched between two small, thin hands obscured by the length of her jacket. She hunched over the table, her booted feet resting on the lower rung of the chair, a woman trying to hide in plain sight. She was small, that much Alazar could tell. He made out the gentle slopes and curves of her profile, as well as the unnatural shadows cast beneath her eyes. Dark waves hid her cheeks, held in place by that knitted cap.

Her frown deepened as Mark spoke. On a few occasions, she shook her head, waved a delicate hand, or turned her face toward the ceiling.

Suddenly, she threw up a hand in a motion for Mark to stop and pressed to her feet.

Alazar looked away as the woman wove through the line waiting to order. He did not miss the glance she cast his way from the corner of his eye. He certainly didn't miss the violent thrum that unleashed inside his body as the soft scent of sweet vanilla followed her toward the ladies' room.

He did not straighten up for a good thirty seconds, giving the woman time to disappear into the bathroom. When he glanced down the hallway, he was surprised to find her standing in front of the door, brows furrowed as she stared at him.

His mouth went sandpaper dry. Small in height and size, she resonated a fierceness that flashed through the stunning gold lacework of her dark eyes. Her generously slanted brows enhanced the gentle tilt of her eyes, but accentuated the dark circles beneath. He would have blamed the lighting in the hallway had he not noticed similar shadows cast along the delicate arch of her cheeks not hidden by the asymmetrical cut of her hair.

Her pouty lips parted. Her nostrils flared and the crease between her brows deepened before she ducked her head and disappeared into the bathroom.

Alazar sucked in a breath, tasting the smoke that had filtered up into his mouth. An alien sensation of weakness teased his legs as he moved through the crowd, his attention on Mark. His Keeper added a packet of sugar to his coffee and stirred, staring into the liquid as Alazar slipped up to the table and glided smoothly into the woman's empty seat.

Mark's head shot up.

Alazar lifted his sunglasses to the top of his head and lounged back in the chair. Damn, it was nice to see his Keeper again.

"Alazar." Mark blinked several times, his lips moving soundlessly. At last, his eyes lit up and his lips curled into a wide smile. "*Alazar.*"

"I'll get my bro-hug on the way out." Alazar smiled back. "Zar saw you at the credit union."

Mark chuckled. "I thought that was Zareh, but I couldn't bring myself to believe it. Here. In Nocturne Falls."

"Believe away." He flicked his hand up and down, motioning to his Keeper. "You look great. Time's been kind to you. Keeping out of trouble?"

Mark chuckled. "That should be the question I propose to you."

"Trouble and I are buddies."

"I see you haven't changed, and that's good."

Alazar hunched over the table, holding Mark's gaze. "Nope. Not a bit. Still the funny guy with a gold addiction."

"Ahh. Although the funny façade hides a dragon with tremendous layers."

"An onion to the core. So, tell me. What have you

been up to?" Alazar lifted the cup that belonged to the woman to his nose and inhaled the scent of mocha, strong espresso, and female. "What have you been hiding?"

Mark's hand paused with his coffee halfway to his mouth. He stared back at Alazar for a long moment, then lowered the cup to the table.

"You know," Alazar continued. "I have this thing about being woken up from a dead sleep to find my jewel in a stranger's possession and my Keeper willfully refusing to speak with me."

"She's not a stranger."

Alazar tipped his head and pressed out his bottom lip in a motion of "maybe, maybe not." Before he'd laid eyes on the woman, he wasn't happy Mark shared the jewel with her. Now, he was intensely curious because his dragon confirmed all of his unspoken suspicions.

"To you, perhaps not. To me, yes. She is. So, who is she?"

"My niece."

Alazar laughed quietly. "That's not possible. You had one brother and he died when the slayers attacked The Hollow." He pushed the mocha concoction aside. "So...?"

"Mike didn't die. I was able to get him out before the magic melted our home. We barely escaped. One of the dragons who lost a Keeper and who died shortly after the attack carried Mike from The Hollow. I told Mike to run, and keep running. It took me two years after we split up to locate him again. He had found a woman, married, and they were expecting a daughter." Mark's expression softened, his gaze shifting away from Alazar. "Ariah. My niece."

Alazar could barely control the rush of his dragon's excitement as he lifted his gaze to the woman who had paused a few feet away. The moment his eyes connected with her dark gaze, irises flickering and swirling with gold veins, the breath in his lungs ceased and his world shook.

The lifemate pull exploded inside his mind and unleashed a powerful current of raw emotion within his dragon.

Protect. Cherish.

Smoke and bones, I'm done for.

Chapter 6

The subtle scent of wildfire laced through her nostrils on her way to the bathroom. With the scent came a fierce warmth that extinguished the endless chill in her blood. She didn't think anything of it at first. For all she knew, it could have been a mixture of coffee, espresso, and burnt milk. Nothing would have come of the scent and the sensation had the stranger propped against the wall beside the hallway not caught her attention.

The man was pretty darn hot. Oh, forget that. He was impossibly gorgeous, with a tapered jaw shadowed by a hint of scruff and thick waves of russet hair he had pulled half back in one of those messy man buns. She wasn't a long-haired-man kind of gal, but it was perfect on him.

Aside from the split-second assessment she performed as she skirted him, she couldn't shake a sudden influx of weakness. It made her dizzy and she caught herself with a hand against the wall to reorient her shaken body.

Think it's time to eat yourself back to a healthy weight.

She turned back as the man rolled off the wall and peered down the hallway. *He's looking for you.* A preposterous thought, but deep down she knew it was true. The lingering gaze from behind his dark sunglasses *pulled* her in.

She escaped into the bathroom, not only from Uncle Mark's persistent chatter about dragons, but now from the effects of the stranger. There was nothing else to do to prevent making a fool of herself. There was no possible way that guy had any interest in her aside from vaguely noticing her walking by.

It took her longer than she cared, and a few extra splashes of cold water on her face, to compose herself. From the moment she and her uncle stood in front of the cozy coffee house—even though they had eaten a short time earlier, she always had room for coffee on a brisk day—a strange tingle teased her spine. An unusual sensation of being watched refused to release her from its grip. She tried to ignore it, blaming the unnerving encounter with the couple at the credit union for upsetting her state of mind. She had even opened her mind to try to capture any thoughts that may have pointed to a cause for the sensation, fine-tuning the dials in her head to fade out nonsense.

In the end, she turned off the thoughts, coming away empty.

"You need to relax," she whispered to the pale face in the mirror. "Just...relax. And stop using the bathroom as an escape route."

Ariah left the bathroom and headed back to her uncle. She stopped short when she saw who had taken her seat.

For the briefest moment, she felt like she was being tossed in a raging sea, her body tilting and turning over and over. When the man lifted beautiful amber eyes to her, she all but fainted. The proverbial gut punch left her breathless and her heart racing to provide oxygen to her brain.

Her world stopped.

"Smoke and bones. I'm done for."

Ariah blinked as the thought filled her head with a deep, rich sound. Her knees wobbled.

"Ariah, honey, is everything okay?"

Her uncle's concerned question barely resonated through the violent rush of blood in her head, sounding hollow and distant. She tried to swallow, but her throat had gone dry.

The strange man was beside her in a flash, strong arms wrapped around her before her legs completely gave out. Heat pulsed along the thin fabric of her shirt, cocooning her in a blanket of secure warmth she never wanted to escape. Her nostrils filled with the delicious aroma of fire and spice.

A dragon's scent.

Yes. He smelled like what her uncle described a dragon would, *if* dragons were real. The scent was as comforting and reassuring as the arms around her.

The man led her to her seat, guided her to her butt, and pulled up an empty chair from another table. He straddled that chair and folded his arms casually over the back. His eyes narrowed on her before he cast her uncle a hard glower.

"She's unwell," the man groused.

Ariah's brow furrowed. Gorgeous or not, he would not pass judgment on her so blatantly.

When she opened her mouth to say just that, her uncle cut her off.

"She's been through tough times."

The man scrutinized her uncle. By the time he turned those heart-melting eyes back to her, there was nothing but tenderness glowing in them.

Ariah lifted a finger. "I've no idea who you are, but don't talk about me like I'm not sitting here. That's obnoxious."

"Ariah, this is Alazar Brandvold."

Ariah regarded the stranger for a small eternity. *This* was the man who would be unhappy because she was skinny? Sweeping a glance over the guy, she could possibly see why. She was a stick compared to his tall, lean, and definitely more muscled form. His dark blue jeans hugged nice legs and his leather jacket stretched over the wide berth of his shoulders. He could snap her with a breath.

A soft whisper of instinct promised her he would bring no harm to her, stranger or not. The soft glow of his eyes reinforced that promise.

"How do you know my uncle?"

Alazar watched her but addressed her uncle. "What have you told her?"

"Everything," Uncle Mark said.

"Sure doesn't seem like everything." Alazar tipped his head and looked over his shoulder. "Here isn't the best place to discuss family matters. Too many humans milling about." He flashed Ariah a devastating smile. In that moment, she craved to have his arms around her again. "You shoot pool?"

Ariah arched a brow. "Pool?" She cleared the knot from her throat. "Um, sure. Yeah. Every now and again. Why?"

"Al, she's not a gambler."

"Come on, Marky. Give me some credit."

She couldn't help but snicker at the way this thirty-something-year-old hunk made her serious uncle blush and brought him down a notch with nothing more than a humor-laced comment and a nickname. Her uncle rolled his eyes.

"Nothing like a little fun to break the ice."

"Ice is nonexistent around you."

"True, true." Alazar chuckled, another sinful sound that left Ariah a puddle of melted mush. She wasn't quite sure about the exchange between this stranger and her uncle, but whatever was happening, she could detect no threat. "It's a problem when maintaining a higher core body temperature."

Ariah's face heated under Alazar's pointed attention. She grinned and rubbed the back of her neck, wishing the blood she felt warming her cheeks would leave her face. A long time had passed since she earned such potent and genuine attention from a man, and never one so handsome. Despite his rather sharp, angular features, down to the hollows of his cheeks, the slope of his dark brows, and the slant of his eyes, the light in those eyes and his amazing smile softened his dangerous edge.

"You know, the Vampire Bites are pretty delicious. I can grab a few for you to try," Alazar offered. "A close friend of mine can devour a bag in record time."

Ariah took a deep breath and dared to meet the guy's gaze. Her eyes faltered on his grinning mouth and super kissable lips. She didn't need his body warmth to heat up areas inside her that had lain dormant for far too long.

"We ate not long ago, but I couldn't pass up the offer for a great cup of coffee." Ariah motioned to her mocha latte. She shifted in her seat. Her body's reaction to Alazar was beyond normal and yet way too natural. The only problem was the awkwardness of her uncle sitting at the table. It was about as strange as having a sex talk with her father. "Thanks."

Mark tapped the table with his fingertips before scooting his chair back and rising to his feet. "I forgot something in my car. I'll be right back."

"Uncle—"

He smiled and clapped Alazar's shoulder. She caught the whitening of his knuckles as he squeezed. "You're safe with him. I'll only be a couple of minutes."

Ariah pressed her lips together and watched her uncle weave through the crowd before disappearing outside. A muted sound escaped her throat, heat flushing her cheeks. Well, she was certainly making an impression, and probably a poor one at that.

"Well, um, so what do you do?" she asked. As soon as the question left her mouth, she cringed inwardly. She talked to people on a daily basis. Why was it so difficult to start a conversation with this guy?

He's gorgeous, and sexy, and you're the equivalent of an upscale street rat.

Alazar's gaze turned away from his inspection of the patrons filling the coffee shop and focused on her. "I fly."

"You're a pilot?"

Alazar pushed off his chair, angled it to face her, and settled in the seat. He propped a foot on the bottom rung of her chair, lounging back casually. His ease helped to settle her awkward nerves. She found extra strength in cupping her latte between her hands. It steadied the tremors that shook her fingers.

"Not quite." A devilish grin touched the man's mouth. "I breathe fire, too. And I have a gold fetish."

Huh. Flying fire-breather who has an affinity for gold. Ariah wondered how much of an influence her uncle had on his friend when it came to his dragon obsession.

"I don't suppose you're going to elaborate on that."

"Elaborate on why you think of yourself as a street rat first."

Ariah gasped, the cup slipping through her hands. Alazar caught it and placed it on the table. His fingers brushed over the back of her hand as she stared at him in disbelief.

There was no logical way he could have heard…

"We're beyond logic. And, yes, I can hear your thoughts. Just as you can hear mine, if you wish."

He leaned closer, the lightheartedness that cloaked him growing heavy and warm. Ariah tried to swallow, but found the motion impossible. Her heart kicked up a few beats, drumming mercilessly against her sternum.

"Right, Ariah?"

He drew his knuckles along her jaw. It was a whisper of a touch, but enough to melt her mind and leave her gasping. Never in her life had she felt such a pull, a call, as she did to this stranger. His presence embraced her, erasing the hustle and bustle, the clinking and clanging of the world around them. His thumb brushed over her lower lip. His nostrils flared.

Ariah stared into the warmth of his gaze and beheld the impossible. Fine threads of yellow-orange snaked through the warm amber of his irises. Tendrils of flames that evolved from an unknown source. Some thickened until fire licked along his pupils. The soothing scent of bonfire intensified and a faint curl of light gray escaped his nostrils.

"Oh. My."

No. This was absolutely absurd. There was no way her uncle had been telling her the *truth*.

"You are…*beautiful*, Ariah." Alazar's quiet compliment squeezed her lungs tight. She was falling uncontrollably for a man she'd known no more than ten minutes.

Alazar groaned and sat back, rubbing a hand over his face. Ariah sank into her seat, trying to shake the delightful tension that wrapped her up in a dream. She could barely focus on anything other than the lingering scents imprinted in her nostrils and the silent pull that led her to stare at Alazar.

The fire had vanished from his eyes. Other than a faint stroke of pink that highlighted his cheeks, he appeared as laid back and relaxed as he had when she first returned to the table.

A far cry from her own predicament.

"Back to the rat thing. You have no tail, no fur, so I declare you are not a rat," Alazar said, flicking a hand up and down from her head to her feet.

Ariah couldn't help but laugh. It broke the strange rigidness between them, a feat she was utterly grateful for. His smile was as heartbreaking as it was genuine, and worked a small miracle on the anxiety the last twenty-four hours dropped on her shoulders.

"However, you could use a few dozen donuts. I was afraid I'd break you when I helped you to your seat."

Yeah, okay. I get you think I'm too skinny. Not my fault.

Something dark flashed in his eyes. Ariah groaned.

"And you heard that, too."

"It's kind of hard to ignore when you project something straight at me." Alazar held out his hand. Ariah stared at his strong fingers beckoning her to accept the small, secure gesture. "Are you happy, Ariah?"

"Entirely," she said, flashing him a wide, exaggerated smile.

"Ahh, sarcasm, is it?"

Ariah toned down her smile until it became a natural reaction to the man waiting patiently for her hand while responding with a lightness she found refreshing. After another stretch of silence, Ariah tentatively rested her fingers over his. The comparison was drastic, her pale, slender hand against his tanned, work-roughened one. He closed his fingers around hers and stroked her knuckles with his thumb. The subtle caress continued to soothe her, melting her anxiety and worry until she felt...free.

For the first time in years, she felt free.

"Maybe I was being sarcastic." Oh, man. Did her voice really need to get all thick and husky right now? Heat tickled her face. "Or maybe not."

"I'm aware of your sarcasm, Ace."

Ariah tilted her head, narrowing her eyes on the handsome man. "Ace?"

Alazar winked. "Yes. Ace."

"Ah. Just put me on a card and play me for a win, huh?"

The humor vanished from Alazar's face. His eyes widened and he straightened up on the edge of the chair. "Oh, heck no! That's certainly not what I meant. Aces are usually coveted in card games. I meant it as an endearment. A coveted woman."

"You're digging a hole." Ariah laughed and shook her head as Alazar's expression of horror intensified.

"I'm kidding." She gave his hand a squeeze. "Calm down."

"Now that's not advice Alazar receives. He's usually the one dishing it out."

Ariah glanced up at her uncle as he side-stepped them to reach his chair. His gaze dropped to their entwined hands and a faint grin touched his lips. Ariah began to pull away, but Alazar's fingers tightened. He brought her knuckles to his lips and pressed a gentle kiss to the back of her hand. The motion unleashed hundreds of butterflies inside her belly and left her momentarily lightheaded.

She honestly believed he could see straight through her hard-shelled ruse to the vulnerable softness she protected deep down inside.

"Yes, Ace. I can."

Ariah blinked. Alazar lowered their hands to the table and sat back in his chair. She received his thought in a direct fashion that did not jive with how she usually heard thoughts. It was more like he *spoke* to her, telepathically.

His deliberate, short nod confirmed her suspicions.

Holy crap, I've been dumped in a fairytale.

"I'll warn you that chivalry has not died with him, despite what he claims. Right, old pal?" Uncle Mark punched Alazar's shoulder. Alazar snickered, tossing a glance toward her uncle.

"Pleading the Fifth." Alazar shifted in his chair until he was seated properly, able to see both Ariah and her uncle. "What are your plans for the day?" He turned his attention to Ariah. "Have you seen Nocturne Falls yet?"

Ariah shook her head.

"Well, if you'd do me the honor and allow me the opportunity, I'd be more than happy to show you the gems this town possesses." Alazar's grin quirked in a devious manner. "Of course, that is if Mark approves."

Mark cast a lingering glance between Alazar and Ariah. Part of her wanted to jump at the offer to spend time with the sexy man. Part of her felt some reserve about walking around a strange town with someone she didn't know. One thing was for sure. Spending time in Alazar's company would keep her mind off her father.

"I'll return her to your home by dinner time," Alazar added, facing Mark squarely. "A few hours to get to know the woman you've hidden from me isn't too much to ask, is it?"

"We've all been hiding, Al. For good reason."

"Um, why do I sense a not-so-good meaning behind that cryptic statement?" Ariah asked.

"Because it's not so good," Alazar confirmed. "But I'll protect you."

"Honey?" Mark shrugged. "I'll leave it up to you. You will be safe with him. That's a promise I can place my life on."

Ariah sighed. Alazar slipped his hand from hers, gave it a gentle pat, and stood up. "I'm going to grab a coffee and some Bites to go. I'll let you two discuss your plans. Don't feel you must take me up on my offer, Ariah. I'll understand completely if you choose not to."

"Thank you." Ariah couldn't help but appreciate Alazar's gracious understanding. She watched him cross the coffee shop and settle in at the back of the line before turning to her uncle. "Who is he?"

"Who? Or what?"

Ariah moved to Alazar's open chair and leaned close to her uncle. "Both."

Mark brushed a wave of hair that had fallen over her cheek. "He's my dragon."

"Really. You still think dragons exist."

"I don't think, honey. I know." Mark's lips curled into a thoughtful grin. "As I know you are his lifemate."

Ariah nearly choked. Her jaw dropped. "Excuse. Me?"

"Yes, my darling niece. He's your lifemate. Your dragon soulmate. And one day, when I'm gone, you will be his Keeper."

"Oh, geez, this fairytale keeps getting better."

"It's not a fairytale. Perhaps to the rest of the world, but not to us. This is our reality." Mark traced her cheek as she tried to process the information. Hearing it from her uncle was hard to digest, even if she thought she saw fire and smoke and smelled the scents her uncle described to her in Alazar. "But with the reality comes danger. We have enemies. Bad enemies. Enemies your father may have seen last night. If they located the jewel and tried to get hold of it, and your father stopped them."

She'd entertain this silliness for a few minutes. "Who are these bad guys? What would happen if they got hold of the jewel?"

"Here isn't the best place to talk about this, honey."

"So, it's not true."

"To the contrary. It's very true. A truth you must take caution with." Mark's gaze shifted to a point over her shoulder. She glanced back to find Alazar texting on his phone as he waited in line. "He is one of eight left in the universe. Eight. There were close to two dozen before the attack that almost wiped out our kinds. He is a rare breed, even rarer now. So rare that the legends paint them as myths."

She lowered her voice to a harsh whisper. "And you *trust* him?"

Mark nodded. "I trust him with my life because I know he'll sacrifice himself to save me. And he'll do the same for you."

"You're worrying me."

"You have nothing to be worried about." Mark rested a hand over hers. "Why don't you spend the afternoon with him? Get to know him. He's a character, that's for sure, but his heart is big."

"Uncle Mark, you're encouraging me to go off with a stranger. What if he tries to...*do* something?"

"Do you want to go with him?"

Ariah opened her mouth to state her denial, but the word caught in her throat. Truth be told, she did want to go with Alazar, as crazy as it sounded.

Mark nodded. "Ahh, you're trying to talk yourself

out of it. Understandable." He leaned back and retrieved his wallet from his pants, flipped it open, and pulled out four crisp hundred-dollar bills. "Here. To put your mind at ease, although I doubt he'll let you use it."

"I can't believe you're pawning me off on this guy." Ariah folded up the bills and tucked them into the pocket of her jeans. "Seriously."

"Tell me you don't want to go and I'll send him off."

"This is crazy," she muttered. "I don't understand it."

"By tonight, sweetheart, you'll understand everything."

CHAPTER 7

Confusion, caution, and skepticism permeated the air immediately surrounding Ariah. He got it, he did. He was a stranger claiming to be something read about in fantasy novels, without directly saying it. Mark, on the other hand, gave her the nutshell rundown while Alazar waited for his coffee and confections.

When he returned to the table, Ariah stood up, grabbed his wrist, and dragged him from the coffee shop. Alazar barely had a moment to throw a questioning glance back at Mark before patrons of the Hallowed Bean obscured him from sight. His Keeper certainly appeared amused by his niece's forward action. Alazar had to wonder what he was about to face at the hands of the small woman who was too thin for her frame and wallowed in murky thoughts.

He liked her fire. Really, really liked her fire.

Ariah started pulling him down the sidewalk, abruptly turned, and pulled him the opposite direction, earning curious glances from those admiring the shop windows along Main Street. She brought him back to Black Cat Boulevard, pulled him around the corner of the building, and spun on him, poking a finger at his shoulder.

"I want the *truth*. I want to know what the heck is going on. My uncle, a man who is grounded in reality, has lost it. What is this joke?"

Ariah's attention moved around them, keeping an eye on the pedestrians passing by. Her voice was low, but the punch of demand behind each word swelled Alazar with a sense of pride. His lifemate was not a pushover. That was a relief.

"And what do you have to do with it?" she demanded.

"Well, first, it's not a joke. Second, Mark is still grounded. His Armani shoes have stakes for heels that get pretty deep in the dirt. Third, I think he already disclosed what I have to do with it." Alazar held up the bag of Vampire Bites. "Snack?"

Ariah's scowl was endearing. It made her cute nose scrunch and the gold in her eyes flash. Oh, those eyes. He could easily lose himself in her eyes for days.

She shook a finger at him, her sloped brows lifting. "You're smooth."

"Like butter."

Ariah's next comment was lost on silent lips. She stared at him, her eyes widening. Alazar smiled and shrugged.

"Ace, I've got a comeback for everything."

He caught the twitch at the corner of her mouth.

"Don't laugh, girl. Don't do it. Find out what the heck is going on first."

Alazar took a sip of his coffee, keeping his attention locked on the spitfire before him as he fought the urge to break out in laughter from her thoughts. Each passing second, he found himself drowning deeper in her wild spirit. She had the same fierceness in her eyes as Mark, the same arch to her cheekbones, the same defiant thrust of her chin when determination took the reins.

As a lull in foot traffic followed a group of tourists, Alazar opened himself to his unfurling dragon. Ariah's beautiful face changed as he stared through his dragon's eyes. Although she still remained gorgeous, he detected the heat rising beneath her skin. The outline of her body turned to hazy strokes of blacks and grays. When she moved, a ghost of herself trailed behind, the smudged colors like a slow-motion film.

Her gasp struck his ears like spears.

He pulled the dragon back, his vision returning to normal as he beheld his wide-eyed lifemate. She slapped a hand over her gaping mouth.

Alazar took another sip of coffee, adjusted the bag of donut rounds in the crook of his arm to retrieve one, and held it out to her. "Here, Ace. Nothing a little sugar can't cure."

She didn't move.

She didn't blink.

Alazar waved the donut in front of her eyes. Nope. No reaction.

"Don't make me resort to archaic means of resuscitation."

Alazar dropped the donut round back in the bag and placed it and his coffee on the brick shelf protruding from the building beside them. He dusted his hands together before gently pulling—or rather, peeling—Ariah's hands from her mouth. He fought to tamp down the rush of desire that erupted inside him at the simple contact. The same desire singed the inside of his body and fed his dragon an elixir he'd never tasted as he cupped Ariah's face between his hands, tipped her chin up, and pressed his lips to hers.

A faint sound preceded the hitch in her breath.

Alazar swallowed down the urge to test her acceptance with a sweep of his tongue. The hunger burned at his throat, but he pulled back and smiled when Ariah blinked several times. Her cheeks darkened to rose, a beautiful hue that complimented her sweeping bone structure. She touched her lips with the tips of her fingers.

"You…kissed me."

"And you woke up. Just like in those fairytales you keep mentioning." He wanted to kiss her again. *Really* kiss her. He cleared his throat. Unfortunately, when he tried to catch her eyes, he got stuck staring at her lips. "Still believe it's a fairytale? Or do I need to completely transform?"

He'd lost all appetite for anything that wasn't part of Ariah. It was nothing more than a measly brushing of their lips, but the doors that opened inside him begged to differ. He finally convinced his brain to stop pining after those succulent lips and focus on more proper objects, like her eyes.

He couldn't resist adding, "That would require me to get nekid. In the woods."

Oh, goddess, help him. Even his funny prodded the hunger. Ugh.

Ariah lifted her chin, the quirk of her lips easing his concern that the woman would bolt. No. Not his Ace. She was stronger than that.

"Nekid, eh?" She let out the sweetest sound, a breath of relief with a musical connotation. A laugh that cinched the beating organ in his chest. "Naked in the woods is not my thing."

Alazar couldn't help himself. He cupped the back of her head and drew her close to press a light kiss to her forehead. He was vaguely surprised, and quite elated, when Ariah's hands gripped the edges of his jacket and held fast. She leaned into his short kiss, accepting his forward motion with the hint of a grin.

"Neither is it mine, Ace. For the record, when we shift, our clothes melt into our scales and our skin. No surprises. This guy won't flash you unless you ask. Promise." He allowed his fingers the freedom to sink into the silky strands of her hair that the knitted cap didn't cover. "So, what do you say? I'll show you around this crazy Halloween town and bring you back to Mark's house in one piece before dark."

"What about shooting pool?"

"Ahh." Alazar leaned back, curled his hand around

the top of her jaw, and lifted her head. "Think you can take me on?"

"Nope, but I'll try for good fun."

"Want to place a bet now?"

Ariah's eyes narrowed. "Bet?"

Alazar chuckled. "Good fun, that's all."

"You know, my father has a terrible gambling habit. I'm not fond of gamblers." She stepped back, dropping her hands from his jacket. "It's a thorn in my life."

Alazar raised his hands in surrender. "It's nothing monetary, if that's what you're worried about."

He gave a one-shoulder shrug and pursed his lips. He'd have to keep her feelings in mind going forward. He loved a good game and a challenging gamble—but not for the reasons everyone thought.

She stared up at him, her expression laced with skepticism. "I'm glad, because I have no money."

The lightness that consumed him drained away as he got a glimpse of the true despair that surrounded his woman. "You're here with Mark. And myself. You'll never have to worry about money again."

He lowered his hands to her shoulders, slipping his thumbs up along her neck. A frown claimed her mouth. A subtle pinch creased her forehead.

"Ariah, I want to learn everything about you. Everything, from the stories you so desperately revolt against to the reason you think of yourself as a lowly street rat. None of it makes sense to me, why you hold this darkness inside of you when all I see is fire and strength. Your life's trials will not sway me in my perception of you, but I need to understand what you've been through so I don't inadvertently hurt you."

"Like I just did."

He projected the thought without using telepathy, just leaving his mind open for her to read. He wanted to give her the choice to hear him or not.

Ariah tilted her head a hairsbreadth, just enough to press into the gentle back and forth motion of his thumb against the underside of her jaw. When her hand came around his wrist and held him a moment before her face relaxed, his dragon reared its protective head. No one would hurt his Ace. The marked pain he caught in her eyes would vanish. He would make sure she knew happiness, true happiness, with him.

"You didn't hurt me, Alazar. I've lived as the product of that lifestyle for far too long. I'm tired of it. I don't want it. I want to be free of the burdens, the debt, the endless cycle of seeing the few bucks I make cross over my palm before they go to pay off some guy or guys my father owes money to. I...I can't do that anymore. I can't do the motels. I can't do the vending machine meals."

Her small confession constricted his chest, but he kept his ire at bay. On his next breath, he detected the potent scent of tears. Ariah curled her lips in and pressed them tight.

Dealing with her father would be discussed with Mark, not Ariah.

"Hey, you will never have to worry about those things again. I promise you that."

Ariah sniffed and straightened her head, rubbing at her eyes with the heels of her palms. As much as Alazar wanted to draw her into his arms and comfort her, he sensed a faint resistance. A warning that she would not be receptive to comfort at this moment.

"You know, there was a time when I was younger that I believed in perfect lives and happily ever afters. I did. I could see the spectacular world my uncle talked about like I walked it every day of my life. When things went bad, I clung to that beacon of hope and those beautiful stories, thinking that maybe the better wouldn't be lush forests and clear waterfalls, but a mere sense of security within myself. As the years passed, the images faded. I accepted reality."

Alazar drew a knuckle under her eye, wiping away a single tear before it escaped down her cheek. The pain and shame that rolled off her in waves stole his breath.

Ariah laughed through a sniffle and stepped back, bracing her elbow on an arm tucked around her chest. She ducked her head, tugging at the strands of hair along her cheeks in a subtle motion to hide her face.

"I'm sorry. This is ridiculous. I mean, you don't know me and here I am, pouring out my pitiful story to you."

He tried to conjure up something funny to say, something to disperse the dark emotions that had thickened the air between them in the last few minutes. The humor had dried up for the time being.

"Ariah, come here."

He opened his arms, beckoning her to accept the support he desperately wanted to provide. He waited, counting each second in his head, ticking off the possibility she would shun him when she may very well need him the most. They may be strangers, but his dragon recognized her in the same fashion her spirit recognized him. The bond was indisputable, silly to try and deny. The longer he stood by her side, the stronger that bond became.

At last, Ariah stepped into his arms, pressing her face to his chest, and releasing a weighted sigh. As he wrapped his arms around her, he felt the tension in her shoulders melt. Alazar held her tight, saying nothing, absorbing her conflict like air into his lungs.

A few more moments passed and Ariah slipped her arms around his waist, settling deeper into his chest. He pressed another kiss to the top of her head, stealing a short breath of her vanilla-scented hair.

"If you could do one thing today, what would it be?" Alazar asked after several quiet minutes. Ariah's arms tightened around him, her face pressing harder into his chest. If she wanted to stay like this for the rest of the day, he'd be more than happy to oblige her.

"Get lost in a fairytale."

Alazar smiled against her cap. "I'll make it happen."

CHAPTER 8

The adult in her felt like a fool. Get lost in a fairytale? Really? She was beyond those years, beyond that flicker of hope.

Alazar had asked. There was something in his question that connected with her and nudged her to be open and honest, no matter how absurd her request sounded. So, she gave him her answer and his response ignited a lost giddiness inside her heart. She was ready to spend an afternoon with a dragon.

A dragon.

There was no way to explain the illusion she'd seen him perform a short time ago. His eyes changed first, his amber irises filling up the sclera, his pupils stretching until they were vertical slits, like a cat's. An impossible wave of deep red scales tipped with black formed over the backs of his hands. His nails elongated until they were lethal, dark-brown talons.

The sight almost left her in shock. When she came to—*he kissed you!*—the first thing she thought was that she had cracked. Alazar the Dragon Man had gone back to Alazar the Human, dealing a blow to her reality as well as to her protective barriers against his charm.

Now, she sat in the passenger seat of Alazar's Mustang and stared at a familiar SUV parked in a driveway in front of a house on a street called Crossbones Drive. There were plenty of large, luxury SUVs in the world, probably even plenty in this town. A quick glance at the neighbor's driveway doused her mental assurances when she saw a not-so-big-and-luxurious pickup truck parked there.

Didn't matter. What were the chances this SUV was the same one from the credit union?

Slim.

Alazar rounded the front of his powerful Mustang and opened the door for her, taking her hand and helping her to her feet.

"Is this your place?" Ariah asked, drinking in the modest two-story home.

"You can say that. Zareh and I bought it a little over a year ago when we came to Nocturne Falls."

Ariah cut him with a curious glance as she followed him to the front door. "Zareh?"

"Good friend. Second oldest Firestorm dragon alive. He and Kaylae are having a house built up in the boonies. They'll be abandoning me in a few months." He wagged his brows. "I'll be looking for a roomie."

Ariah snickered. "This is a lot of house for one person."

"That's why I'll be looking for a roommate, preferably a lifemate."

"Wanted ads might help with that."

Alazar paused on the stairs to the small stoop and faced her. "Aren't you the comedian."

Ariah gave him a playful shove. Alazar snatched her around the waist, pulling her close as he stumbled back a step.

"I go down, you go down with me," he murmured. Despite the good-natured banter, being intimate and close to this dragon left her dizzy with a tidal wave of need.

The heated moment shattered when the door opened. Ariah looked up to find herself staring into a very familiar face.

"Hey, Zar. Poor timing, buddy." Alazar kept his arm secured around her waist as they faced the tall, imposing man filling the doorway. The man gave her a once-over before a hint of a grin softened his otherwise fierce expression as Alazar said, "Found her, no thanks to you."

"You were at the credit union earlier," Ariah stated the obvious.

"Yes. Releasing Alazar from grounding."

Ariah quirked a brow. Alazar laughed. The guy he called Zar rolled his eyes.

Ariah looked up at Alazar. "Grounding? Your friend grounded you? How old are you?"

"Five hundred and seventy-one. And no, I wasn't grounded."

"You're *how* old?"

"With him, age really is only a number," Zareh said, stepping aside and motioning for them to come in. He closed the door once Alazar and Ariah were inside the small foyer and held out a hand to Ariah. "He's got more kid in his heart than a five-year-old. Name's Zareh."

"Ariah." She shook Zareh's hand. "I'm stuck on the 'hundred' part of that age," Ariah said, trying to turn the conversation back to the nonchalant disclosure of Alazar's age. "Actually, not a single number in that line-up jives with you."

To her entertainment, Alazar tapped the corner of his eye. "No wrinkles, my friend. I'm aging well. Better than any of those injections and creams could do."

"Yeah. Those fine lines around my eyes are all thanks to you." Zareh chuckled and shook his head.

"Would you like something to drink?" Alazar asked, drawing Ariah's attention once again. She'd take any excuse to stare.

"I'm good for now. Thanks."

He gave her hip a gentle squeeze and stepped away. "I'll be right back. Don't let him frighten or frisk you."

Ariah went wide-eyed as Alazar hurried up the stairs. She snapped her attention to Zareh and took a small step away. Zareh motioned to the living room.

"Not going to frisk you, have no worries. I save that specifically for Al."

"Uhh…"

Zareh lifted his hands and waved in denial when he realized what he said. "Oh, no. Not like that. The woman you saw me with earlier is Kaylae. She's my lifemate. You've nothing to worry about."

"So, you're a dragon."

"Last I checked."

"And Alazar, too?"

"There are times I wonder if he'd make a better peacock."

Ariah burst out laughing. She slapped a hand over her mouth. Zareh snickered.

"Sorry. I can't see that." Ariah shrugged, lowering her arm to her side. "I think he would make a great dragon."

Zareh leaned toward her and nodded once. "You know something? You're right. He makes a damn fine dragon. And he'll make you a damn fine lifemate. Beneath the comedian, he's an incredible man."

"I'm getting that." A strange warmth simmered in her chest. Her logical self told her it was way too early to have any sort of feelings for Alazar while the hopeful child in her dished out love-at-first-sight propaganda to her wistful mind. "It's been a while since I've laughed. He's made me laugh a lot today, like he knew that's what I needed."

"It's amazing how we can sense what our partners need most. You're meant to be in tune with each other. It's natural."

Alazar returned, flipping through his wallet before stuffing the thick leather book into his pocket. "I'm going to show Ariah around Nocturne Falls. Give her the exclusive tour and all. You and Kaylae have plans?"

"We need to head over to the construction site and

make sure the house is coming along as planned. Pandora offered to bring us to Melworth's Kitchens and More to guide us in some countertop choices and hardware for cabinets, then on to curtains. Again." Zareh scratched at the shadowed scruff along his jaw. "Doe insists I help make the decision, although I told her I'm not the best with interior design."

"Doe?" Ariah asked.

"Kaylae," Alazar and Zareh answered in unison.

"Wow. You two really have a...connection." Ariah wagged a finger between the men and smiled. "Endearing."

"Let's get moving before Zar starts into his sob story about curtain shopping. It'll make you twitch." Alazar slung an arm around her shoulders as she stifled a laugh. "We're high-tailing it. Enjoy comparing paisleys and damasks."

"Does Kaylae's father live around here? Is that how she and Zareh met?"

Ariah thirsted for more information about Alazar and the dragons. Actually, she wanted solid, impenetrable confirmation that she wasn't still asleep and dancing around in a dream. The man sitting behind the wheel of his sports car, looking like a compelling bad boy with a sucker-punching smile, was certainly dreamy. Even her own actions—going off with a stranger after seeing scales on his hands—was dreamlike. Uncle Mark's push for her to remember and embrace her childhood stories was certainly a depiction of an alternate reality.

For some reason, Alazar's lingering grin fell at her question. She instantly regretted mentioning the other woman.

Dream shattered.

"Talius was Zareh's Keeper and Kaylae's father. He was killed a few months ago by the Baroqueth slayers in search of Zareh's dragonstone." Alazar laid off the accelerator a bit and sighed. A rush of unease settled in Ariah's chest. She was all too familiar with sensing trepidation, from hearing the strain in a person's voice to reading the body language. "Kaylae followed a trail of cryptic messages that led her to Nocturne Falls, and into Zareh's arms. Literally."

"Oh my. That's terrible." Curiosity clawed at her. "About her father, I mean. Her meeting with Zareh sounds almost too perfect."

"Quite the contrary. She was treading madness. Her father hid who and what she was from her, so she didn't know how to control hearing people's thoughts. She thought she was going crazy. Then Zar hit her with the dragon thing. And the lifemate thing. She took it in stride and now they're planning their happily ever after."

"Incredible, really. I should be thankful, then, that my uncle had the foresight to teach me how to control the thoughts." The corner of Ariah's mouth twitched as she looked over Alazar's impressive profile. Even in his serious state, the guy had a warming effect on her. She wanted to reach over the console and sidle up against him. Allow him to shield her from all the bad in the world. Said world knew she needed the shield. "What are these slayers you mentioned?"

"Ancient sorcerers. A few centuries ago, the head of the Firestorm *tatsu* clan had a Baroqueth Keeper. The Keeper wanted the dragon's power. The dragon refused, and hence ignited the first war between Baroqueth and Firestorm. Wiped out most of our kind, both dragons and Keepers. Rebuilding was slow. Female Keepers are rare. Extremely rare. The only time they seem to come along is when our bloodline is on the verge of extinction. About thirty years ago, the Baroqueth invaded The Hollow in an attempt to siphon power from the dragons. Eight of us dragons were able to escape with our Keepers. We abandoned our homeland and came here, to your world. Dragons separated from Keepers to protect our more vulnerable counterparts. We all went into deep hiding and the hiding worked until the Baroqueth found Talius and somehow tracked Kaylae here to Nocturne Falls."

"Please tell me these bad guys are finished. Kaput." Ariah's heart sped up at the prospect of escaping one dark life only to find herself falling into the waiting embrace of another, very possibly a Reaper of, dark lives. "Please."

Alazar's hand closed over hers. She hadn't realized her fingers were fisted until the heat of his skin and the simple contact relaxed her. Every tense muscle along her shoulders and her back eased as she flexed her fingers, allowing his to fall between her own.

"The three who came here were entrapped in stones that Cade, our leader, took back to The Hollow. Our land is a land of magic. The magic used to entrap the sorcerers here was strong, but I would not doubt that their buddies would sniff them out and release them. Those three are in a very secure dragon jail."

"So, there *are* more bad sorcerers?"

Her mind reeled. Her father claimed to recognize a threat and her uncle suspected their enemies were after the jewel. Had these sorcerers been at the auction house?

Alazar frowned and gave a slight nod. "Yes. The exact number is unknown. They've had thirty years to grow their numbers and their powers. After the attack on Kaylae to get to Zareh, I question the safety of staying separated from our Keepers. Zareh still grieves Talius's death. He thinks that if he had been closer, he could've prevented it." He paused at a Stop sign and rested his head against the headrest, releasing a long breath. "I've sensed Mark close by since we arrived in Nocturne Falls, but kept my distance. Even after the attack, I continued to keep my distance, although I tried to pinpoint his location. It wasn't until last night when you two opened the dragonstone's box that I was able to trace him to his home."

"What does the stone do?" From what she witnessed last night, it did nothing. It sat pretty on its velvet bed. "Does it really *do* anything?"

"That jewel must be guarded. It's your proverbial baby, Ariah. If it fell into Baroqueth hands, it could mean my death, Mark's death, potentially your death, and the destruction of the Firestorm dragons as a whole. The responsibilities that come with being a Keeper are ingrained in a Keeper from birth. Mark was born into the position as firstborn to his line. His father was my Keeper before him. Mark fathered no children of his own, but his brother sired you. Not only are you next in line to be Keeper"—he rolled his head against the headrest and caught her gaze—"you're my lifemate."

The intensity in his gaze, the glow of his eyes, poured warmth straight down to her toes. She didn't care for all the drama with the sorcerers, but she certainly liked the sound of being a lifemate to this particular man. It gave her the first sense of security in her tumultuous life in over a decade.

The responsibility that came with being a Keeper, however, seemed daunting.

"How do you know I'm that person?" Even as she asked the question, her heart ached at the thought that Alazar and her uncle might be wrong. "Is it permanent? Is it something that we choose? What happens when I get old and die and you continue to live for a few more thousand years, like the dragons in my uncle's stories?"

"There's no denying the pull between us. I know you feel it. It can be overwhelming at times. In the hour since we've been formally introduced, I can't bring myself to think about parting ways." Alazar twisted enough to look out the back window. Ariah couldn't help but follow his gaze to the car pulling up to their bumper.

Stop sign conversation has ended.

Alazar waited for a car to pass before turning onto the two-lane street that bled into Main Street. He held her hand, maneuvering the shifter in a fluid switch of gears. Ariah saw a few storefronts down the road, followed by the busy main thruway of Nocturne Falls. The fancy streetlights caught her attention momentarily. She smiled. The festive cobweb brackets added a very authentic touch to the celebratory town.

"You didn't answer my other questions," Ariah pointed out as the silence stretched.

"Nope. Don't suppose I did, huh?" The humor had returned to his voice and the telltale grin on his wicked mouth conquered his frown. "The dragonstone is a piece of pure magic. It contains the blood of every single Keeper I've had, down to Mark. By bleeding into the stone, it creates a bond, a connection between dragon and Keeper. The stone is a means for the Keeper to communicate with the dragon at a distance. It also acts as a looking glass for me."

Ariah rubbed her forehead as she processed this bit of information. "Okay, so if you look into it—"

"No. I don't look into it. I see *through* it. When the box is open, I can see through the stone." He lifted their entwined hands to her chin and gave her a playful pinch. "I saw you in the wee hours of the morning when Mark had you open the box."

Ariah's eyes widened. "*That's* what he meant when he said it was time 'he' saw me. He was talking about you because he knew about this lifemate thing and all."

"That's what I got out of it."

Alazar guided his car into an empty spot on a side road and cut the engine. Ariah kept the ache of his hand slipping away to herself, focusing on the throngs of people trolling the storefronts. She couldn't get over the spirit of these tourists, most of whom were dressed up like witches and vampires, or wore eccentric Victorian gowns and impressive pirate garb.

Ariah glanced down at her flimsy black thumb-hole shirt, black tank top, and hooded sweatshirt jacket. Her jeans were fitted down to her ankles, worn and faded, and her black hiking-style boots were scuffed and untied.

At least I'll fit in here. A Halloween costume of sorts.

She climbed out of the car before Alazar reached her side to help her, earning a narrow-eyed glower and scowl before the scowl melted into a smile. He crooked his arm after she closed the door. She gladly slipped her arm through his and sidled up close to his side. The car alarm engaged and Alazar led her toward a small shop with pink and purple striped awnings. A craggy tree branch poked out of the faux cracked brick façade, and red-eyed crows perched on it. The swinging stressed-wood sign creaked in a creepy wrought-iron bracket. Two black wrought-iron wall lights flickered in an unseen breeze and flanked a rickety wooden door that looked like it would turn into a pile of splinters if poked.

"Into the Woods," Ariah read on the sign. She looked up at Alazar. "Keeping with the fairytale theme, are we?"

Alazar chuckled and pushed open the door. "This is a close-kept secret that locals flock to."

Ariah followed Alazar into the dimly lit store. The door shut, closing them into a lobby that led to another wooden door. Ariah soaked in the atmosphere of the small enclosure. The walls looked as though they had been carved to form serpentine tree roots, knotted and twisted. A single dangling lantern cast drab yellow light over the lobby.

"I think the locals can keep their secret place." Ariah leaned into Alazar, seeking his security.

"Wait, Ace." He flicked up a latch lock and pushed the interior door open. Ariah's jaw slackened as he led her into an open, two-story room with dazzling chandeliers and filled with the subtle aroma of wildflowers. Candles flickered in strategic placement on shelves piled with clothing. More items hung from the numerous racks. Shoes were on display toward the back of the store. Linen-lined tables displayed unique shirts and fancy bottoms. "Still want them to keep their secret?"

Ariah stepped up to a table and fingered the line of stones decorating a trendy tank top. She turned over the price tag and almost choked.

"Um, why don't we check out something a little less extravagant?" Ariah's cheeks burned. She stole one last look around the store and turned back to Alazar. A confused pinch marred his brow. Darn, didn't he look cute. She swept her hand against her body, motioning to her outfit. "I'm pretty plain when it comes to my choice of clothing. One of those small-scale department stores will do."

"Huh." Instead of leading her from the store, Alazar drew her deeper into the luxury she could not afford. He pointed to an oversized plush chair. "I'm going to sit down and watch you peruse the clothes."

"But—"

He tsked.

"Look. Browse. Try things on. Peek at a single price tag again, and I'll buy everything in this store for you. Got it?"

Ariah stifled a gasp. She'd have to get used to this telepathy thing.

Alazar gave her bottom a playful pat. She jumped at the bold motion as Alazar settled in the chair. He waved her off.

"You're impossible."

"I'm giving you what you deserve." Alazar's smile dimmed and a flare of sincerity lit his eyes. "What you should have had all your life. Now go. Enjoy. And keep your money in your purse. Actually, better yet…" He held his hand out, wiggling his fingers. "Let me have it. I'll give it back to Mark."

Ariah scowled. "I can't accept—"

"Ariah Callahan."

"Full name basis, are we?" She laughed and shook her head, digging in her pocket for the bills her uncle had given her. "Here. Don't lose it."

Alazar lounged back in the chair, slipping the bills in the pocket of his jeans, and folded his arms behind his head. "I propose a challenge, since you don't like wagers. I challenge you to put a dent in my wallet while in this store. Let's see what damage your shopping can do."

Ariah rolled out her shoulders, pulled her bag over her head, and tossed it at Alazar. The dragon caught it without a flinch.

"The bet is on."

CHAPTER 9

Had it been anyone else, Alazar would have walked out of the store. Thirty minutes was his limit in a clothing store. He'd accompanied Kaylae and Zareh shopping once and since swore off the activity.

An hour and a half later, he was as content as a child in its mother's arms, basking in the borrowed excitement that ensconced Ariah. Into the Woods had acquired two more patrons, and he was happy to oblige his sweet lifemate's requests to give her an honest opinion of the clothes she modeled for him.

Not exactly modeled, but to him, she was putting on a private fashion show. The comfort and ease she felt in his presence fed confidence to his dragon, among other things. However, he did notice there were certain items she would not let him see on her. Items that either dipped low in the front or showed too much of her arms or belly. One shirt she came out in hid nothing of her frail chest and prominent collarbones. Whether she noticed the flare of his frustration over the evidence of negligence to her health, she made sure after that to be careful with what he saw.

He stirred in a sea of turmoil, one that mixed anger with a fierce need to protect Ariah. Keeping his mouth sealed in the store was as hard as refraining from the desire to surprise Ariah inside the changing room and kiss her mad. Yeah, he wanted to kiss her, taste her, learn her like he would have years ago if the situation between the Firestorm and the Baroqueth were different.

Now he definitely understood why Zar and Kaylae spent as much time secreted away in their room as they did.

"I think this is the last one."

The white peasant shirt embroidered with gold vines hid her delicate frame but gave her a sweet appearance he could see trapped beneath the results of hardship. It lightened her face and drew his attention to her gold-laced eyes. The shirt slipped off her shoulder a little, but otherwise, she was covered. Paired with the long black, slitted skirt and pointed pumps, the ensemble left him in danger of combusting.

"That's a keeper, Keeper." Alazar braced his elbows on his knees and nodded. "Definitely in the buy pile."

Ariah made a circular motion with her finger around her face. "You look a little flushed." She cut a pointed look to the huge pile of clothes on the table beside him. "This really isn't necessary. Sure you're okay with this?"

"Yep. Internal thermostat decided to conk out on me. Don't be surprised if I start breathing sparks."

"Oh." Ariah's brows cinched in a cute way, giving her an almost innocent look had her eyes not been cast with shadows. A faint kiss of rose touched her cheeks. "Yeah. Got it. Remind me to invest in a fire extinguisher."

"Not happening. I never acquired a taste for chemical foam."

Ariah laughed and disappeared back into the dressing room. Alazar pushed to his feet, snatched up Ariah's bag, the stack of clothes, and headed to the checkout counter.

The owner of the store, a dainty pixie named Dalila, rounded the end of the counter in a graceful, dancing manner. Her brown eyes sparkled when she saw the pile waiting to be rung up.

"Is there anything else I can help you with, Alazar?"

"Building a new addition to my house to hang all of this stuff. There is one more outfit coming, but you can start with this," Alazar said. Dalila giggled and began the task of folding the clothes and preparing the tags to run through her computer system. He'd be surprised if she finished by dinnertime.

"Alazar?"

He twisted around and smiled. Pandora, the queen of real estate in Nocturne Falls, hurried down the half-circle staircase. How she managed the narrow staircase in those heels without face-planting was beyond him.

Probably some witchy spell to stay vertical.

101

"I thought you and Kaylae had a date to torture Zar over granite or marble, dark wood or light."

Pandora laughed and lifted an arm draped with trendy shirts. "I promised Kaley I'd pick these up for her while she was at school. Teenagers nowadays. Needing to feel cool to fit in." Her green eyes shifted to the pile of clothes. A curious wrinkle crossed her forehead, disappearing under a lock of red hair. "I see you're doing Zareh a favor, too, I suppose?"

Ariah emerged from the dressing room and came toward him. Her attention settled on Pandora. A faint ripple of tension pulsed off her when Pandora turned and graced her with a professional smile.

"Ah. I see."

"You see?" Ariah licked her lips, throwing Alazar a questioning glance before holding out her hand. "Ariah Callahan."

Pandora shook. "Pandora Williams." She gave a small shrug, her smile brightening. "I sell real estate here in Nocturne Falls. So, are you new to town? I haven't seen you around." Alazar scoffed when Pandora winked at him. "I'm sure I would've heard something if Alazar was hanging with a lady friend."

"Um, not everyone has a nose, or a snout, in my business," Alazar said, concern rising in him as Ariah's expression grew more curious. He laughed, waving a hand at Pandora. "Real estate equals know-all."

"Benefit of interacting with society on the level I do." Pandora eyed the pile of clothes Dalila had barely made a dent in. "I think it's safe to say you've made Dalila a very happy business owner today."

Dalila giggled, pausing in her folding long enough to flash them a smile. "I can count on most of you to make me happy."

Alazar reached a hand out for Ariah. Ariah placed the remaining clothes she'd chosen over his arm and dangled the straps of her pumps from his fingers, then took her bag from his hand. He lost his smile, tossing the items on the mountain of purchases, and hooked his arm around her waist, tugging her to his side.

"That's what I meant," he murmured against her ear, giving her hip a gentle squeeze. Pandora's shaped brow lifted when he straightened up. "Dalila, could you ring Pandora up? Don't want to hold her up and leave her clients feeling abandoned. I don't want to hear the whining all night long."

"Oh, of course. Of course."

Pandora gave Alazar a pat on the shoulder and handed her far shorter pile of purchases to Dalila. "Thanks, Al. You're a doll."

"You're on edge. Why?"

Ariah's gaze lingered on Pandora. At last, her shoulders settled, releasing the tension that rode them. *"Not edgy."*

"Uhh, maybe I'm reading you wrong, but I doubt I am."

Ariah shot him a stubborn look. "Aren't we being...overconfident."

Pandora laughed and hitched a thumb at Alazar. "That's him to a T. Until Zareh has to swoop in and save him from a bad gamble."

"Really, Pandora?" Alazar groused.

"Gamble? Is that so? Seems to be a running theme," Ariah said. The tension returned, a hundred times over. "How often would that be?"

"Ace—"

Ariah whipped up a hand, silencing him. He groaned, begging that Dalila would stop stalling and send his darling friend on her way before she said something super damaging.

Pandora tapped a finger on her lower lip. "Well—"

"I gave it up about a month ago," Alazar intervened.

Heck, his entire future balanced on this tenuous high-wire and he was already tripping over his feet. The way Ariah's lips quirked to the side and her brows disappeared beneath the waves of bang that framed her face promised him a fight to earn her trust. Which was fine. Really, it was. Completely fine. Entirely okay.

Who am I fooling?

He wanted her trust *now*. He wanted that twist of her lips to reform into one of her bright smiles. He wanted the doubt in her gold-laced eyes to fade into the abyss of darkness.

Was it such a bad thing to want her to snuggle up against him and, well, maybe kiss him?

"Come to think of it, Bridget hasn't seen you hanging around the pool tables in a while." Pandora handed her credit card to Dalila and leaned a hip against the counter. "I guess passing time gets boring. Ivan does that wrestling gig and doesn't need to do it for anything other than self-gratification. When you have an infinite lifespan, what's a little gamble here and there, right?"

"Digging the hole deeper, Pandora," Alazar warned through a tight-lipped grin.

"Don't make it obvious, Poker Face," Ariah said, then sighed. Alazar's heart soared when she finally leaned into him. "Guess I can understand it from that perspective. Now I'll know when he's bored."

Pandora took the bag Dalila handed over the counter, followed by her card and receipt, and flicked an index finger toward Alazar.

"I have a feeling he won't be bored anymore. Have a nice day."

Alazar exhaled the anxiety that had mounted with each second during the conversation between Ariah and Pandora. He had nothing to hide from her, but not even the fact they were lifemates could guarantee Ariah would accept him and stay with him. Eons ago, the bond between lifemates was seen as a sure and secure relationship. Times had changed, though, and now the choice was left up to the woman instead of the dragon.

He'd grovel if he had to. He'd dance around in a tutu if Ariah asked him to. He'd eat a bowl of—*gulp*—kale if it would earn her trust and her heart.

Alazar glanced down at Ariah. "Do you like kale?"

Ariah snorted, a hand flying up to her face. The gold shimmered in her eyes once more. "Excuse me?"

Alazar shifted on his feet and shrugged. "Kale. Do you like it?"

She giggled behind that hand, a sound so musical and airy that Alazar wanted to bottle it up and listen to it whenever they were apart. "That's the poorest pick-up line I've heard."

"You've already been picked up. So?"

"You're serious?"

"I'm preparing myself."

Ariah blinked before tilting her head and narrowing her eyes on him. "For what? A bunny war?" When he didn't answer, she shook her head. "No. I don't like kale. Then again, I've never had it cooked in a decent manner."

Alazar's relief swelled. He wouldn't have to worry about facing the repulsive greens.

By the time Dalila finished ringing up and bagging Ariah's new purchases, a sense of fulfillment settled in his chest. He paid with cash and tucked his wallet into his jeans, helping his little lifemate with her bags.

"Well, Ace." He lifted his arms, each draped with two oversized paper bags. "You do lovely damage. Congratulations."

Ariah tugged her lip between her teeth. "I think I went overboard. I don't know what got into me. I shouldn't have taken advantage of your offer, or accepted that challenge."

"Nonsense. You earned every article of clothing in these bags. You won. So, since we've paid Dalila's rent for the month, what would you like to do next? More shopping? Ice cream? Spinach and kale shake?"

Alazar held the doors open for Ariah. The bright sunlight nearly blinded him. Ariah went into a sneezing fit. She turned into him and curled her head against his chest as she sneezed a couple more times.

This was something Alazar could get used to.

Nope, already used to it. Want to keep it now.

"How about we get you a pair of sunglasses and I'll take you to the park?" Alazar bowed his head, unable to refrain from kissing the top of her forehead, and added quietly, "I'll show you what a *real* gargoyle looks like."

Alazar despised the streaks of red, pinks, and purples in the sky, since they signaled the afternoon had gone by in a blink. After he purchased a swanky pair of sunglasses for his girl among other accessories, followed by milkshakes at the I Scream Shop, he led them to the park that split Main Street. The peak of dinner hours thinned the crowd of tourists who flocked around the gargoyle fountain. A few patrons sat in the numerous benches provided throughout the stretch of stunning green with splashes of colors from different flowers. Strategically planted trees had matured enough to provide umbrellas of shade against the fiery glow of the setting sun.

Ariah stared at the gargoyle statue in the center of the magnificent fountain. "I still don't believe you."

"I think his name is Maxim. Ask him something," Alazar urged.

A few of the bystanders were prodding the gargoyle with questions. Although tourists to Nocturne Falls believed the statue to be just that—a statue—with incredible animatronics involved, the supernatural residents knew otherwise. Alazar's next-door neighbor, Nick Hardwin, was a gargoyle. He liked the guy, especially when it came to their fun coin bets.

Ariah sipped her milkshake, eyeing the statue and the small flock of humans. Alazar glanced at his watch and sighed inwardly. The day was coming to a close at breakneck speed, and he had no way of stopping the inevitable parting once he brought Ariah back to Mark.

"I don't think talking to a robotic stone is my cup of tea."

"You also didn't believe the vampire charming those teenage girls was real."

Ariah twisted enough to give him an "are you serious" look. "The sun's out. Aren't vampires allergic to UV rays? And, he wore"—Ariah motioned to her torso—"*glitter*."

"Magic and marketing strategy."

Alazar lifted his thumb to the corner of her mouth and wiped away a small drop of ice cream at the same time the tip of Ariah's tongue licked it. The feel of her tongue on his flesh stirred the fire in Alazar's belly to unbearable proportions.

He had no conscious intention of leaning down, and certainly no intention of brushing his lips over hers. The brief, airy caress was nothing shy of electric, urging him to test her willingness to kiss him back.

Slowly, he kissed her again, flicking his tongue along the seam of her lips.

She dropped her head and fidgeted with the straw in her cup. "I, uh, I think maybe we should head back home. It's getting late and my uncle is probably waiting to eat dinner."

If *that* wasn't a sword through his heart.

Alazar straightened and cleared his throat. He shouldn't have pressed his luck. He certainly overstepped his boundaries. Here, he wanted more time with his woman, and instead he gave her an excuse to leave his company.

Ariah finally lifted her gaze back to his. The turmoil swirling in her beautiful eyes prodded the dragon within him to try and calm it. He didn't want to see Ariah, the woman he wanted to protect and cherish, in such a state. She held a strong front, but the fragile soul she protected shone through.

Alazar managed a half-smile. "Of course. Anything you wish."

"Thank you."

The sudden shift between them set him on edge. Had it been something he said? Was it the talk about gargoyles and glittery vampires? Everything seemed to be going just fine up until that little thumb-tongue exchange.

An unsettling coolness licked at his spine as he slipped his hands into his jacket pockets and walked beside Ariah toward his car. A few of the stores shimmered beneath a display of fairy lights, adding a magical touch to an already magical town. A couple of fortunetellers were setting up their tables on the outskirts of the park. A pair of witches began displaying their magical talents for tourists who had gathered to watch.

It was part of the beauty he wanted to bring to Ariah, and yet a subtle warning of resistance fed the cold that had managed to break through his fiery walls.

"I'm sorry, Ariah. I shouldn't have taken the liberty—"

"Don't apologize," she said quietly.

Okay. That had to be a good sign. "Do you have plans for tomorrow?"

Ariah shrugged a shoulder, still playing mindlessly with the straw. She was taking in the town as night fell, but her expression was a mask of indifference. So unlike the woman who packed the backseat of his car with bags of clothes, laughed over the names of the ice cream offerings, and had spitfire comebacks for vampire Julian Ellingham's harmless flirting.

He feared the strength in this special woman's foundation had fractured and she was about to shatter.

The turn of mood was so fast, so abrupt, Alazar didn't know how to respond. He did the only logical thing. Gave her a bit of space.

Maybe things were going too good.

One thing he learned over the last few hours: His darling lifemate was not one to be coddled. Problem was, he didn't know if that was because of something in her past, or because she feared accepting support from another. She wouldn't give him any indication.

It tore him up inside.

"Is there any other place you'd like to see in town?"

Ariah sighed. "I don't know."

Alazar bit the insides of his cheeks, refraining from asking more hollow questions. He wasn't going to get an answer of worth and feared he'd shut her down even more if he pressed her.

They made it to his car with nothing more spoken between them. He held open the door for her, received a hushed thanks, and rounded the car before falling into the seat behind the wheel. As tempted as he was to brush the outer circles of her mind, try to calm her with a gentle whisper of assurance, he refused to invade her in such an intimate way. Her thoughts were schooled, completely closed off to him. Mark had taught her very well on the magic of her mind—a blessing and a curse at the moment.

"Is there anything, Ariah, that I can do for you?"

At last, she gave him a lopsided grin. It wasn't much, but it was something. He'd take it. "I think you've done plenty for me today. Thank you."

"There is so much more I'd like to do."

"I think you've over exceeded. As it is, I'm probably not going to be staying here long."

Alazar's attention narrowed on the road ahead. This was a complete one-eighty from the silent acceptance he received from her earlier, and he had no doubt it was not connected to his misplaced kiss.

"Will you tell me what happened to you?" He started to reach for her hand. She knotted her fingers together in her lap and he rested his palm on the shifter, licking his suddenly parched lips. The dragon was breathing fire up his throat.

"There's nothing to tell."

She had completely shut.

He endured the painful silence during the remaining twenty-minute car ride. The occasional screech of the straw against the plastic lid raked down his scales as he tried to quell his swelling frustration. Not at Ariah. Certainly not toward his lifemate, but toward the secrets she refused to share to help him understand. The things that happened to her that she couldn't trust him to know.

Whether the trust was lacking on his part or hers, he wasn't sure.

Alazar pulled up behind the beat-down Toyota in Mark's driveway and cut the engine.

Ariah was halfway out the door before he had his hand on his door handle.

"I'll get the bags. You go on in," Alazar said with a smile, trying to smooth the rasp in his voice. Ariah nodded once and headed away from the car, shoulders hunched, one hand punched deep into her jacket pocket. He watched her, a storm of confusion, questions, and lust whipping around inside him. "I wish you'd tell me what's going on," he said too softly for her to hear.

With a disheartening sigh backed up by determination to learn the truth, Alazar began unloading Ariah's purchases.

Tonight. He'd learn the truth tonight, whether it be from Ariah or Mark.

One way or another, he was not going to let his Ace slip through his fingers.

CHAPTER 10

"Are you positive you don't want to stay for dinner? Miriam went out with some of her friends tonight, so it's only Ariah and me. I ordered take-out. You won't be subjected to my terrible cooking."

Alazar tried to laugh at Mark's joke, but couldn't find the humor inside him to muster even a chuckle. Standing in the grand foyer with its elegant crystal chandelier, beautiful marble mosaic floors, and massive half-circle staircase—complete with an impressive dark wood banister carved into a miniature dragon at the end—should have elicited Alazar's love of all things grand.

Instead, he found his dragon reaching out for his lifemate.

Ariah stood somewhere nearby, most likely listening in on the conversation. The avoidance ate at him more than her silence, especially after the day they had together. She could hide her thoughts like a pro, but the darkness, the pain of her secrets lapped along his scales like foul water falling from storm clouds.

"I know my skills can't compare to yours."

Alazar forced a grin. "You haven't forgotten, huh? Still love cooking up a good meal at the house. I think I missed my calling as a chef."

"I think you'd burn the place down at some point or another."

"Possibly." He'd given Ariah more than five minutes to come out and join them. He hoped she would insist he stay for dinner. That hope waned, leaving him uncertain in his own clothes. "I need to speak with you, Mark. Privately."

Mark's smile faded and his shoulders straightened. Alazar held his Keeper's dark gaze, impressing on him the seriousness of the situation. Mark swallowed, released a long, controlled breath, and nodded.

"Of course." He spread his arm toward a set of double doors at the bottom of the stairs. "We can speak in here."

Alazar followed Mark into an opulent office, impressed by Mark's taste in décor of dark wood, dark area rugs, masculine leather furniture, and shelves packed with fabric-bound books and a few ancient leather-bound volumes Alazar recognized. An oversized dark cherry wood desk sat in front of the bookshelves, files and papers organized neatly in baskets.

Mark pulled the pocket doors closed.

"Don't lock it," Alazar said as Mark started to place the lock latch. He gave Alazar a quizzical glance. "Not necessary."

Mark nodded once and crossed the room, slipping his hands into the pockets of his tailored pants. "What do you want to discuss?"

Alazar circled the desk, admiring the different dragon statues scattered on the shelves. It had been a very long time since he last fought against the ugly essence of anger. He hated the way it churned in his gut, reaching its claws up into his chest.

"You have the dragonstone in safe keeping?"

"Of course. When I designed the bookcase, I had several secret compartments integrated into the shelving." Mark pointed to the far top corner shelf. Alazar crossed his arms over his chest and pressed his lips together. "It's designed around riddles, a proverbial treasure hunt. One must figure out where the next mechanism is in order to get closer to the compartment. It's secured in the wall behind shelves that will not move until they're unlocked."

"Engineering mastermind." Alazar turned away from the bookcase and pinned Mark with a hard look. "Tell me what happened to her."

Mark blinked once, then lowered his head. His fingers danced absently over his blotter. "Do you believe it is my place to disclose her secrets to you?"

"Are they secrets? Is it that bad?" Smoke curled out of his nostrils. He snorted, trying to get the scent out and succeeding in sending up a small gray plume. His dragon was rearing in light of his growing frustration. "She shut down, Mark. So, yes. I think I need to know what is going on. Or do you not know?"

"Would you like me to tell her about your past without your knowledge?" Mark retorted. He lifted his gaze to meet Alazar's. "Not the gambling past."

Alazar stiffened. "If it was coming between us, yes." He shook himself free of the icy tendrils creeping along his spine. "But my past is not and will not. And you know as much as I do that I did everything I could to save him."

Mark nodded. "But it left scars."

"Death always leaves scars. It leaves gouges that never heal." Alazar scowled, rounding the desk. He approached Mark, fire licking at the back of his throat. When he next spoke, the dragon's deep growl entwined with his own voice. "What happened to her?"

"Put your scales away, Alazar. I'm not the threat. I would never hurt my niece. She's practically a daughter to me."

"Then tell me what happened. She's my lifemate, and you kept her hidden from me all these years."

"We were all hidden from each other."

"She's a female!" Alazar smacked his hand on the desk. Mark's eyes widened. "She's in danger. She's *always* been in danger. If anyone found out what you are, what she *is*, her life would be sacrificed to keep our bloodlines from continuing." He spun away, pulling the reins taut on his riled dragon. "Why didn't you use the jewel before last night? Why didn't you tell me about Ariah?"

"I didn't have it."

Alazar twisted so fast he left a trail of smoke circling

around his head from the plume that erupted from his mouth. His vision pulsed, human sight melting into dragon sight. Mark straightened in the face of Alazar's dragon self.

"You *what*?"

"I didn't have it. I had a cabin in Upstate New York and it was robbed over ten years ago. It was one of the things that went missing. Mike and I tried to track it down together, but couldn't locate it."

Talk about trust. The bookcase was overcompensation for a prior failure. "You let my dragonstone get stolen over ten years ago and never told me?!"

Mark threw up his hands. "I didn't let it get anything, Alazar. *I* was robbed, and it was taken. I guarded that stone with my life. The one evening I went out to the store without it, my cabin was broken into and ransacked."

Every bad outcome of this news rushed through Alazar's mind. It must have shown on his face, because Mark grimaced. Alazar glanced down at his hand. His talons had extended, gouging the smooth wood surface of Mark's desk.

He left his talons right where they were. He'd probably gut the pretty leather chairs if he didn't. His anger flared.

"How does Ariah play into this? How does all of her pain and her scars play into the loss of the jewel? I need to know so I can protect her."

Mark's lips curled back, his face distorted by the orb-like projection of Alazar's dragon eyes. "I sure hope you plan on protecting her better than you protected my father."

The battle to keep her chin from quivering and her tears from spilling took a toll. Fatigue plagued her. Her mind was exhausted, her emotions depleted.

Something inside her chest ached the moment she stepped into her uncle's house. She escaped his concern with a flashed smile and a wave before running up the stairs to her room.

Her conscience haunted her. Her secrets thickened like black smoke, suffocating her the more she fought to be free. For the first time in the last ten years, she experienced the warmth of hope. That fine, flickering beacon of light in the distance that somehow attached itself to Alazar.

He was her greatest hope. He was her greatest fear.

He would either save her from this dark abyss or drown her in its deepest trench.

When she heard Alazar come into the house, she couldn't help but slip out of her room and walk softly to the end of the hallway before the landing leading to the stairs. She pressed her body to the wall and listened to the conversation between Alazar and her uncle. As they moved into her uncle's office, she crept down the stairs and stopped outside the closed doors. Guilt swelled, but curiosity drew her closer, tilting her head and angling her ear toward the crease between the two doors.

She listened, every muscle in her body tightening in apprehension as their conversation escalated from calm questioning to fury-fueled. She dared to open her mind, reaching for Alazar and her uncle, and received a flood of potent thoughts that left her sick. Alazar's voice had changed to something deep and growly. A faint scent of smoke touched her nostrils.

She could barely make out what her uncle said a second before her mind was pummeled by body-splitting agony and anger that exploded from—

"Alazar."

She threw open the doors and rushed into the office, heart threatening to pound through her sternum. Uncle Mark spun around, his hardened expression melting into one of shock.

Her attention turned to Alazar. Her good-natured dragon man had grown a few inches, thickened a few sizes, and cast black-tipped red scales along the bone structure of his face. His eyes were both frightening and magnificent. The amber took on a fluid fiery color with a slashing pupil straight down the center. Smoke plumed from his nostrils on each exhale.

Fearless of the creature, Ariah stepped up to him, placed both palms flat on his chest, and stared up into his eyes. "Don't hurt him. Please."

"He won't hurt me. He's pissed, is all," her uncle groused. Ariah didn't take her eyes off Alazar when he added, "He puffs up when we discuss certain things."

"You were never one to aim below the belt, Mark. I'm surprised by your less than honorable jab." Alazar closed his eyes. Ariah watched in absolute awe as the man she spent her afternoon with regained control. The scales faded away and he shrank back down to size, although he was still an intimidating head taller than Ariah. When he opened his eyes again, his pupils had returned to normal, but the fire remained. He sucked in a deep breath and let it out, smokeless, before looking over her head at her uncle. "That was unnecessary and you know it. How much guilt rides on your shoulders?"

"Too much."

"He doesn't know everything about my past, Alazar. He only knows what I've chosen to tell him," Ariah said. Her fingers curled around the lapels of his jacket. She hadn't realized how powerful the darkness inside her had become in only a few minutes until Alazar tentatively covered her hands with his and infused familiar heat into her blood. She looked over her shoulder at her uncle. "You have nothing to feel guilty over. Nothing, Uncle Mark. It was my father's choice, and ultimately mine. I could've left him and gone to college. I could've left him to deal with his problems on his own and my life would have been different."

Mark frowned. "No, honey. You couldn't have. That's not the way your heart works."

Ariah ran her tongue along her dry lips. As much as she wished her uncle to be wrong, he knew her too well. She loved her father and abandoning him was not in her genetic makeup. She'd sacrificed everything to care for him.

"Where's Miriam?" Ariah asked abruptly, forcing the wretched name from her lips without a vile tone.

"I'm not expecting her home for another couple hours." Her uncle rubbed the back of his neck, returning to the office doors and pulling them closed again.

Ariah turned back to Alazar. The dragon had disappeared, leaving a concerned, handsome man in its stead. "I was scared. I'm sorry. I'm sorry for pushing you away, but I was...scared."

"Why?" Alazar's brow creased. He lifted a hand and cupped the side of her face, his thumb stroking along her cheekbone. She absorbed his warmth, his strength. "Was it something I did?"

"No. You did nothing, I promise you." She sighed, her shoulders dropping. "I'm not used to the luxuries you showed me today. That's all."

Her uncle grunted, earning Alazar's sharp attention.

"You have something you'd like to add?" Alazar asked the man, but Ariah shook her head.

"He has nothing."

Unfortunately, Uncle Mark must have made some indication that he did. Alazar's dark brow arched. When she glanced back at her uncle, he was rubbing his beard in his signature conflicted manner. His dark gaze turned to Ariah, then back to Alazar. He crossed his arms over his chest.

A ripple of tension skated down Alazar's fingers, the smooth motion of his thumb on her cheek jerking momentarily. She could have sworn the hot surface of scales brushed her cheek, but in a breath, his skin was all that pressed against her.

Alazar broke his gaze from her uncle and focused on her. "Will *you* tell me what happened?"

Ariah tried to form a reassuring grin, but knew it fell short of anything substantial. Staring into the flames licking in Alazar's eyes, realizing the fierce dragon reflected behind his irises was for her and only her, coaxed her into a place of comfort. Still, she couldn't find the words to put to her lips. The strength to face her shame continued to slip through her fingers.

"It's been hard the last few years. I've worked a lot and had to take care of my father. So, today was a gift I wasn't expecting and it kinda caught me off-guard. There's really nothing to tell."

Alazar stared at her for an excruciating minute. In that minute, she swore he was picking and peeling at pieces of her mind, trying to find out the truth in her hollow assurance.

"Okay." The corner of his mouth twitched. "Okay." He placed a kiss on her forehead. The soft breath that escaped his nostrils was hot against her skin, almost scorching. "I should be going. You had a long day and need to rest."

"You certain you don't want to stay for dinner?" Ariah asked.

Alazar's thumb strummed her lips before he dropped his hand. The loss she felt as he stepped back was unbearable. She lowered her hands to her sides, unable to wrap her head around the powerful connection thrumming between them. Dragons, lifemates, magical dragonstones. It was real, she believed that now, but she never expected the pull to this handsome dragon man to be so...so overwhelming.

"I know you'll be safe with Mark for the night." The cutting side-glance toward her uncle made her believe he had doubts about that. Her uncle puffed out his chest as though offended. The unspoken battle of wills continued. "May I come by tomorrow to bring you back to town?"

Ariah silently begged him to stay with her longer, but she managed a nod. "Sure. I'd like that."

Alazar brushed a knuckle over her cheek and headed toward the office doors.

"I'll walk you out," her uncle said.

"I think I can find my way."

Uncle Mark followed Alazar from the office, pulling the doors closed behind them. Ariah moved to the doors and cracked one open to watch the two men in their awkward walk to the front door.

"Al, I didn't mean what I said earlier. I know you did everything you could."

"Hey, it's all good. Nothing I can't handle." Alazar chuckled and clapped her uncle's shoulder. "I've got tough skin, remember?"

Ariah chewed her lower lip as a faint pulse of

shuttered pain caressed her mind on a far softer scale than it had before she burst into the office. Whatever her uncle said to ignite Alazar's mental agony was somehow linked to his apology. Something that involved Alazar.

What happened?

Hadn't that been the question Alazar asked of her minutes ago? And she froze. The words, the explanations, everything froze somewhere in her throat.

Ariah moved away from the door, leaving the two men to exchange their quiet words. A short time later, her uncle returned to the office.

Uncle Mark observed her in his closed, quiet manner for a long moment. "I think you need to fill me in on a few things over dinner."

Ariah nodded, lowering her head as she knotted her fingers at her belly. Her uncle crossed the room, took her by the shoulders, and pulled her into a bear hug. His tenderness and protectiveness threatened to bring her to tears, but she stubbornly fought them off.

"You need to get this out of you, honey. Start with me. Trust me. At some point, you'll find it in your heart to trust him, too."

Trust. The very element of a relationship. The key factor in a family unit.

She had trusted her father. It earned her a gun to her head with only a cryptic explanation.

Could she trust the man who destroyed her father's soul?

And Alazar. A near stranger who she felt she knew better than her own father and uncle.

Could she give her trust to a man, a dragon, who had his own dark secret?

Guess it's time to find out.

CHAPTER 11

"Looks like you're *really* off your game, my friend."

Alazar glanced up from the spread of pool balls over the green felt table. Bridget Merrow, werewolf and owner of Howler's Bar and Grill, held out a tumbler filled with his usual bourbon on the rocks.

Damn, did he need the drink right about now. After leaving Mark's house—*Walking away from Ariah without any more understanding about her shadows than when I first met her*—he all but stewed in the smoky residue from his confusion. Mark knew more than he let on. Ariah had lied to him. He felt the shift of evasion in the air, caught the slight downward glance as she spoke. That invisible connection between them resonated with a lie.

He didn't understand it. They were lifemates. Twenty-first century or not, a match was a match. Didn't Kaylae learn to trust Zar in a day?

What luck. He sucked at gambling. Why not relationships, too? Weren't they a gamble?

"Hey, Al. You're drifting. Very unlike you. Wanna talk?"

Bridget hitched her hip on the edge of the pool table and crossed her arms over her chest. Her wild auburn hair brushed her golden eyes. She was in jeans and a tank top with the bar's logo printed on the front, a dish rag tucked in the side of her waist apron.

Alazar accepted the drink and straightened up from his next shot. He'd missed the pocket anyhow. He missed the pockets more than half the time, hence the losses Zareh usually saved his sorry butt from. There was a time he and Zareh could throw down a suspenseful challenge.

Once upon a time, long, long ago...

He swirled the drink, ice clinking the sides of the glass, and took a sip. The alcohol didn't burn his throat as it might a human's. Then again, he breathed fire. Last he checked, flames were more damaging than liquor.

"I'm always off my game." Alazar propped the pool stick against the floor and leaned on it like a crutch. Bridget's brows rode up her forehead, her lips quirking. "Ah, screw it. I have no game. I suck at pool."

"And darts."

"Yeah, that, too." Another sip. "And chess."

"You play chess?" She gave his shoulder a playful punch. "I can't see you playing chess."

"I play for entertainment purposes." Alazar saluted his glass toward her. "The entertainment of others at my expense."

Bridget laughed. Alazar found it in him to smile behind the rim of his glass.

"You're a great guy. You're going to make one lucky lady very happy one day." Bridget pressed up to her feet and shook a finger at him. "Like, belly-aching-from-laughing happy."

Alazar gave a dramatic bow at the waist. "I aim to please."

Bridget clapped his shoulder. "Don't we all?" She flicked the glass in his hand. "That's on the house. Maybe it'll help loosen up your shoulders so you can pocket some balls."

Alazar glanced at the table. He'd started his solo game twenty minutes ago and only succeeded in pocketing two balls. His thoughts were so skewed he couldn't focus on the pockets. Certainly one of his worst nights.

"Thanks for the drink."

"Let me know if there's anything else you need."

Alazar put his glass on the edge of the table and set up his next shot. He aimed for the corner pocket, a straight, simple shot, drew back, and hit the cue ball.

The seven deflected off the corner of the pocket. Alazar scowled. He was a dragon. Precision was ingrained in his DNA. He should be able to pocket an entire rack with his eyes closed. The harder he tried, the more he missed. The more he concentrated, the more he messed up.

"Just like with Ariah," he muttered, lifting the glass to his lips for another sip. "Just like Micah."

Coming to Howler's probably wasn't his smartest move. Not in this frame of mind. Taking to the sky to release his tension might've been better. There was nothing like spreading his wings and letting the rush of air over his scales take away the vile memories of his lethal failure.

Precision.

When one of the Firestorm's key characteristics failed him most.

Another sip, another missed shot, another scowl.

Fifteen minutes later, he managed to pocket one ball and finish his bourbon. He drank the liquor for the taste and nothing else. It would take a case of high-proof liquor to give him any inkling of a buzz. Firestorm dragons didn't get drunk. The alcohol metabolized before it had a chance to settle in the stomach. The fire in his gut often burned off the rest of the alcohol lucky enough to make it that far.

After another several missed shots and turning down a human's offer of betting a hundred bucks on a game—if he lost to a *human*, he'd need that case of high-proof liquor—a server came over with a fresh glass of bourbon and a basket of fries.

Alazar flashed Bridget a smile and a short wave of thanks. He came to Howler's way too much. He didn't even need to order his usual before it arrived.

He popped a fry into his mouth and lined up for another miserable shot. One ball bounced into the pocket by sheer luck. He watched, brows drawing together, as the second ball slowed at the edge of another pocket, teetered, and tipped into the pocket.

"You've got to be kidding me."

He set up for another shot. He hit the cue, splitting two balls. Both sank into pockets.

"What the heck?"

"Wow, you *are* pretty good."

Alazar spun around. The pool stick slipped as his fingers slackened, and he fumbled to keep it from crashing to the ground.

Ariah rubbed her index finger nervously against her lower lip in an absolutely adorable way he could easily become enthralled by. The motion brought his attention straight to her mouth, and reminded him how soft those lips were and how he had yet to fully kiss her.

"You caught me on a lucky shot." His dismal mood soared until a bout of skepticism wedged its ugliness into his head. "What are you doing here?"

"I, um…"

Her cheeks flushed and her eyes glowed. She looked so beautiful. The soft scent of flowers struck him, as did the shimmer of her hair, still damp from a shower. The pretty waves caressed her cheeks, her bangs swept to the side. She had changed into a pair of dark jeans that hugged her legs, and one of her new sweaters that teased him with a peek of her shoulder. No knit hat. No overly baggy clothes.

The corner of his lip curled.

You're starting to feel comfortable with me.

Ariah dropped her arms to her sides, hooking her thumbs on the pockets of her jeans, and tapped the toe of her boot against the floor. Man, what he wouldn't do to wrap her in his arms and kiss her crazy.

Crazy. Just like the idea.

"I went over to your house and your neighbor told me I could probably find you here. The really pretty blond with strange"—Ariah's eyes narrowed and made a single pointed gesture to her ear—"you know."

"Ahh, Willa." He chuckled. "Yeah, you saw right. Told you to believe me earlier."

Ariah tilted her head, a wavy lock falling over her eye. "That glitter? Yeah, not buying it."

"I told you it was a marketing strategy. Nocturne Falls is a paranormal town with paranormal creatures who hide behind the perception that they are playing a part in the town's overall Halloween theme. In essence, they're real paranormals pretending to be human pretending to be paranormal."

"Yeah? Any paranormals here now?"

"I think you're looking at one."

Ariah's glossed lips lifted and a spark lit her eyes. Her pupils dilated. "I think I see a handsome guy playing pool by himself."

"Not too bad of a guess." He tapped the pool stick against the table. "Can I interest a breathtaking young lady in joining me in a game?"

Ariah snickered. She grabbed a pool stick from the wall-mounted rack, rolled it over the table to check the stick's condition, and chalked the tip. She handed him his glass of bourbon with a pointed look. "How many in are you?"

"This is number two, and it doesn't affect me the way it affects others."

"Hm." She gave a nod to the table. "I warned you earlier, it's been a while since I've played."

"Let's see what you still have then."

Alazar put his drink on a high-top table and leaned against the pool table, unable to take his eyes off Ariah as she checked out her options. He drank in every small detail of his Ace, from the way her brow creased as she thought to the way she chewed her lip. He wondered if she took into consideration her drooping neckline as she leaned over the table and positioned the stick on her fingers in preparation for a shot. Despite the camisole she wore under the soft gray material, he caught the frailty of her sternum. It reignited his determination to find out about her past.

Ariah took her shot. The cue ball cracked into a side-by-side pair, splitting the balls apart. One ball fell into a pocket. The second bounced off the rail.

"Reactivating luck?" Alazar asked. Ariah laughed. "Well, you're not a beginner."

"No. I used to play when I would pick my father up from bars because he was too drunk to drive." She came around the table, her eyes moving between the cue ball and possible shots. Alazar straightened up as she approached him and gave his hip a tap. "Excuse me, sir. You're blocking a perfect shot."

Alazar crossed one booted foot over the other, and wrapped both hands around his pool stick. "Perhaps I should stay here."

"I have another option, just a little trickier."

"How often did you play?"

Ariah sized him up before she brushed around him, her arm sliding against his side. He followed her with his gaze, willing to take the bait in this unspoken flirting session.

"Too often." She leaned over the table, set up for her shot, and hit the cue true. Two balls fell into pockets. Alazar blinked. "Unfortunately."

Despite the sensual smile she slid him, he couldn't miss the sadness in those three words. "Where is your father now?"

She took her eyes off the table long enough to impale him with a lingering look of despair before going back to the game.

"Jail."

He lost his smile and cleared a sudden lump from his throat. That certainly wasn't the answer he was expecting.

"Would you like to fill me in?"

"Not here. It's still pretty fresh in my head." She took her shot. The ball missed. She sighed and straightened up. Alazar was impressed by her strength to keep her smile, but the light in her eyes had dimmed. "Your turn, hotshot."

Alazar laughed and rounded the table. She watched him closely, her attention heating up his skin as he closed in on her.

"Ace, you're on fire. Not me." He tapped the top of his stick against hers. "So, seems what goes around comes around. I see a perfect shot, but I would need to ask you to move to take it."

Ariah lifted a brow and mimicked his stance from a few minutes before. "And I think I'll stay where I am."

"Very well." Alazar gauged the line-up between the cue, the ball, and the pocket.

Then he set up for the shot with Ariah's slender body tucked between his arms, his head pressed to the side of her belly, and his leg braced behind hers.

"Alazar!"

Her laughter was contagious. He took the shot.

To his utter shock, the ball rolled into the pocket.

"Holy cow. You actually made it."

Alazar stretched up on his feet, trapping her against the edge of the table. Ariah's chest rose and fell on short breaths, hunger conquering humor in her eyes.

She licked her lips before they parted.

He nearly came undone. "My Ace."

"I'm sorry to interrupt." Alazar swallowed down a growl as he glanced over at the server. "Bridget asked me to get a drink order for your friend."

Ariah dipped her head as her cheeks turned pink, rolled away from the table and out of his arms. Alazar chuckled and tossed a glance toward the bar. Sure enough, Bridget made a blatant look at Ariah before turning her gaze back to him and lifting her hands in a "well?" motion.

"Poor manners on my part. Ariah, what would you like?"

"I'm good." Ariah placed her pool stick in the rack, drawing his curiosity. She turned back to him and shrugged. "I really don't drink much."

"Let Bridget know I'll be cashing out my tab in a moment."

The server nodded and moved to another pool table. Alazar motioned to the rack. "Throwing in the towel?"

"I think that last shot showed me what I'm up against. I don't stand a chance."

Once again, he sensed her fighting the urge to shut down. Only this time, he refused to allow it. Not when she'd obviously come looking for him.

Alazar hung up his stick and started racking the balls so they'd be ready for the next players. "How about we go for a walk?"

He was briefly surprised when she came up beside him to help place the balls in the rack. He looked at her, caught her shy glance, and grinned.

"I'd really like that, Alazar."

CHAPTER 12

At ten o'clock, foot traffic along the main portion of Nocturne Falls was almost as busy as it was during the day. Numerous street performers and live acts were in progress, drawing astonished crowds of onlookers. Even though it was a Thursday night, music pulsed in the air from a nearby club and other bars. What Alazar called "fairy lights" twinkled up and down Main Street's storefronts, enhancing the magical appearance of the town. Vampires dressed their parts and engaged groups of tourists with dramatic tales and flashes of fangs—fangs that were the real deal, Alazar assured her. A magician created a bouquet of flowers from a puff of purple smoke.

The night was wild, the air filled with vibrant energy that sank into her soul with that elusive promise of happiness.

Ariah tugged the supple leather jacket tighter around her body to ward off the chill of the late September night. Georgia or not, fall nights could lend a surprising bite, foresight she had lacked when she left her uncle's house in a dash to find Alazar.

She had barely shivered when he peeled his jacket off and draped it around her shoulders without question or comment. His scent surrounded her, warmed her twice as much as the leather, and settled her nerves.

Maybe the man walking close beside her helped, too. As laid back and funny as Alazar appeared, there was definitely something dangerous and beastly about him. His height was eye-catching and comforting to her smaller five-five stature. He was muscular beneath the simple black T-shirt. The fabric stretched over his chest and appeared to melt into his biceps. The angles of his face were fierce, but his ever-lasting smile and laughter, along with the soft glow of his eyes, smoothed every razor-sharp edge. His hair, now completely pulled back in one of those strange trendy man buns, fit him perfectly. She had to bite back her request for him to let it down.

Three times.

A gold chain glinted above the collar of his shirt. His watch looked like one of those crazy expensive gold timepieces she'd expect to see her uncle wearing. She didn't doubt the price tag of Alazar's was anything less than astronomical.

Alazar cut her a glance with a knowing smile. "You're staring at me."

Her cheeks burned and she laughed.

"Busted," she said, knocking him in the arm with her elbow. "Like you don't stare."

"I have. You just haven't noticed."

She noticed, all right. Every time his attention focused on her, she wanted to melt. Her heart would start racing and breathing became a chore. A flutter teased the base of her throat. Her skin tingled. Her legs, not just her knees, turned to mush reinforced by toothpicks. Alazar's effect on her was profound, to say the least.

"Or, have you?"

Ariah tsked. "I think I'll let you simmer in your own ideas about that."

"Darling, I've been simmering. Boiled dragon isn't a delicacy, I assure you."

She laughed. "You have a way about you that can make people feel so comfortable."

"Except for the one who matters."

Alazar sidestepped a group of teenagers dressed up like skeletons. Ariah didn't miss the way he cocooned her without encapsulating her in his arms. She wouldn't have minded his embrace.

"I am comfortable. It's just…hard to face certain things."

"What is it you fear, Ace? How you'll sound? How I'll react? How you'll react when you hear yourself say out loud whatever it is you have to tell?"

D. All of the above.

Her biggest fear, though, was having this new spark of hope snuffed out. She still pinched herself every now and again to make sure she wasn't dreaming.

"My uncle. He hasn't told you much, has he?"

"The first time I've seen Mark in thirty years was earlier at Hallowed Bean. He wouldn't tell me anything in his office. Maybe because he couldn't. Ultimately, it's up to you whether or not you want to share your past with me."

She looked up at him. "Will you share yours?"

A shadow crossed his face. For a moment, she wasn't sure if it was from the lighting of the streetlamps until she caught the very tip of scales along his chin disappearing. Their presences was ghost-like, leaving her to wonder how much of Alazar was the dragon and vice-versa.

Who controlled whom?

"I control the dragon. Not the other way around. That's asking for an increase in unexplained fires." He slowed down and brushed aside her bangs. "And yes. I'll share my past with you."

Ariah caught his hand as he lowered it to his side, folding her fingers between his. "Thank you."

He raised their hands to his lips and kissed her knuckles. "Anything you need."

"You mean that."

"I can be serious when I need to be."

She didn't doubt that for a moment. She wondered how others perceived this magnificent man walking beside her if he had to make such a statement.

"You know, we were under the impression that your father was killed at The Hollow."

Ariah inched closer and placed her head on his arm. "Is that the magical land my uncle used to tell me about?"

"Possibly."

"Was it destroyed?"

Ariah listened to the somber sigh that left his lips. "No. Not the way you think. The heart and soul, the essence of the land has been stained by death and deception. The world itself is a living entity. It has recovered and is more beautiful than ever."

Ariah dug out the memories of her uncle telling her about a mystical world that existed beyond human reach. He had described certain aspects in such stunning detail that Ariah could picture herself standing riverside, listening to the birds sing and the rocks sluice the water falling from the cliffs. She could smell the fragrances of rose and jasmine, or a hybrid of the two, and see silky white petals fall from tree branches like summer snow. The grass was emerald green and fields swayed with wildflowers of every color imaginable. Mountain peaks rose up from valleys, draped in ivy and blooming vines.

"He told me stories." She cleared the husk from her throat. "Mark."

"From the projection you gave me, seems he did a pretty good job."

Ariah turned her eyes up to find Alazar staring down at her. "Really?"

Alazar stroked her cheek and nodded. "Yes."

His sincerity drew her in by the heartstrings, fanning those sparks of hope to life. If she wasn't careful, it would become a blaze in no time.

She couldn't afford to let that happen. Not right now.

"So, you thought my father was dead."

"We had no indication that he survived the attack on the home he shared with your uncle. The Baroqueth launched a surprise attack on The Hollow in the middle of the night. Keepers tried to herd families to safety while we fought the sorcerers from the sky. It was a nightmare in the most literal sense of the word. We watched our brother dragons fall from the sky after being struck by deathblows of Baroqueth magic. The slayers went through the villages, melting homes with dark magic. The remaining dragons fought to get the survivors out of the Hollow. Dragons and Keepers were separated if one, the other, or both weren't killed. Cade, our leader, proposed the separation of dragons and their Keepers in this world and we all went into deep hiding."

"Oh my. How horrible."

Her heart tore from the short glimpse of memories he projected to her. Fire. Apocalyptic fire everywhere. Sheer, unimaginable horror and destruction.

"Wasn't my first battle. Most likely won't be the last. It's that universal balance thing. Everything needs balance, although I haven't figured out what kind of sick entity thinks annihilating an entire species is 'keeping the balance.'" He shrugged one shoulder, disrupting the comfort of her head against his arm. "But the discovery of female Keepers and lifemates is definitely a balancing technique I'm all for."

"And why is that?" she teased.

"Oh, I know a few reasons off the bat."

"Care to share?"

"For one, it's nice to know someone can understand you, accept you, and allow you to be true to yourself. Devotion for lifemates can't be broken down. It's something that blossoms intensely in a short period of time. A whisper deep inside your soul connecting with another. It's a sense of security. An element even the strongest of us need."

When Ariah finally looked around them to see where they were, she smiled. The lush grounds of the park were not nearly as crowded as they were earlier, with only a few small groups of walkers taking a late-night stroll. A few had gathered at the fountain to talk to the stone gargoyle, waiting for the statue to actually speak.

"Ah, looks like Nick's on duty tonight."

"Who?" Ariah glanced around before she followed Alazar's gaze to the fountain.

"Nick. Our neighbor. The gargoyle you thought I was joking about."

"You're telling me that huge stone statue is actually a real gargoyle?"

Alazar led her to a park bench close to the fountain and motioned for her to sit. She accepted the invitation, as well as the strength in the man who sat beside her. Close beside her.

"I've been telling you that all day. I'll introduce you to him later when there aren't humans around. He enjoys surveillance. Not much of an interacting kind of fellow."

"Guess the idea gargoyles are real shouldn't be too hard to accept, considering what I've seen in you."

Alazar stretched an arm across the back of the bench behind her, and rested his ankle on his opposite knee. "You still have the dragon in whole to see."

The prospect excited her. "I'm sure I will."

"Oh, Ace. You will." He cast her a side-glance. "Tell me why your eyes are haunted."

It was coming. She knew it was only a matter of time before she couldn't steer the conversation away from the very reason she came out again tonight. She was a mess. A hot, rattled mess.

"Perhaps I am haunted. Feels like my closet is full of skeletons."

"Ariah, we all have skeletons. A skeleton is what provides support to each of us." Alazar's expression was serious and thoughtful. Ariah opened her mouth with a comeback, but he continued. "Without skeletons, we'd be flaccid blobs of skin and tissue. No matter how deep you try and hide it, remember it is part of who you are. Your experiences, your triumphs, and your failures. From those secrets you lock up to the experiences you share to help others. Every part of your skeleton, however dark, however haunting, is the seed to something beautiful, if you nurture it."

Ariah stared at this philosophical Alazar in awe. The depth of his argument was both breathtaking and raw.

He had a valid point. The skeletons she tried to hide were the very essence of the person she was. Hard as it was, almost impossible at times, she fought through and made it out, stronger than before.

Ariah drew a leg up beneath her and contemplated whether or not to lean against Alazar. His arm came around her shoulders and pulled her close a moment later.

Decision made.

"Remember that perfection does not exist. Even in the most perfect of creatures, there are imperfections you don't see." Alazar pressed a kiss to the top of her head. She was beginning to regret getting spooked earlier before she had the chance to finally experience his kiss. She only hoped she hadn't screwed that chance up for a future attempt. "So, the stage is yours, my darling Ariah."

"You can steal it back from me."

"No. I can't. You came out tonight for a reason."

"I did." She resigned herself to whatever outcome their talk produced. Sooner or later, she'd have to tell him because a relationship of any kind could not survive on secrets and lies. "I guess I'll start when things got bad. Before that, I spent summers with Uncle Mark while my father worked overtime.

"My mom passed away when I was a baby. I don't remember her and my father never gave me details surrounding her death. Uncle Mark was a second father to me. He paid for my activities at school, my dance lessons, anything that helped me excel and become the best I could be. He taught me how to control the outside thoughts and tune them out while protecting my own thoughts from those who might try to pry into my head. He gave me history on your home and the dragons. I believed him. I believed in everything against logic because he made everything so *real*."

She smiled sadly as she thought of the simpler days when she only had school and her clubs and activities to worry about.

"You lost your belief."

Ariah sighed. "How could I hold onto something that was obviously nothing more than a fairytale? I knew how absurd the very notion of dragons and other worlds was before I turned eight, but I couldn't let myself lose belief until reality set in."

"How old were you when this new 'reality' came about?"

"Seventeen. I was in my senior year of high school. I had a goal to graduate valedictorian. I had offers to universities, mostly Ivy League schools. I had my entire life ahead of me. A bright, promising life."

For a split second, she allowed her mind to wander to the "what ifs." What if Miriam had never come into her father's life? What if she accepted one of the offers to a top university and left home? What if?

"What, or who, was the trigger for this new reality?"

"My father had been dating a woman for a few months, but it got serious fast. She was a self-proclaimed witch. My father met her at some silly party for one of his coworkers where they brought in a bunch of fortunetellers and such. I was at Uncle

Mark's, so when I returned home after the summer break to start my junior year, my father introduced me to Miriam."

Alazar twisted, his eyes piercing through her. "Miriam. Mark's Miriam?"

Ariah scowled. "The one and only. Courtesy of my father." Her stomach churned at the memory. "She accompanied us to Uncle Mark's the summer before my senior year. I have no idea what happened, but by the end of the weekend, my father and my uncle both had chips on their shoulders and Miriam was walking around like a preening swan."

"She's a witch."

Ariah snorted. "I already said that."

"No. She's *really* a witch. There's a magical vibe in Mark's house that is completely disconnected from dragons, Keepers, and lifemates. It's not a really nice vibe either, but since I haven't met the woman, I wasn't going to pass judgment on her."

"Judge away, Your Honor. She's pure evil."

"Apparently," he said with a touch of exaggeration. Ariah huffed, pulling her other leg up onto the bench. "So, Miriam came between your father and Mark."

"Pretty much. She destroyed my father. Destroyed him. She conned him, deceived him, you name it. He did everything for her. He bought her everything she wanted. If she commanded him to sit, stay, crawl, he did it in that order with his tongue hanging out of his mouth."

"Sure she hadn't cast a spell or a curse on him?"

"It never occurred to me, but I wouldn't put it by her."

"Sounds a bit suspicious. But why jump from your father to Mark?"

"Mark is loaded. He's got more money than he knows what to do with."

"Uh-huh. Truth."

Ariah shifted, pushing up higher against Alazar's side. "What do you know of his fortune?"

"I provided it."

She pushed off Alazar, catching his humored gaze. "You what?"

"Ace, Firestorms provide for their Keepers. Our fortunes can't be measured. Remember how old I am. I've been collecting for a few years." His half-grin dropped away. "I'm certain he shared a portion with your father."

"Well, if he did, my father wasted it away gambling, drinking, and paying back-owed debts after Miriam left him for my uncle. I was a teenager. I watched my father spiral out of control. He began binge drinking and spending weekends at local casinos. He was hospitalized for alcohol toxicity, detoxed, and went right back to it after discharge. Had a small stroke, detoxed again, went to rehab, went back to drinking, then tried to kill himself. Ended up in a psych ward for two months for counseling and detoxing. Medical bills were piling up. He had no insurance. The money he didn't throw away went to paying bills until we had nothing left.

"Halfway through my senior year, I was working two part-time jobs to keep us afloat while he moped around at home, most of the time mumbling to himself. I withdrew from my clubs, stopped dance classes because I didn't have the time and couldn't afford the activities. I tried to find out from my uncle what had happened, but his cell phone was disconnected and Miriam answered every time I called the house. After a month or so, I couldn't reach anyone on the landline."

"I think I'll be having a cozy heart-to-heart with my dear Keeper."

Alazar's anger startled her, the growling undertone of his voice resonating in her marrow. Fire licked at his eyes again.

"Don't, Alazar. It's past."

"I don't think it's as much in the past as you claim." His eyes narrowed. She lowered her gaze. "Or am I wrong?"

She pressed her lips together for a long moment, trying to sort out every ending to this debacle. She should've kept her mouth shut about Miriam, but the woman was the trigger to her father's self-destructive path that ultimately carved a new, less bright path for Ariah.

"Don't do anything that'll come between you and my uncle. My uncle hasn't changed since I was a little girl. I have to believe that he truly did, and does, love her. Uncle Mark had always been alone as far back as I can remember. I just wish it wasn't *her*. I didn't like her with my father, and I don't like her with my uncle. But,

Miriam hasn't changed him. He's stronger willed than my father."

"And you were stubborn to sacrifice your future to stay by his side."

"He's my father. My only surviving parent. Watching him destroy himself tore me apart. I pulled through the rest of the year at school. *Not* valedictorian. My grades slipped. My focus had turned from school to wondering what would be our next meal if I didn't work an extra hour or two. Child labor laws were tricky to skate around until I turned eighteen toward the end of the school year. As soon as I graduated, I picked up a full-time job at a diner because I couldn't get anything else.

"Shortly after that, our house went into foreclosure. My father hadn't paid the mortgage in months, and I was unaware of how dire our situation had become. We lost everything. For years, I worked two, three, sometimes four jobs, scrounging for each dime to make rent wherever we ended up. We were half a step above homeless. There were nights we slept in the car because I didn't make enough...money for another night in a...motel."

Her chin quivered uncontrollably and her eyes blurred with tears. A softball-sized knot swelled in her throat and refused to go down when she swallowed. She started to press her forehead to Alazar's chest in hopes of hiding from the devastation that was her life, but he caught her face in his hands and lifted her head, forcing her to look him in the eyes.

He brushed tears away with his thumbs. A quiet cuss spat from his lips. "Show me. Project into my mind. You don't have to speak. I'm here, Ariah. I will not let anything happen to you."

She did as he suggested, cutting through the cords that held the story of her sad, pathetic life and let the last ten years pour into Alazar's mind. Everything, from the derogatory treatment she received from customers to suffering excruciating hunger pangs and eating a meal tossed in a garbage can just so she could stand up straight without pain. Her frail body was due to the effects of months of surviving on scraps.

She couldn't slow the memory of the night before it hit Alazar. The memory of her father holding a gun to her head, threatening to kill her if people didn't do what he demanded. Her escape. Finding the box in her purse. Calling her uncle.

Arriving in the town next to Nocturne Falls, where her childhood hopes, dreams, and imagination sparked to life once more.

Alazar gathered her in his arms and pulled her into his body, holding her close as she sobbed quietly. He said nothing, but the turmoil he battled impressed her.

Several minutes rolled by before she gained enough control to wipe the tears from her face with the back of her sleeves and sit up.

"Ariah, look at me."

Ariah hesitated, wishing she hadn't lost control. She had made her choices and lived with the consequences. She didn't want pity. She didn't want coddling, although having a rock of a man to support her was definitely a nice change.

At last, she composed herself enough to meet Alazar's open and brutally honest gaze. He held her hands in her lap.

"You are incredible. Never believe anything less than that. You are strong and beautiful, a true fighter, an honest soul. You are everything I could have ever hoped and dreamed for a future Keeper. For a lifemate. You've learned valuable lessons during your hardships. Keep those close to your heart and never forget them, but from now on, you will never have to worry about anything. I hope you choose to accept me. Even if you don't, I will provide you with any monetary needs, protection, and safety. Your life will change. Has changed. A new start."

"Hope."

Alazar nodded. "All your hopes and dreams will become your reality, sweetheart. I promise you."

Ariah reached for a grin, but the faint quiver still attacking her chin wouldn't allow it to come. "Thank...you."

Alazar leaned down and kissed her forehead, then her cheek. "I will do anything for you, Ariah. Anything. Don't ever forget that."

CHAPTER 13

Alazar could sit like this for the next ten years, Ariah curled and tucked against his body, her voice softening as exhaustion finally settled in. As the night progressed, the moist chill bit deeper. He turned up his internal furnace and provided extra warmth for his Ace when his jacket couldn't do the job. Shortly after her heartbreaking crying jag, he made the decision to hold off on revealing his past, his skeleton, for another day. Although the burden on Ariah's shoulders had eased, he really didn't want to bring more devastation to their night.

Besides, the sweet gem under his arm had begun yawning consecutively, managing just a few words before another yawn battled past her lips. Those few words that did escape were slurred at best.

He glanced at his watch and blinked when he realized the time.

"I think the night's gotten away from us," he said during another one of her yawns. She curled tighter against him, slinking her arm around his waist. *Way to make this an easy parting, Ace.* "Ariah, sweetheart. You're falling asleep."

"Hmm?"

Why couldn't this be happening, say, on his living room sofa?

Alazar shifted, regretfully disturbing Ariah's balled-up form. She groaned and rubbed her hands over her face, mumbling something into her palms. Alazar shook his head.

"I don't think you need coffee. I think you need a bed." He caught Ariah's chin and lifted her rosy face, noticing her sleepy eyes. His dragon protested the very idea of letting her drive home. Even as he watched her, her eyelids drooped until she blinked several times, opened them again, only to have them slide lower and lower. "I can't let you drive home like this. You'll fall asleep at the wheel."

"I'm okay." She lifted a hand to her mouth and yawned. Her head grew heavy in his hold. "Once I...walk."

"Why don't you stay at my place? There's a spare room you can have for the night. I'll call Mark and let him know so he's not worried about you. We'll get your car in the morning and you can go home then." Alazar scooted to the edge of the bench and adjusted his hold on Ariah. "Unless, of course, you'd prefer to hang out with me."

The darling woman tried to laugh, but the sound that left her lips was anything but humorous and everything sexy. Alazar grunted, weaving an arm beneath Ariah's and hoisting her to her feet. He happened to glance toward the fountain, quiet and free of tourists at this late hour, and received a curious tilt of Nick's stone head. He simply flashed his friend a smile, focused on Ariah's jellied legs, and started moving them back toward Main Street. By the time they made it down the first block, Ariah had woken up enough to appear sober, which was a good thing when a police cruiser slowed down alongside them.

Sheriff Merrow rolled down the passenger window and leaned over the console. The werewolf jutted his chin toward Ariah. "Damsel?"

Ariah's sleepy switch shut off. She scowled. "Far from a damsel." When she picked her head off Alazar's chest and saw who she had snapped at, her eyes went wide. Alazar chuckled when Merrow's brows arched at her meekly added, "Sir."

"Yeah. She's anything but," Alazar concurred.

"Apparently." Sheriff Merrow settled back in his seat. "Things going good?"

"For the time being. You know how things can change at the flip of a coin." Alazar adjusted his arm around Ariah's waist when she swayed on her feet. Sheriff Merrow's eyes narrowed. "She's tired."

"Huh."

"I'm tired," Ariah said, and yawned the proof.

Sheriff Merrow chuckled. "I'll let you go. Take care."

As the cruiser pulled away, Alazar steered Ariah across the street. She tripped over the curb.

"They need to stop jumping out at people," she muttered.

"I can't imagine it jumped on purpose."

Ariah smiled. "I like you."

Alazar wasn't certain what to make of that. "Like" could go one of two ways. Like as in friend or like as in attracted.

He knew his idea of "like" went the way of the latter.

"I think I might like you a bit myself."

"Probably a good thing we like each other if we're spending time together, huh?"

"Definitely makes the time together more pleasurable."

Alazar cursed himself when Ariah tipped her face up to him. Her gaze lingered over his mouth for an excruciating moment before she lay her head back on his chest. Alazar rolled his eyes to the sky.

Hey, whoever up there thinks this is a joke, it's really not that funny.

He wasn't sure how much longer Ariah would have lasted on her own two feet. Arriving at his car couldn't have happened fast enough. He unlocked the doors and eased his half-sleeping woman into the passenger seat, buckled her in, and closed her door. The parking lot was empty except for stragglers and staff from the bar, and Ariah's beat-up car in the far corner.

He climbed behind the wheel, started the car, and headed to his house. He warred with the idea of driving her home, knowing it would have been the honorable thing to do. He couldn't bring himself to place her anywhere near Miriam. Not after hearing and feeling the extent of her hatred for the woman. Ariah had suffered enough over the last decade. Even if it was for a few hours, he wouldn't let her suffer in the same house as the witch.

By the time he pulled into the driveway, Ariah was slumped against the door, breathing steadily in sleep. The soft waves of her hair obscured her face from his sight, and his jacket drowned her smaller frame. His heart thumped with emotion.

Only a couple of months ago, he wondered if his lifemate was out in the world somewhere. Zareh discovering Kaylae had given Alazar hope that he, too, had a treasure that measured more than all the gold in his hoard. He once told Zareh he would give up his hoard for a lifemate.

His lifemate.

Sitting in his car, trusting him enough to protect her in this vulnerable state.

"I would give up *everything*," he murmured.

After a long moment of watching Ariah sleep, Alazar unfastened her belt before he rounded the car to her side and gathered her in his arms. The neighborhood was quiet, the only sounds coming from the chirping of crickets and the occasional howl of a werewolf on a run. The houses along Crossbones Drive sat in darkness, lit only by the street lamps with a muted yellow glow.

Alazar locked up his car and carried Ariah into the house, keeping quiet. His honed hearing picked up the deep breathing of sleep from Zareh's room—a surprise, since there was seldom a night that silence came from that direction. Maybe Ariah wouldn't be disturbed, if luck held out.

Alazar delivered Ariah to the guest room without so much as a stir from her. He had to lay her on one side of the full-sized bed in order to pull the covers down. He moved her over, shucked her boots off and rested them on the floor beside the bed, then pulled the blanket up to her chin.

Her eyelids fluttered open to slits. "Alazar."

He lowered himself to the edge of the bed and brushed her hair from her face. "Yes, Ace?"

"Thank you. For today. For tonight."

Alazar smiled and pressed a kiss to her cheek. Tipping his mouth to her ear, he whispered, "You're welcome, sweetheart. Get some rest."

Deep down, part of him hoped she'd ask him to stay. If she extended that invitation, he'd be helpless to reject it. As much as he wanted to have her in his arms, he knew she wasn't ready. Maybe tomorrow. Or the next day. But not today. Not tonight.

Only when he was assured she had fallen back asleep did he take his leave, moving stealthily to his room. This internal battle was wearing him to the bone. He wondered how the heck Zareh was able to leave Kaylae at that dead-and-breakfast the first night.

Alazar wasn't sure he'd be able to let Ariah go come morning.

For the first time in months, Ariah woke from a dreamless sleep feeling refreshed and renewed. No aches poked at her body. No dread settled in her chest. Despite the overcast sky that hid the sunlight from the world outside the window, her soul burst with light.

"Wow."

She stretched her arms over her head, arched her back off the soft mattress, and sighed with a smile. As her senses rose from slumber, the faint aroma of something delicious teased her nostrils, making her stomach grumble. Instead of hopping out of bed and following the scent trail, she remained tucked under the blanket, still ensconced in Alazar's leather jacket, and observed the guestroom. It was the size of her last motel room, but furnished far more palatably. The décor was simple, essential, with a couple of general pictures of forests and flowers. The gold-and-cream color scheme absorbed the little light from beyond the window.

It exuded warmth and comfort, a similar warmth and comfort to what she found curled up in Alazar's arms.

"Time to face the day."

Ariah climbed out of bed and checked the time on her cell phone, which was on the bedside table. Alazar must have taken it out of her jeans pocket.

"Holy crap." She flipped the phone open to double check she was seeing the time correctly. Yep. It was almost one in the afternoon. There were three text messages from her uncle, asking her to call when she woke up. "Crap."

She sent a quick text back, promising to call in the next ten minutes, that she had just woken up, and scrambled to find Alazar. When she pulled the bedroom door open, she dodged a fist to her head from the woman she'd seen with Zareh at the credit union.

About to knock on the door, the woman laughed in surprise. "Sorry about that. Alazar thought you were awake. I see that he was right." She held out her hand. "I'm Kaylae."

"Ariah," she said, shaking the woman's hand. "Um, I don't mean to be rude, but where's the bathroom?"

"Follow me." Kaylae led her down the hallway. "I ran out to the store this morning to pick up some things I thought you might want to hold you over."

"I, um, thanks."

Kaylae tossed her a friendly smile. "Whenever you're ready, join us in the kitchen." She pointed toward the archway a little farther down the hallway. "Right through there. You won't miss us. If you need anything, just call."

Ariah opened the bathroom door and saw a small plastic basket filled with toiletries sitting on a dark marble vanity. Her lips twitched, an overwhelming gratefulness swelling in her chest.

"I don't know your past, Ariah, but I can see it's

been hard on you," Kaylae said, sympathy clear in her voice. "Mine was hard, too, but I'm certain for different reasons. It will get better from now on, I promise you."

Kaylae folded her hands in front of her, the smile and the glow in her pretty blue eyes shredding any reservations Ariah may have held toward the stranger. It was her mind's automatic defense mechanism, but it failed with this woman. For a split moment, she felt like she was standing face-to-face with a sister she had never met. In that moment, she realized that even if Kaylae was a stranger, something powerful connected them.

They were both lifemates to dragons.

"Maybe we can commiserate," Kaylae suggested. "Share our stories. It'll be nice to have another woman around who understands."

Ariah nodded, her grin quivering. Okay, these overwhelming emotions were so *not* like her. With a deep breath, she said, "I'd like that." Hitching her thumb to the bathroom, she slipped through the door. "Thanks for the things."

Kaylae left. Ariah packed away the sudden flood of emotions and went through her morning routine without burning eyes or a shaky chin. She wished she had something else to wear, something that may have hidden a little more of her body. She wasn't sure what she was thinking when she chose the outfit last night.

"Yeah, you do," she whispered to the reflection in the mirror. The cautious smile on her lips did wonders to lighting up her eyes. The dark circles that had become a permanent feature beneath her eyes had faded. Even her cheeks had a healthy brush of color she hadn't seen in years. "I think he's good for you, Ari."

More than the reflection agreed with that. The heat that swirled to life in her belly and made her all weak and dreamy reminded her of the potent reaction she had to Alazar.

"He still has a secret," she reminded her glowing reflection. A secret she would ask about today. The relief she experienced after unloading her past to Alazar was indescribable. When she feared what he might think of her for the choices she made, he showed her the fear was sown in futile soil. "Thankfully."

Freshened up and ready to face what was left of the day, she followed Kaylae's directions to the kitchen, which wasn't hard to find at all.

Kaylae and Zareh, seated at the counter, laughed over something. Alazar leaned against the counter beside the stove, which had pans and pots sitting on live burners.

Ariah swallowed, hard. Could the guy tamp down the degree of gorgeousness a tad? Her poor body couldn't handle this.

Alazar's gaze shifted from the couple to her and his smile widened. He pushed off the counter and held out his hand. "Good afternoon, beautiful lady. Come here. We were just discussing adventures in house-building and new ways to torture Zareh."

Ariah rounded the island and accepted his hand.

She gasped when he tugged her close and graced her with a signature kiss on the top of her head. If one thing grew in the last twenty-four hours, it was definitely her appreciation toward this guy for being a gentleman. He hadn't tried to take advantage of her when she was at her most vulnerable. That alone made her heart flutter.

"I couldn't hold off breakfast. There was a hungry dragon threatening to burn the house down if I did. However, there is lunch," Alazar said, loosening his arm around her waist so she could peek at the pots and pans. To her, it all looked like a mess of ingredients scattered over the stove. "What would you like? Meatball hoagie? Pasta primavera? Chicken Milanese with salad?"

"Is there a lunch party you didn't tell me about?" Ariah asked. Zareh chuckled behind her. Alazar shrugged. "Geez, did you seriously make all of this?"

"Alazar loves cooking," Kaylae said. "He cooks up some mean cuisine from scratch. I still don't know how he does it."

"Please tell me none of you've eaten yet. That this isn't all just for me." Ariah looked at Kaylae, then Zareh, and finally landed on Alazar. Alazar tapped the tip of her nose. "Seriously."

"We were waiting on you for lunch. So? What will it be?"

A typical breakfast for her would have been stale toast or scraps from plates. If she was lucky, one of the cooks at the diner would slip her an egg or two. She wasn't certain she could handle a meal this size immediately after waking up.

"Hesitation means indecision, which means a little of everything." Alazar gave her hip a playful pat before she could argue, and maneuvered her to stand to the side. "Zar, mind giving me a hand? We can pamper the ladies."

"I pamper all the time, right, Doe?" Zareh said as he slid off the stool.

Ariah couldn't help but notice the affectionate glide of his hand over Kaylae's shoulders and the chaste kiss to her temple. A subtle yearning stretched inside her, wanting that same affection. Tenderness and adoration.

"You're whipped, buddy. You're going to reinvent the meaning of pampering and have every male on the planet hating you for it." Alazar laughed as he removed a sheet of chicken cutlets from the oven and placed it on hot pads.

"I'm not whipped. 'In love' is a nicer term."

"Call it what you will. You're whipped so tight you're blind." Alazar pointed to the fridge. "Grab the salad and the dressings. I'll need plates, too."

Kaylae motioned for Ariah to follow her to sit at the long table in the connected dining room. Ariah snickered as the two men continued their playful banter and left them to their devices. As she sat down across from Kaylae, she hitched her thumb toward the performance.

"Is this normal for them?"

Kaylae rolled her eyes. "Yep. They've been close

friends for centuries. The two are practically part of each other. Alazar is a perfect balance for Zar, who can be quite serious. Al has a gift for breaking down tension. I don't think I've ever seen the guy angry. It's not in his nature."

Ariah tipped her head and watched Alazar plate food, his smile never dimming. Yet she knew there was more hidden beneath the ease and laughter. She had seen his anger and felt his anguish.

He fit a meatball into a hoagie roll and whipped the prongs up, splashing sauce on Zareh's shirt. Zareh growled, smoke escaping one nostril.

"Come on, brother. What the heck?"

"You've got a dozen of the same shirt in the same color. I did you a favor." Alazar twisted, catching Ariah's gaze for a brief moment before cutting across to Kaylae. "I'll bribe you with more Vampire Bites if you'll do something about his wardrobe."

"First the bed, then your keys, now his wardrobe. I've gained five pounds since I moved in with you two. I think I need a Vampire Bite diet." Kaylae shook her head, her grin widening. "Ariah, have you tried the Vampire Bites from Hallowed Bean?"

Ariah shook her head. "I think he intended to introduce me, but it didn't happen."

"She's still a Bite virgin. I left them on the building ledge after we reenacted Snow White."

Ariah's cheeks warmed as Kaylae's attention intensified on her. "He showed me scales and I kinda went into shock mode. He pulled the chaste kiss stunt."

165

"Brought you back, didn't it?" She didn't hear him approach until he braced a hand on the back of her chair and slid a plate in front of her. As decadent as the food smelled, Alazar's scent captivated her more. "Enjoy, Ace." To Kaylae, he said, "What will it be, since your man abandoned your plate to change his shirt?"

"The chicken and salad."

"Coming right up."

Alazar tipped his head, brushing his gaze with Ariah's. The fierce pull latched onto something unseen and unknown low in her belly, reeling her into the liquid amber of his eyes. He drew his knuckles over her cheek before returning to the kitchen. Ariah looked at the huge plate of food he managed to arrange with restaurant-quality talent and couldn't find it in herself to take a bite. Her stomach and throat were tied up in knots.

Kaylae reached over to rest a hand over Ariah's. Concern etched the woman's face.

"Everything okay?" she asked quietly.

Ariah blinked and cleared her throat. When had her hands started trembling? The heat that filled her face had tripled from the faint whisper of warmth a few minutes ago.

And the delightful hum that traced along her muscles and her nerves...

"I, uh, I..." Ariah tried to clear her throat again. "Um, I'm sorry. I'll be right back."

Ariah hurried from the room, hoping the escape would give her reprieve from this incessant reaction.

She knew the only way to keep it at bay, and she wasn't willing to give that up. Give *him* up.

You don't even have him.

"Ariah."

She'd barely made it halfway down the hallway to the guestroom when Alazar's fingers caught her forearm in a gentle grip, staying her. She squeezed her eyes shut, willing away the redness from her cheeks, hoping whatever had transpired between them passed enough that she wouldn't look like a desperate fool when she faced him.

"Ariah, what is it?"

If his voice could sound any more soothing, it would lull her into a trance. He spoke softly, slowly, coaxing her to open up and be honest.

"I forgot my phone in the room."

And...you lie.

A sharp breath left her lips and she turned to face her hopes and fears all wrapped up in a perfect male package. He regarded her with a mixture of concern and skepticism.

"No. I didn't forget my phone. Well, I did, but that's not why I left." She was a wreck. Tugging her fingers through her hair, she groaned. "This. This is all too much. Too perfect. It's a fairytale, Alazar, and fairytales don't exist in real life."

"Neither do dragons," Alazar said, releasing her forearm to regard her through narrowed eyes. There was no threat or anger in his expression. Only thoughtfulness. "Which would mean neither do I."

"You do exist, obviously." She waved a hand up and down his form. "You're standing right here."

"Yes. And?"

Ariah struggled to make sense of her thoughts, her emotions, enough to put them into words. Her brow furrowed and she held Alazar's gaze to impress upon him the importance of her next statement. "I can't buy into this. It's not what would happen to me. Don't you see? My life is not a fairytale."

"You don't say."

She scowled. "You're mocking me."

"No," he said, drawing out his single-word answer, cutting down the defenses Ariah tried to enforce before she could get them erected. For a long moment, they stood in the hallway, simmering in a quiet hum that would not release her from its hold. His expression held no guard, no anger. She watched as something brewed in his head, something she couldn't sense, couldn't hear, and he wouldn't share. "But is running away from everything you *think* you don't deserve really the answer?"

Ariah opened her mouth. Silence answered his inquiry.

"Do you honestly believe you don't deserve to be happy?" He took a small step toward her. "That you don't deserve to be treated like a woman should be treated? Have you lost all hope for yourself and accepted the life you lived as the only possible reality there is?"

Ariah's fingers curled into her palms. "Damn you."

A short breath of a laugh fled his mouth. "I get that when I'm pretty spot on."

Ariah clenched her teeth and turned her head down.

"I know what you need."

"I'm not sure you do." She flexed her fingers and crossed her arms over her chest. Tight. "I'm not sure *I* do."

Alazar brushed by her and disappeared into the guestroom. A moment later, he came back with her boots and her phone. "Here. I'll pack up lunch." His brows lifted when she hesitated to take the items. "Trust me. I know *exactly* what you need."

CHAPTER 14

"Are you certain this is safe?"

Ariah moved a frustrated glance between her uncle and Alazar. An hour after Alazar insisted he knew what she needed, she found herself standing in the woods on the outskirts of Nocturne Falls. A light rain had started, plastering her hair to her head and face, and starting a chill that touched her bones.

So far, Mr. Know It All was way off his guess.

"Will someone please tell me what the heck is going on?" Ariah demanded. She eyed the strange leather contraption her uncle had draped over his arm. It resembled a saddle without the seat. Actually, it looked more like a harness with lots of loops.

Alazar turned his handsome face toward the sky. She hated herself for allowing the sight of rain streaming over his skin to melt her aggravation a bit. She was still raw from his brutal assumptions at the house and this super duper secret cure for her acceptance issues.

You're angry that he hit the nail on the head.

It had been a long, long time since someone was able to call her out the way he did. The last person to do so was a friend from her school days, and that was after years of knowing each other. Alazar's keen sense of knowing what was going on inside of her before she put the puzzle pieces together irked her.

"Perfect weather," Alazar said. He dropped his chin and his attention to her uncle. "Once we're above the cloud cover, it'll be smooth riding."

Ariah's eyes widened. "What did you say?"

"'It'll be smooth riding.'"

"Riding?" Oh, heck no. She wasn't riding anything anywhere in this rain. "Yeah, no. I'll take a rain check."

Alazar's lips curled as he strode several long paces away from them. "Ace, it's raining. I checked." He pointed to her uncle. "You remember how to put that on?"

"Pretty sure I do."

"You're going to have to protect her with your riding coat until I can have one made for her."

Uncle Mark tugged at the ankle-length leather coat covering his body. "It's large enough that I can encompass her in front of me."

Ariah threw up her hands. "Hey, wait! I'm standing right here. Will you please include me in this conversation? What are you talking about? What is this riding coat business? What is *that*?" She jabbed a finger toward the harness thing. "And what are you protecting me from?"

"Hold those thoughts."

Although the last twenty-four hours had proven to be the roller coaster ride of a lifetime, nothing could have prepared her for what she witnessed in the next minute.

A ghostly gray haze curled around Alazar, expanding and growing as the form of the man she knew stretched and thickened. Limbs grew from a torso that rounded and puffed out. Her jaw dropped and her eyes widened as the haze melted into glinting black tips that blended into burnt red and lightened to a dark red closest to the enormous body. Scales. Hauntingly beautiful scales. Wings budded from the widening body, enlarging until they flapped, sending a burst of air, rain, and leaves flying against Ariah and Uncle Mark.

Ariah threw up her arm, protecting her face from the debris. Her uncle stepped up beside her and pulled her into his arms, using his body as a shield until the *whoosh-whoosh-whoosh* of those wings flapping subsided.

When Uncle Mark stepped aside, Ariah reached for his arm, desperate for the support as her legs weakened.

"Oh...my..."

"I never lied to you, honey."

Alazar. In full dragon form.

All she could do was stare at the magnificent creature of myth and lore.

"Come back to me, Ace. Kissing you Snow White-style right now wouldn't be a good idea."

Ariah shuffled back a step when Alazar's large head came around to her on a long, thick neck that snaked over the ground.

"Easy, sweetheart."

He tilted his head slightly, watching her out of one giant eye, and held his head a few inches from her as she took in the broader details. Geez, just his dragonhead was almost twice as big as her entire body. His scales were smaller along his head, smoother, with only a hint of black along the tips. Those scales darkened around his eyes, highlighting the intense amber color and thick vertical pupil that dilated when her fingertips grazed his jaw above a spiny beard. A sound that resembled a stifled growl rolled through her ears and the scent of fire filled her nose.

Her heart thundered in her chest, the surreal experience leaving her lightheaded. She flattened her hand against his scales, absorbing the heat that poured off him, her skin sliding with ease over the hard, wet coat. Alazar's crest was both frightening and beautiful, black bony horns linked by hard webbing. Small spines enhanced the dangerous ridge over his eyes.

A faint sting touched her eyes. "Real."

"It's certainly not a dream."

He pressed his snout down, gently nudging her side before his massive form lowered to the ground. Uncle Mark moved to Alazar's side and tossed the harness over his back. Alazar partially extended a wing. Ariah stared, too enthralled by the ease with which her uncle maneuvered a boot onto the spike at the tip of the wing and hoisted himself onto Alazar's back.

Energy, alive and electric, thrummed in the air around them. It resonated along Ariah's skin and sang to her soul, the lost little girl she stowed away. Her uncle moved with fluid grace, born to move over a dragon as he fit the leather straps through the spines along Alazar's back.

"You have no idea the gift you're granting me, Ace. To see the magic sparkling in your eyes... I have a feeling not many have been lucky enough to see it."

Ariah peeled her attention away from her uncle and turned to the glowing orb level with her head. Alazar stretched his wing out, lifting the thin skin over her head to shield her from the rain.

Without hesitation, she stepped up to the dragon's head and pressed herself against the warm scales covering his face. She closed her eyes and smiled. "Thank you."

Ariah must have lost time against Alazar's cheek. When she opened her eyes, Uncle Mark was walking up to her, brushing his hands together. He reached out a hand for Ariah.

"Come with me. Al, be easy," Uncle Mark warned.

Alazar snorted, smoke pouring from his nostrils and from between his lips. Ariah caught what she thought was him rolling his eye before she accepted her uncle's hand and followed him to the fastened harness. He gave a strong tug on one of the leather loops that flanked one strap.

"Climb up. I'll be right behind you. I'll get us settled. Figuring the seat between the spines can be tricky."

"I can't believe this," she whispered. Finding her grip on two of the loops that served as rungs on a ladder, she locked one foot into the lowest loop and pulled herself up. The climb was slow as she traded out loops between hands and feet until she reached the line of spines and stopped.

As she lifted her head, a smile slowly claimed her mouth. She stood easily two stories above the ground. Far in the distance, through the trees, she caught a glimpse of a waterfall. The canopy of the trees seemed almost within reach, although they were still far from reachable.

"Pretty incredible, isn't it?" Uncle Mark asked.

"Such a poor choice of words, Uncle Mark. This is so much more than incredible." Ariah glanced down when her uncle patted one of the spines. "How does this work without being impaled?"

"You lean to the side of the ones in front of you. The one you will sit on will help give you leverage and help secure you to his body in flight."

"So, sit?"

"Yes."

Ariah slid her leg between two spines and waited for her uncle to settle behind her. He leaned forward and wrapped one hand around a grip in the top strap.

"These are your hand grips. This harness is tight, so it won't slide. Get a good hold, then fit your feet into the stirrups on the lower strap. I'm going to secure the belt around our waists."

Uncle Mark reached around her, grabbed a belt from the straps connecting the upper and lower harness together and fitting around the spines. He adjusted the size and pulled it around them as she fit her hands into the grips, followed by her feet in the stirrups.

"How's it going up there?"

Her uncle leaned over and shifted her to the left of the line of spines.

"Guess we'll see once we're airborn?"

"You feel like a natural."

"And why do I sense something not so innocent in that comment?"

A deep, rumbling growl was her response.

"Do not panic once we're in the air. You've Keeper blood in you and your body will adjust to the altitude and air quality. The connection you have with Alazar will protect you from some of the elements. You must be one with him and not allow your conscious mind to instill fear. This is who we are, Ari," Uncle Mark said, testing his grips. "I'll protect you until we have a coat made for you."

"All right, Ace. I've got the okay from Mark. Are you set?"

Ariah tried to ignore the frantic beat of her heart and the twist and turn of her stomach as excitement and anxiety battled for ground. She sucked in a breath and let it out slowly.

"I'm trusting you, Alazar. My life is on your back."

"I've got precious cargo."

Ariah couldn't get a scream out of her throat when Alazar launched himself from the ground like a missile, breaking through the forest canopy, spiraling up, up, up with powerful strokes of his wings. She squeezed her eyes closed and turned her face into her shoulder, the force of air rushing over her body near painful. Her uncle pressed tighter against her back, disrupting some of the force. The thickness of the rain-swollen clouds made it hard to breathe.

The first spark of panic lit in the back of her mind.

"Ariah, take a breath. You can breathe. You do not have the restraints a normal human would."

A flood of heat poured up through her belly and legs, a pulse of security from the dragon beneath her. She fought to stamp out that spark of panic and tried a breath.

Air filled her lungs without a hitch. A second breath proved just as easy as the first.

Then they broke through the cloud cover. Alazar's wings shot out, jolting their ascent and bringing them horizontal. Ariah grunted when she smacked back down onto Alazar's back.

She opened her eyes.

And gasped at the view of the world far below them through patches of clouds.

Alazar filled her with heat against the colder temperature at this altitude. Her uncle provided another barrier of protection as the air rushed over them. Alazar flapped his wings a few times, then went into a glide. She had no idea how fast they were going or where they were going.

All she knew was that she had found a new addiction to flying on the back of a dragon.

"Alazar! Stop!"

"Easy, Ace. Trust me."

Ariah fought beneath her uncle's iron hold and the insane kamikaze dragon she was attached to. "Uncle Mark!" She staved off a spring of tears as she watched the solid wall of mountains come up on them at an impossible speed. "Tell him to stop!"

"Ari, calm down!"

"No!" She released one of her hands from the grip. Uncle Mark snatched her wrist, casting them off balance as Alazar gained speed. "We're going to die!"

"Stop! Get your grip back and stop!"

"Ariah, I need the speed to break through the magic. Woman, chill."

"Chill? Chill?!"

She seethed beneath her panic. Her uncle managed to raise her hand to the grip against the force of the wind from their flight, securing them to the suicidal dragon.

"You're dead! You're dead if you don't kill me first!"

"I'm willing to make a bet that I won't be dead. You make me dessert if I win."

Ariah's entire body tensed as they came up to the jagged side of the mountain. She curled tight beneath her uncle, squeezed her eyes shut until her head hurt, and let out a high-pitched scream, expecting to be a bloody smear on the rocks at any moment.

Darkness surrounded her. A strange sensation of static rippled along her body from head to toe. The scents of moist earth and fresh snow filled her nose. The air against her face went from cold to cool to warm in a matter of seconds.

Dead. I'm dead.

A slight jerk accompanied the rustle of Alazar's wings as he thrust them out, slowing their flight.

Ariah trembled, her body in a death-press against his scales.

Her uncle's weight lifted off her back.

"Open your eyes, Ariah."

"No."

"Ariah."

"Screw you."

Uncle Mark touched her shoulder. "Honey, open your eyes."

Ariah gritted her teeth. *"Wuss. You're using my uncle to get through to me."*

"If you won't listen to me, then yes. Would you like to see if your visions from your younger years hold true or not?"

Okay. She'd bite.

Slowly, she peeled open one eye. She received an eyeful of wing at first. As she lifted her head and opened her other eye, she forgot her anger at the

179

creature carrying her over a land bursting with beauty and colors and magic.

"Where are we?"

"Welcome to The Hollow, Ari."

Ariah glanced back at her uncle. She had never thought the man capable of tears until that moment. His dark eyes shimmered as he beheld a home he'd abandoned decades ago. As she turned back to this strange new world, she could understand why. No streets. No cars. No skyscrapers. No modern-day pollutants. Mountain peaks reached into the sky as far as she could see. The land below rolled with hills and pastures cut by veins of crystalline rivers and ponds. Trees of all sizes filled patches, thickened in other areas. Vibrant swathes of color spread like a sea of swirling paint. In the distance, mist billowed from the foot of a spectacular waterfall that spilled between two peaks.

Alazar wove through a few peaks before circling a field tucked in the valley at the base of a sloping moss-and-flower covered rock.

A whoosh of air that ruffled her hair across her face jerked her from her awe.

Ariah lifted her hand and pointed to a second dragon that put Alazar's impressive size to shame. "Uhh, Uncle Mark?"

"That's Cade. Don't let his size fool you. He's a big, huggable monster."

How reassuring.

Alazar glided to a perfect landing in the field. He

lowered himself to the ground as the second dragon approached, enormous wings flapping as his hind legs reached for the ground.

The sight was fantastic.

"Come." Her uncle dropped the belt from their waists and slid out from behind her. "Same method climbing down."

Ariah took her time securing her feet and hands with each step closer to the ground, casting glances toward the other dragon her entire descent. His coloring was similar to Alazar's, a little darker and more smoky, and his crest was larger with a few more horns.

Overall, he appeared far more ferocious than Alazar. She wondered how much of that had to do with what she knew about Alazar's laid-back attitude.

Ariah judged her position on the last stirrup before hopping to the ground. As she turned, a formidable man appeared around the tip of Alazar's snout. He had dark red hair and a matching beard, as well as probing eyes set beneath hard slashes of brows. He was huge and muscled and definitely *not* huggable.

Instinctively, she shuffled back until she bumped into Alazar. Her uncle twisted from his position on his knees, loosening the harness.

Alazar released a low, grumbling sound accompanied by streams of smoke from his nose and mouth. The strange, frightening man who could probably squash her between two fingers tilted his head and smiled.

Okay, so the guy could produce a friendly smile.

"Cade." Uncle Mark gave the harness straps a sharp tug, releasing them, and stood up. Ariah still couldn't take her full attention off the guy, who continued to assess her like she was a scientific anomaly. "Old friend, it's nice to see you again."

"The pleasure is shared." The big man stopped his approach a few feet from Ariah, his features softening, if that was possible. "And who is this?"

"Ariah Callahan," Ariah introduced herself, thrusting a hand forward. Cade's hand swallowed hers between thick, strong fingers. The air shifted at her back, a whispering swoosh and the curl of a breeze ruffling her hair. She pulled her hand back and watched as Alazar the dragon shrank and reformed into Alazar the man. He shook the harness off his shoulders and handed it to Mark.

"Think you forgot to finish the job," Alazar joked, coming to Ariah's side. To Cade, he said, "It seems Mike escaped The Hollow and had a daughter."

Cade's eyes narrowed, but his smile remained. It made Ariah's skin itch. "Mark, you have no children of your own."

Mark shook his head, but lifted his chin with pride when he placed a hand on Ariah's shoulder. "Ari is a daughter to me. Even if I bore a child, she is next in line to be Alazar's Keeper. She is his lifemate. I've known from the first moment I met her when she was two weeks old."

Cade's gaze shifted to Alazar, freeing her from his

intense inspection. A quiet breath fled her lungs in relief.

"How did you come to learn about her?"

Ariah listened to her uncle give a shortened version of events over the last few days, including her father's part in stealing back the dragonstone to the possibility the Baroqueth had located the stone, discovered her father, and possibly herself.

Her attention drifted from Cade and to the stunning world surrounding her. A warm breeze blew endlessly, carrying subtle hints of sweetness through the air. The grass in this valley reached up to her calves and swayed with Nature's breath, the vibrant colored flowers of purples and pinks and yellows dancing in an endless mosaic of beauty. Thick moss covered the base of the peak's rocky walls, dotted with pretty white and pink blooms.

She wanted to run and scream with joy and drop to the ground to stare up into the blue sky. The serenity that encompassed not only her senses but her soul left her longing to belong to this special, magical place. She could not imagine anyone or anything wanting to destroy this spectacular beauty.

"In essence, there's a good chance we'll have another face-off in Nocturne Falls?" Cade surmised.

His words were like a finger snap in the face, and Ariah's calm shattered. She twisted back to Cade and found the man watching her with a sparkle in his eyes.

"We're going to try to avoid that," Alazar said. "I

don't want our enemies bringing their ugliness to our friends again. Once was enough."

"It's only a matter of time before they scour that town again in hopes of finding you or Zareh. Since Zar is planning to lay his roots deeper in Nocturne Falls, there will always be a threat of Baroqueth attacks there." Cade sighed. "Seems their hunt for us has become more aggressive over the last few months, especially if what you suspect is true and they went into a public venue to potentially steal the dragonstone."

"It's speculation at this point," Uncle Mark said. His fingers squeezed Ariah's shoulder. "She is not familiar with what they look like, and was unable to tell me if she saw anyone resembling the Baroqueth. I raised her on our history and trained her in her gifts as best I could until Mike and I had a falling out."

"Wasn't a falling out. I believe she's put a spell on you," Ariah muttered, earning herself three sets of curious eyes. Ariah shrugged. "Now that I know she's a real witch, I do. I think she cursed my father and has you under some spell."

"Who?" Cade asked.

"Uncle Mark's wife. Miriam the witch with an affinity for Louis Vuitton and Jimmy Choo." She nudged her uncle in the ribs with her elbow and flashed him a sardonic grin. "You've yet to buy her a yacht."

"Ari."

"How about I show you around," Alazar

interrupted, slipping an arm around her waist and tugging her out from under her uncle's hand. He made a motion toward the open field leading down to a copse of trees with weeping branches of gray-green leaves dripping with flowers. "Why don't we meet up with you two in a few hours? Mark can fill you in on three decades' worth of gossip while I help Ace destress."

Cade nodded. "I'll have a spread prepared for your return. Do you plan on spending the night in your home?"

Ariah looked up at Alazar to find him watching her.

"I need to get back," her uncle said. A note of sadness touched his voice. Ariah frowned at him despite his sad smile. "Perhaps another time? I sure do miss this place."

"I think we all do," Cade agreed. "Soon. Our home calls to us to return." He waved a hand to Alazar and Ariah. "Enjoy your time."

"Thanks." Ariah tucked her head against Alazar's shoulder as he led her away from Cade and Uncle Mark. "As much as I hate to admit it, I think you were right."

Alazar chuckled. "About what, Ace?"

"Knowing what I need."

Alazar nudged her head, turning her face up to him. Despite the small smile on his mouth, something far more sensual coasted across his expression. It set off every flutter and tightened every knot from lunchtime, the sensation intensified by a factor of one hundred.

Had she not felt the watchful gazes of the two men they left at their backs, she might have finally given in to the relentless urge to kiss him.

"If you thought this was what I meant, you're sorely mistaken. Just wait." He leaned down, pressing his lips to her ear. "I'm delivering you to your fairytale."

CHAPTER 15

The moment Alazar broke through the magical portal between the human world and The Hollow, his entire being thrummed with old magic and energy. He had returned to his home maybe a dozen times over the last thirty years, usually to add items to his hoard or retrieve coins to transfer into currency.

Each trip back to The Hollow, it proved more difficult to leave. In the human realm, his magic leeched away, leaving him with little of the essence that was the very foundation of the Firestorm *tatsu*. Not only were they an ancient race, they were a powerful and magical race.

Nocturne Falls provided a slight taste of magic, but it also made his dragon yearn for his old powers.

With Ariah beside him, he couldn't wait to see her eyes sparkle with glee as they had upon seeing his transformation before their ride. The shadows had been cast out of her gaze, opening her soul for him to read. They were connected—all lifemates were connected—but he craved to witness the earning of her affections.

He craved to kiss her, hold her, promise her everything that had been stripped from her in the last decade and deliver on that promise.

Half an hour after leaving Cade and Mark in the valley, they came up to the first place he wanted to show her. The sound of water cascading over rock blended with the rustle of trees in the warm breeze. The air smelled fresh, summer sweet, and he soaked in the familiar scents with each breath. The dreamy calm that relaxed Ariah's expression, as well as the fluttering thoughts that touched his mind, reassured him she basked in the beauty of his homeland.

Her fingers tightened between his, her other hand wrapping around his wrist. He brushed aside weeping branches laced with flowers. Those same flowers rained soft white petals in the breeze, adding to the allure of The Hollow.

"Have you ever swum beneath a waterfall?" Alazar asked, leading her through the curtain of branches.

"I don't have a bathing suit. I'm not swimming."

"We'll see."

Alazar held aside the last of the branches, opening up a window to the wildflower-covered shores of the crystalline pool. The gentle flow of water pouring over a rock shelf into the pool enhanced the soothing sounds of nature's music.

Ariah brushed by him, her lips separated on a gasp and her eyes glowing with delight. Alazar let the branches sway back into place and guided her down to the pool's rocky perimeter.

188

"This used to be a favorite spot of ours. Kind of like a swimming hole. After a heavy rain when the falls were swollen with water, the sound alone drew us here." Alazar licked his lips, casting aside memories from so long ago. Much had changed since those happy times. When he glanced down at his Ace, he couldn't help but imagine the joyful possibilities and memories he could make with her. "In late spring and early summer, the rocks across the way are lined with vines that produce some of the sweetest berries. Although they bear no fruit now, at night, the blooms open and release a scent that is almost as sweet as the berries taste."

"This is so much more than what my uncle could ever describe."

Alazar drank in her awe and wonder, admiring her ability to release her burdens and embrace simplicity. There was so much he would share with her if she made the decision to accept him as her partner, her lifemate.

"And imagine, this is just a small piece of what you will see in this world." Alazar pushed the sleeves of his shirt up to his elbows. "Swim?"

Ariah glanced down at her clothes, the same outfit she'd worn to Howler's. "I'm not ruining this after what you paid for it."

Alazar rolled his eyes and nudged her boot with the toe of his own. "Take them off."

He hunched over and unlaced his boots, slipping them off, followed by his socks. When Ariah hadn't made an attempt to remove anything, Alazar groaned, grabbed her foot and earned a shriek. Her hands latched onto his shoulders as she hobbled on one foot.

"You are impossible."

"I'm giving you what you need." As he tugged off the boot and sock, he glanced up at her. "A chance for you to *live*."

He removed the second boot and sock, lowered her foot to the rock, and pressed up on his feet.

Ariah's gold-laced eyes peered up at him, a new and vulnerable light shining behind her stunning irises. It soaked into his mind, undiluted and captivating. He stood, cast beneath the spell of his Ace, unable to break free even if he wanted to.

As her hands slipped along his chest to rest on his shoulders, his heart rate accelerated. Part of him, like the entire dragon part of him, wanted to tug her close and take control. But he, Alazar the man, understood his sweet lifemate's need to make this decision on her own.

He just wished she would do it a little faster. For her, it was twenty-four hours. For him, he'd waited centuries for this moment.

Ariah leaned into him, pressing up to her toes. He took her about the waist, easing her closer, raising her higher, until the first hot shock of her lips brushing against his bolted along his skin. An airy touch, a whisper of a kiss, and it sent him reeling, anticipating more. Her slender fingers curled up along his neck until they combed into his hair.

When her lips moved across his, leaving a path of scorching heat in their stead, he fisted his fingers in her sweater, forcing himself to remain grounded. Her breaths were little flutters of air over his mouth. The subtle tremble along her body resonated in his own, as did the rapid beat of her heart against his chest.

Then, she pulled back an inch. Could have been a mile for all the difference it made.

"I, uh…"

Alazar lifted a hand, sank his fingers into her hair, and drew her up, stealing her words from her lips on the kind of kiss he'd burned for since yesterday. A soft moan escaped Ariah, her arms tightening around him, her small body pushing closer. The dragon unfurled, heat pouring into every molecule, hunger unlike anything he'd experienced laying claim to his mind and his body. Conscious thought evaded him, leaving him to drown in the tidal waves of this new, overwhelming sensation of necessity.

Ariah met each sweep of his tongue with an eagerness that both pleased and prodded at his control. She tasted like succulent ambrosia, nectar from the gods, all warm and sweet and utterly satisfying. He drank in each gasp she breathed against his tongue, imprinting her essence into every cell of his body. Her small, fragile frame in his arms provoked another layer of tenderness from beneath his scales, another surge of desire to protect her from the worst.

Right now, he might very well categorize himself in that list of "the worst." He grappled for the slippery cords of calm as their kiss intensified. The quiet little whimpers that wafted from her throat to his ears worked effortlessly to undo him.

When he caught his hand slipping lower down her back, the tips of his fingers cresting the top of her jeans as he skimmed the soft, warm skin beneath her sweater, he buckled down, tapering off this dangerous session before it turned into something along the lines of no-clothing intimacy.

The pool would have been a delightful addition.

Now he understood why Zar's bed rocked more than it lay silent. Every story he heard about the connection between lifemates was true a hundred-fold.

Alazar gave Ariah's bottom lip a gentle tug with his teeth before he straightened up. Smoke and bones, he needed an ocean to extinguish the fire raging uncontrollably inside him. The orb-like distortion of his dragon's sight could not hide the dark, dark depths of Ariah's lust-strewn gaze, her pupils like bottomless abysses calling him back. Her lips, rose and moist, separated as she panted for breath.

When her fingertips traced his brow, curved back around over his cheek, and came to rest against his lips, he couldn't refrain from capturing one tip between his teeth and flicking his tongue over her pad. Her nostrils flared and her cheeks darkened.

"You have fire in your eyes," she whispered.

There's fire in more places than my eyes, Ace.

He kept that to himself, releasing her finger. "Dragon."

Ariah slipped her hand over his chest, resting her palm flat over his throbbing heart. Slowly, he managed to bring his dragon back to heel and his vision returned to normal.

"Why...why did you stop?"

Alazar stared at her for a long moment, contemplating the question and exactly what she was asking.

At last, he leaned over, plucked a purple and yellow flower from the swaying grass, and tucked it in her hair. He drew his knuckles along her silky waves, desperately fighting to keep from sinking said fingers back into her hair. She was too alluring, too tempting, too everything at the moment.

"You're not answering me."

"Since you are reluctant to go swimming without a bathing suit, I doubt you're up for skinny dipping." He gave a small tug at the collar of her sweater as her face flushed. "I think you know where that kiss was headed."

She cleared her throat, glancing away. "Yeah."

"Don't sound so miserable. Come on. Take this thing off, since you have that tank top item beneath it, and hop in."

It killed him to step away, to break the connection as he dropped his hands to his sides. The distance was safe. Any other time, he would have shed his shirt before diving into the water. He kept it on and took the plunge, letting the cool rush of the mountain-fed pool douse the heat permeating his skin.

The water sizzled when he hit it.

When he broke the surface of the crystal clear waters and twisted to face Ariah, his little Ace stared at him, a brow arched, and arms crossed over her chest.

The sweater was still on.

Alazar slapped the water, sending an arc of shimmering crystal blue toward her. "Come on, Ace."

"You smoked, you know that?" She motioned back and forth between them with her finger. "Internal thermostat went kaput again? Or is the water super cold?"

Alazar tipped his head, unable to stop the grin from curling over his lips. "Why don't you dip a toe in and you tell me."

Cautiously, Ariah moved to the edge of the pool and stretched her foot to the water's surface.

The moment her toes touched the water, Alazar unleashed a small ripple of his old power through the pool. Water latched onto Ariah's leg and tugged her away from the ridge, protected her from hitting the rocks, and dropped her into the water.

When she broke the surface with a gasp, her wide eyes shot to him. Alazar smiled.

"You were taking too long."

"Wha...Did the...Did you..." She jerked around, looking at the rocks, Alazar, back at the rocks. "Did you see that?" He was stunned when she began a furious swim, not stopping when she reached where he tread until her entire body wrapped around him like a ribbon. "The water. It-it pulled me in. Is this pool haunted?"

"That was me."

Her head snapped around, those wide eyes gauging him for a long moment. "No. You were here."

"Magic, Ace. All Firestorm have magic in The Hollow. It's stripped when we go into the mortal realm, but here?" He demonstrated another small dose of magic, arcing a thick swell of water up over her head before the pool reabsorbed it. Ariah leaned back a little more, the uncertainty in her eyes melting into awe. Her legs remained wrapped in a death grip around his waist. He shrugged. "Since we are a race of fire dragons, we can control fire the best, but we have some sway over all the elements to a degree. If the Baroqueth were the only ones with power and magic, we'd have been wiped out in the first war."

Alazar enjoyed watching her revel in this new bit of information. She dropped a hand to the surface of the water, touching it like she had never seen water before. The wonder in her expression captivated him. Thankfully, he could hold her and tread water with little exertion. He didn't want to disrupt these precious minutes.

At last, she brought her dream-laced gaze back to him, her lips tugging upward. She reached toward the back of his head and poked the knot of his hair. "You realize that trying to get bands out of wet hair is a pain in the butt, right?"

"Well, I hadn't thought about it when I took the dive." He touched his forehead to hers. "I had some smoking to do." He gave her leg a playful squeeze.

"Keep these wrapped like this, and the water is going to get hot real fast."

"You're right." Ariah took her sweet time peeling herself away. "I don't want you getting the wrong impression of me."

"Sweetheart, that could go both ways. Rest assured, what you're feeling is completely normal."

"Wanting to throw myself at you is normal?" Ariah scrutinized him, her face scrunching in one of her adorable expressions. "I've never wanted to throw myself at anyone."

"Then I'm honored to be your first."

And hopefully your last.

"Let's lighten things up a bit, shall we?" Alazar was willing to make an effort to keep things respectable. Looking at his current predicament, he wasn't sure swimming with Ariah was the smartest idea. "Splash contest?"

Ariah snorted. "I lost that before it even began." She dove under the water, resurfaced, and swam closer to the falls. "Is there something behind there?"

"A grotto."

It also led to one of the three entrances to his home.

The mountain peak that rose into the sky a quarter mile away, where the first plummet of the falls snaked over the jagged rock and into the river that fed this pool, awoke the longing in his spirit to return. For good. If Ariah came with him, he'd be complete.

He twisted to find Ariah had paused at one side of

the falls, squinting against the light mist. She flashed him a smile.

"Can I go back there? Or are you going to do another magic trick?"

She didn't give him an opportunity to answer before she disappeared behind the curtain of water. Alazar rubbed a hand over his face.

"This was definitely not your grandest plan, buddy," he muttered under his breath. Gathering his mental reinforcements, he took after Ariah, realizing this trip to The Hollow was going to have one of two results.

With each stroke closer to the falls, he knew exactly which result was going to come to fruition.

CHAPTER 16

Ariah was living a dream in this twist of reality. Alazar promised to give her a fairytale. He delivered above and beyond anything she could have imagined. She could no longer fight what had been sown in her soul from her earliest years. Everything she had seen so far—and she doubted she saw even a tiny fraction of the whole—from the weeping trees, the music of the wildlife, the spirit-cleansing scents, to the warm breeze and the magic, stole her breath, stole her logic, and left her never wanting to leave.

Then, Alazar kissed her. With that single kiss, he split open her world beyond repair and carried her into a realm of fantasy and perfection.

He stole her thoughts. He stole her strength.

She feared he had stolen her heart before she realized it was capable of living.

That kiss. The fierce hunger in his eyes. The tenderness in his touch.

She felt nothing shy of safe and secure with Alazar.

Crazy as it may be, she felt complete. She didn't want to lose that.

Brushing aside the wet strands of hair plastered to her face after crossing through the waterfall, she soaked in the hollow feel of the grotto and the rays of sunlight that stretched beneath her feet, casting the water in the clearest of blues until it faded a few feet ahead. The rock shelf she passed beneath opened up overhead, the soothing echo of the water behind her hypnotic and relaxing. The walls shimmered as though encrusted with diamonds.

It was magnificent.

She treaded deeper into the grotto, the burdensome weight of her sweater dragging on her arms, until the tips of her toes brushed pebbles. The ground came up beneath her until she stood waist-deep in water, weaving her fingers along the calm surface as she stared in amazement at the walls.

"It's gold."

Ariah grinned, warming as Alazar drew closer. She had become hyperaware of his presence, the way it made her skin tingle and her heart flutter and other places melt. She recognized the effect he had on her when she first laid eyes on him in the Hallowed Bean. Now? The intensity of her reaction to him made her nerves hum.

Water sloshed quietly as he approached her from behind. "The cave is filled with veins of gold. Here." The air around her thickened until she almost couldn't breathe. Alazar slipped a hand beneath one of hers and lifted them from the water. Her hand felt so small against his as he cradled her fingers, palm up. "Trust me."

"I do."

Oh, how natural those words felt falling from her tongue without hesitation. A strange, prickling sensation started along her knuckles, spreading around her hand and across her palm. The prickling turned to a momentary shock of heat.

Tiny flames erupted from her palm. She jerked, eyes widening, jaw going slack. She hadn't realized she had stepped back into Alazar until his other arm wrapped around her waist and his mouth rested closer to her ear.

"There is so much I can teach you. So much I *will* teach you. My fire, Ace, in the palm of your hand. This"—he lifted their hands, the flames growing brighter—"is who you are. Keeper. Lifemate. This will become the flesh to your skeleton, if you choose."

Ariah lifted her head, following the glinting veins of gold in the rock. The firelight brought them to life, live metal in its secured home. It was absolutely stunning.

"I'm speechless," she murmured, angling her head into Alazar's until their noses brushed. "How could I walk away from this?" She slid her free hand along his arm, folding her fingers between his at her hip. "From you?"

"I hope you won't."

Ariah lifted her head enough to catch Alazar's gaze. Sincerity blazed in the light of his eyes. She moistened her lips.

"I'm not strong enough to fight what is happening between us," she whispered. "I don't *want* to fight it."

"It's not meant to be fought, Ariah." Alazar's hand folded hers, extinguishing the flames. "I fight it solely for your sake."

"Don't." Ariah closed her eyes, seeking the warmth of Alazar's breath as she brought her mouth closer to his. "Not anymore. Give me that chance to live."

"Ariah?"

"I'll be your Keeper one day." Ariah brushed her lips over his. "But I want to be your lifemate now."

There was still so much she needed to learn and understand. She had denied herself a life for so long. She would not now deny herself what she needed most. The central pillar to this new life. The arms around her, the body pressed to her back, and the mouth that found hers in a kiss taut with restraint. A need she had only recognized a short time ago.

Alazar. Firestorm dragon. Lifemate.

Completion.

The crackling flames in the fireplace and the subtle flickers from candles lent a calm, relaxing glow to the otherwise dark room. Ariah couldn't wipe the smile from her face as she basked in the afterglow of her spontaneous decision to stop fighting the natural pull to the dragon man lying beside her. She kept her face pressed to his shoulder, her eyes closed, and absorbed the waves of heat that kept the chill of the room at bay. Not to mention the comforting heat radiating from Alazar's body.

"I think I missed the grand tour of your home," Ariah murmured. The airy whorls he drew along her spine worked their own magic, threatening to put her to sleep.

"You received the abbreviated tour." He pressed a kiss to the top of her head. "Extremely abbreviated. Secret-entrance-only abbreviated."

"All I remember is stairs."

"Because I carried you the rest of the way, and I was in a bit of a hurry."

Ariah shifted, propping her chin on her fist, and gazed down at Alazar. The man was incredible in every possible sense of the word. Her entire body sang from the delight he gifted her with skill and tenderness.

"I've delivered on my debt of dessert."

Alazar chuckled, twisting to his side. "Oh, no, Ace. I have a weakness for chocolate truffles, so the debt is still owed." He brushed his thumb over her lower lip. "Besides, you are not a bet, nor are you a prize. There is nothing that can compare to you." Pinching her chin between his thumb and index finger, he drew her closer and kissed her once. "And I *do* know you."

"You've been in my mind."

"You'll be in mine soon enough." He nuzzled his nose against her cheek. "I think I'm going to keep you here. You do wonders for the stagnant air of this place. It can definitely use a woman's touch to make it not so...cave-ish."

"Ahh, so you live in a man cave? I would've never guessed."

Alazar pinched her waist. She squirmed, biting back a laugh until he tickled her in earnest. Ariah let out a cry of laughter, curling in on herself, sinking her hands into the silk of Alazar's loose hair.

"It'll be yours, too." Alazar pressed a crushing, fierce kiss to her mouth before he sat up. Ariah wiped a tear from the corner of her eye and caught her breath. "Everything I own."

Ariah cleared her throat after her bout of laughter and pushed up alongside Alazar. She stayed his hands as they started to pull his hair back and gave a small shake of her head when his gaze landed on her.

"I like it down."

Alazar narrowed his eyes. "You're not a long-haired man-bun kinda gal, Ace. Right?"

The brief shock caused by the realization that he'd picked up on her thought from the Hallowed Bean wore off as quickly as it hit. She smiled, twining a thick lock of russet hair around her finger.

"Guess you didn't catch the last bit of my thoughts." She tucked the lock behind his ear. "The bit about how I really like it on you."

Alazar caught her hand as she lowered it back to her lap. He drew her knuckles to his lips, kissing each one, stealing another string of her heart. In the recesses of her mind, the last ten years tried to haunt her, promising heartache and broken dreams.

Batting away the dreary voices, she rested her head against his muscled arm. "Think my uncle and your leader are wondering where we are?"

"They're most likely chumming it up over stout and steak." He played with her ring finger, his thumb brushing against her skin as if tracing a ring she did not see. "Wonder if Mark ever thinks about coming back here."

"If he didn't make the worst mistake of his life by marrying the witch, I'm sure he would leave everything in Georgia in an instant. I remember how much his eyes would light up when he told me about this place. His heart longs to return, but his obligations keep him Georgia-bound. Ten years of awkward estrangement from my father has not changed that in him. He's still the same man I loved and adored before Miriam came along."

"I'm going to have to meet this Miriam witch and tell her to keep her spells far away from you."

"I can hold my own against the prissy snot."

She hadn't meant for her voice to sound so acrid and hateful, but the half-amused, half-curious look Alazar cast her made her realize how nasty her statement sounded. Frankly, she didn't care. She'd held her own against bigger and badder people than Miriam.

She'd faced the barrel of a gun, for crying out loud.

"You mentioned in the pool that you have magic here because the Baroqueth couldn't be the only ones with power. Were they always enemies?" She needed to get her thoughts away from the woman before it ruined her mood. Learning more about this impending threat was a good detour. "How powerful are they?"

"They weren't always enemies. Some had been Keepers eons ago. But like any epic fall, jealousy and greed came into play. A Baroqueth Keeper wanted his dragon's power and was willing to kill for it." Alazar shrugged. "That was centuries ago. The first battle. The second was thirty years ago. Not sure how powerful they've become since, but after the attack on Kaylae, we realized their powers have increased. Cade's been trying to figure out how many are living, where they are, and how powerful they've become. He's also been trying to locate the Keepers of the other Firestorm dragons and determine if there are more females. We know of two more female Keepers besides you and Kaylae. Since females are rare and provide hope to continue our bloodlines, the Baroqueth will seek to destroy them first, before they come after the dragons. Once we meet our lifemates, Ace, to lose them would be devastating to our minds."

His fingers tightened around hers, whether he realized it or not. He stared into the flicker of the fire, his breathing steady, his face calm. "Now that I have you here, I could never picture my life without you. It's that potent, that quick, and that encompassing."

"You said nowadays, lifemates can choose to accept their dragon or walk away. How can there be a choice when the decision is already made? Did Zareh and

Kaylae contemplate their fate? I mean, you're right. I can't see a future that doesn't include you, either, however foolish it sounds so early in our acquaintance."

Alazar chuckled. He tossed a glance down at the makeshift bed they sat on. "Sweetheart, we skipped the acquaintance phase and went straight to the mate phase." He eased Ariah's head back to his arm when she started to press off him. "Normal for lifemates, so don't start getting all logical and stuff. I'm surprised we lasted the first day without something happening."

"Um, we didn't make it that much longer."

"Well, we've shopped together, you spent a night in my home, I cooked you lunch, and we went on our first mini-vacation beforehand, so I'd say we did pretty good. The only reason Zar made it longer was because Kaylae's situation was far different from yours. She had no idea who she was, no idea dragons were real, no idea about *nada*. Mark taught you enough not to be completely shocked by the reality."

"Does Kaylae know about the powers she has?"

"Yes and no. Zar hasn't rushed into explaining her powers. She'll learn when she's ready. Zar's waiting for that time. I will, too."

"Dragon, you won't have to wait long." Ariah sucked in a breath, held it to ten, and let it out. "Okay. Ready."

Alazar laughed, clapping her knee. "Come on. I've neglected to feed you anything of substance. Quite honestly, I don't need Mark or Cade barging in here."

They dressed, doused the fire and candles, and

followed a narrow stone staircase down into the cavernous mountain. Ariah stayed close to Alazar as he led the way. Thin shafts of sunlight dappled through cracks in the rock, casting thin white rays of light across the narrow space.

Alazar paused on a step and rested his palm flat against the stone wall. Ariah peered around his arm when the screech of rock sliding against rock lanced the quiet. Another narrow stairwell opened up and torches blazed to life in alcoves lining the new path.

"Shouldn't we be going up?" Ariah asked.

"Yes."

"Umm, like to embellish?"

"Nope."

"Alazar.

"Shh, Ace. Patience."

Ariah rolled her eyes and followed her zipped-lipped dragon down the stairs to another strange magical door and another descending stairwell lit by torches. The deeper they trekked into the mountain, the colder and damper the air became. Alazar's warm scent became obscured by that of cool, moist dirt and musty rock.

When they reached the bottom step, Alazar flexed his fingers. Ariah moistened her lips at the sight of his half-extended talons before they disappeared into cracks along the rock. The wall separated on unseen tracks, opening the way to a vision she could not wrap her head around.

"Just in case you think I was pulling your chain

when I said you will want for nothing." Alazar stepped to the side of the archaic doorframe. Ariah tentatively stepped up to the opening and peeked into a room with no end in sight. The torchlight behind them reflected off the mounds of gold piled closest to the door and produced a stream of never-ending shimmer farther back. "Some dragons like to change up their hoards a bit. I keep it gold."

Ariah rubbed her eyes and blinked, trying to grasp the enormity of wealth hidden deep within this mountainous home. She finally gave up and turned to her dragon man. "I'll let you handle the finances."

Alazar's smile made her heart flutter. "Sure you don't want to go in and swim around?"

"Swim?" Ariah laughed, giving Alazar's shoulder a playful poke. "Have you forgotten where the last swim landed us?"

"Exactly." Alazar led her into the abyss of a room and spread his arm toward the riches. "Go ahead, Ace. Choose something. Anything. A reminder that what is mine is now yours."

Ariah glanced over the closest mound of golden coins, bars, necklaces, goblets, and numerous other gold objects. She reached down and picked up a single coin, lifting it for Alazar to see.

"There. A lucky coin." She tucked it into her pocket—one good thing about a fire dragon was how quickly he could dry wet clothes—and rested a kiss on his cheek. "'Cause I'm lucky to have you."

"Aww, Ace. I think it's the other way around."

Chapter 17

Mark nudged him three times to leave The Hollow before he looked Alazar dead in the eye and said, "Leave. Now. I have to get home."

Alazar growled in response, popping the last bit of steak-juice-covered roll into his mouth. He wiped his hands on the napkin draped over his knee, wiped his mouth with the same napkin, and looked at Ariah seated beside him. She smiled, sure, but beneath that calm façade, her sadness soaked into his scales. Next time he returned to his home, he'd bring just Ariah. Alone. No time restraints. No reality tying them to the human world.

There was so much to show her, so much to teach her. He touched the tip of the mountain with her earlier, and received one of the greatest gifts. Ariah's unabashed happiness. Not a single shadow of her past dimmed her joy. He didn't want to take her away from this reprieve.

Cade gave Mark a hand harnessing Alazar in the valley while Ariah nuzzled up against the side of his head. Her fingers drew lazy patterns over the small scales beneath his eye, the simple gesture quickly churning him into a hot mess. His scales were sensitive to begin with, one of the many defense mechanisms of their dragon breed. He could feel the slightest breath in a ripple of air or change in temperature before a Keeper had any clue something was amiss. His coat was both an impenetrable shield and a sensory device.

With Ariah, it was all about sensory overload, from scales to the leathery skin beneath, to every inch of tissue and bone in his body.

His attention focused on Cade as his Viking-like leader came up alongside Ariah. He rested a hand on her slender shoulder. Alazar couldn't help but snort in amusement over the incredible size difference between the two. Standing beside Cade, Ariah defined fragile, delicate, handle-with-extreme-care perfection, even if she was anything but on the inside.

"We will have to give you some lessons in riding. Before you know it, you and Alazar will be soaring the open skies, a match to the hearts." Cade jutted his chin toward Alazar's back. "It was an honor to meet you, Ariah. I will be seeing more of you in the days to come. Alazar, give Zareh a head's up I'll be stopping by tomorrow. We'll need to figure out a plan to get Ariah's father out of jail before the Baroqueth get him first."

Ariah jerked, moistened her lips, and looked up at Cade. "Do you think he's in danger? In a jail?"

Cade nodded. "Jail is great for humans, not for

paranormals. Not when guns and Tasers will provide little to no protection against raw power and magic. Your father is vulnerable in a cell. They can reach him, but he can't escape. He is your uncle's brother, but his Keeper blood lies dormant while Mark is alive. He can't access his powers like Mark can." Cade lowered his chin. "Like you can."

Ariah's worried gaze turned back to Alazar.

"We'll get him out, Ace. He'll be safe."

She nodded, tugging her bottom lip between her teeth. She pressed her forehead to Alazar's cheek, then straightened up and held a hand out to Cade.

"Thank you."

Cade stared at her hand, his brows coming together over his nose like dark red slashes of fire. He opened his arms instead. Alazar watched as his woman was swallowed up in Cade's embrace, patches of color and pale skin the only sign that Ariah was in his hug.

When Cade placed her on her feet, she shuffled back a step. Alazar received a rush of disorientation before she could compose herself.

"You take care of her, Alazar."

Alazar twisted his head on his long neck and glowered down at Cade. Like he wouldn't do exactly that. His leader patted the taper of his lower jaw, flashed a white-toothed smile, and led Ariah to Mark.

Ten minutes later, he was sky-bound with his precious cargo and his Keeper holding tight. The sun had begun its magnificent descent to the west, the fiery orange-yellow orb drenching the world in a spray of vibrant colors. He wished he could turn around and settle on the shelf of his peak with Ariah tucked in his arms, and witness the pure magic of his home instead of barreling toward the portal door into the mortal realm once again.

The rain had stopped in Georgia, leaving the Earth damp and soft as he landed in the woods on the outskirts of Nocturne Falls. Night creatures chirped and skittered beneath the darkening blue sky. Leaves fluttered to the forest floor in the increasing breeze, branches rustling and lending a succulent undertone to the night's symphony.

Alazar lowered his belly to the ground and waited for Mark and Ariah to dismount. Mark unfastened the harness much faster this time, patting his shoulder to signify Alazar could transform.

"Mark, I'm not a horse," Alazar said as soon as he reined in the last of his dragon on a puff of smoke and stood on his booted feet. He moved up to Mark, who smirked, and clapped his Keeper's shoulder. "Giddy up back home before your wife poisons your food out of spite."

Mark flashed Ariah a hard glance. "Ari."

She threw her hands up in the air. "I swear I didn't say anything I haven't said before." Her hands lowered and a guilty expression trickled over her face. "Well, maybe I said a few more things."

A sharp breath fled Mark's mouth as he crossed his arms over his chest. "Ariah Callahan. My apologies will never fix the last ten years, but she is my wife.

You do not have to like it. All I ask is that you respect it."

Alazar did not interrupt, observing the flare of anger that lightened the gold in Ariah's eyes and the way her stubborn jaw locked as she clenched her teeth. Her fingertips curled into her jeans pockets. Alazar caught her pulsing thoughts like she was screaming them in his ear.

"I don't. I won't. You can't force me. I have so many colorful things I'd love to spew at you right now."

Alazar cleared his throat. He feared Ariah was about to lose her cool. The volatile hatred she felt for Mark's wife was a force that knocked him like a fist to his gut. It was potent, raw, and unsettling.

He definitely had to meet this lady.

"Hey." Alazar dared rest a hand on Ariah's shoulder. Instantly, the tension melted out of her muscles and she leaned into him. The hard contours of Mark's face softened and a ghostly grin touched his lips. "Whoever she is, both of you, you two are family. Mark, Ariah is part of who you are. Your bond between each other is stronger than most human familial bonds. Witch, wife, stepmother, some other bright and shining descriptions, whatever you want to label her, Miriam can*not* come between you. She has no power to break what you two have."

Mark's chin lifted as he regarded Alazar with a spark of appreciation. Yeah, he'd gotten that look a few times before when he spouted philosophical mumbo-jumbo that no one expected to come out of his mouth.

To keep to his farce, he wagged his brows once. "And if she tries, crispy diva ends up on the local menu."

Mark's appreciation died. He groaned and rolled his eyes. "I can always expect an explosive ending to a meaningful chat with you." He cast the harness over his shoulder, looping the ends over his forearm so they didn't drag on the ground, and nodded toward the road where their cars were parked. "Ariah, can I expect you home this evening?"

Ariah glanced up at Alazar, who shook his head. "I think I'll keep her another night. Or two. Or forever. Of course, if she'll have me."

"I'll need to get something to wear for tomorrow." Ariah tugged at her sweater. "This has been slept in, swam in, and fire-dried. I think it needs a break. And a wash."

"Clothes it is, then. Mark, you lead the way."

A half-hour later, Alazar pulled his Mustang into the driveway behind Mark's sleek Jaguar, and cut the engine. This time, Ariah didn't try to jump out of the car before he had a chance to open the door, which satisfied the gentleman inside him.

"We still need to get my car," Ariah said, keeping in step with Alazar as they followed Mark up to the front door. "I don't need a ticket."

"How about I torch the car and buy you a brand new one?" Alazar suggested, only half joking. The hunk of metal was certainly unsafe. He'd feel more comfortable if she were driving around in something reliable and more fitting to her style. "Anything you want."

"It still runs. It's fine for now." Her arm tightened around his as they drew up to the front door. Ariah might appear tired and content on the outside, but her turmoil and reserve beat against his mind. He'd seen Miriam's coyness through Ariah's thoughts and memories, but he feared there was something deeper to her that no one was privy to. Hatred this dark was soul-eating and dangerous. "Between Uncle Mark and you, I'm sure it's fair to say I have a backup."

He quickly nodded as they followed Mark into the foyer. Ariah broke away from Alazar and took the stairs to the second level, two at a time. Her determination and hurried strides had both Mark and Alazar sharing a concerned glance.

"Is there something I should know about your lovely bride?" Alazar asked, keeping his voice low. The pulse of magic in the mansion alerted him to Miriam's presence. Tonight, she wasn't out with friends.

Mark scanned the lower level from where he stood before motioning to his office. "Let's keep things controlled tonight, okay?"

Alazar followed him into the office and partially closed the doors, leaving them open a crack. "Hey, I'm chillaxed, Mark. Just don't press sensitive buttons."

"Bourbon?"

Alazar flashed a wicked smile. "Man, you've got me all figured out. On the rocks."

Mark chuckled as he crossed to a sideboard and poured two tumblers of bourbon. Alazar met him beside a leather sofa facing a marble fireplace across from the desk. The hearth lay cold and gray. Alazar contemplated lighting up the fresh logs, but refrained.

"Miriam has always been jealous of Ariah. She's a witch. I know she can read auras. I don't know if there is something in Ariah that she's latched onto and envied, but the two are oil and water. Their jabs are anything but subtle behind their smiles. Ariah's anger toward Miriam is understandable. I don't blame her. Nor do I blame her for her anger toward me."

"You took your brother's woman, Mark. That is so unlike you."

Mark sighed, sinking down into the sofa. "It is and trust me, I live with the guilt of it to this day. I fought the attraction for a month after I met her, but I finally caved. I couldn't fight it anymore. In those first few weeks before Ariah became aware of the issues between Mike and me, Miriam seemed to adore her. She often suggested Ariah live with me permanently. Then Mike and I had our falling out. He took Ariah from me and I couldn't track them down. I tried calling her, but she wouldn't pick up. In those first few years, she didn't call me at all. It killed me inside."

Alazar perched on the arm of the sofa beside Mark, hunched forward with an elbow on his knee, and caught Mark's regretful gaze. "Actually, she did try to call you on several occasions. Someone interfered with your communication lines."

Mark stared at him for a long moment. "What are you saying?"

"I think you know exactly what I'm saying. I saw the last ten years of your niece's life from her own mind, Mark. She let me in and I saw everything. You have no clue what my lifemate went through, and she is too ashamed to talk about it. Stronger for it, but beat down because of the life she lived. She tried calling you when your brother spiraled out of control and she was lost. No money, no home, barely a job because she would have to call out sick too often to take care of her father."

Alazar straightened up and sipped his bourbon. Then, he raised his glass to the room. "Posh luxury all around you. Never a worry. Never a need. So, do you think there is magic at work in your own home? Because, hey, I can certainly feel something."

"Al, I get the protection thing. I do. I know you will do anything and everything you can to make Ari happy. I know you will try to strip the pain of the past to let her live her future. What you didn't see, what she didn't know, was that I searched for her. I tried to locate her. I hired PIs and touched base with connections I have along the east coast. I started a programming business as a façade for my wealth. Mike moved around so much that every time I thought I was on his trail, I lost him. I wanted to make amends and, by the blessing of the gods, I wanted my niece back. At least I knew she was capable of protecting herself with her gifts, her powers. I worked hard with her on all of that before Miriam came along. She could obscure her aura to protect her Keeper blood from detection."

"Perhaps Miriam gets mixed signals from her and that's where the touchiness comes from?"

Mark shrugged. Alazar tossed back the rest of his drink and sighed. His Keeper's expression twisted and his dark eyes, stark with helplessness, shimmered. He didn't like the unease that settled in his gut as he ran Ariah's memories against Mark's claims. Neither lied to him, but the invisible wall that stood between Mark and Ariah for ten years until the other night didn't fit. He was missing something. They all were missing something.

"If Ariah didn't have your number, how did she get in touch with you?"

"She called the house phone. I happened to be home. Miriam was out with friends when she called."

"She wasn't around to intercept the call. How convenient." Alazar made a nonchalant circular motion with his hand. "So, is your relationship with this woman good? Are you happy? You two never had kids."

"Not for the lack of trying, at least in the beginning. It's now a platonic relationship." Mark shrugged and knocked back his bourbon in a single gulp. "It's a civil, respectful relationship. More companionship at this point."

"Not worth the troubles the woman caused."

Mark leaned back into the sofa and let out a long, resigned breath. "You know it's hard for Keepers to find a match. Our genes won't allow for a woman to conceive unless her genes can withstand our mutations.

When we were thrown into this world, loneliness became a reality. Mike was lucky. He found a woman who was able to conceive a gift to you. I have always imagined being a father. It was a dream of mine. Ariah became the child I never had."

"She will continue to be, but we do need to figure out a way to get her father out of jail before the real threat finds him."

"I'll give my contact a call and see if he's made headway on the case."

Alazar gave a one-shoulder shrug and rose to his feet, swirling the ice in his glass. Mark's expression turned from self-pitying to cautious curiosity.

"You have that look about you, Alazar. What are you thinking?"

"Oh, nothing."

"Uh, no. It's not nothing."

"Two words. Put them together. Jail." He rested his tumbler on the sideboard. "Break."

"That's brilliant. Not only will my brother be a fugitive with local law enforcement and the FBI after him, nothing screams attention to our enemies like a potential connection to our breed's sudden escape from jail. And where do you think he should go?"

"Home."

He spoke his answer telepathically, and almost immediately felt a strengthening in the house's magical presence that left him uneasy.

"I'm going to check on Ariah." He glanced at his watch. "I want to stop at Delaney's on the way home to pick up some truffles. I'm craving sweets. Where's Ariah's room?"

"I'll show you."

Alazar kept his eyes peeled and his senses honed for any sign of the witch stalking around the house as he followed Mark up the grand stairway and down a hallway until they came to the second door. He was surprised by Miriam's lack of welcome for her husband's friend, at least pretending to be a good hostess, but hey. He really didn't care. His concern was Ariah, and he would be lying if he said his negative impression of his Keeper's wife hadn't been swayed. Distance between them might be a good thing.

Mark knocked on the closed door. "Honey, you need a hand in there?"

The door pulled open a moment later. Ariah stood in a towel, her skin damp and her hair dripping around her shoulders. Her face was rosy from the heated water. The delicious scent of flowers and apples filled Alazar's nostrils. He leaned against the wall and cast his eyes to the floor.

He did not need to see her like this right now. All the sweetness he needed stood a few feet away.

"I'm sorry. I wanted to jump in the shower. I have everything packed up for a couple of nights." Ariah's bashful gaze burned into his head until he looked up. "Just in case."

"Good thinking," Alazar said, unable to temper the gravelly husk of his voice. He cleared his throat. "Want us to grab your things now while you change?"

Ariah turned back to the room, leaving the door open. Alazar headed in, but Mark stayed in the hallway.

"I'll meet you downstairs."

Alazar nodded as his Keeper closed the door. Ariah had disappeared into the adjoining bathroom, thankfully, leaving him to handle the consequences of her appearance. He looked over the room, decorated with a basic appeal to any guest. The bags of clothing and accessories he had purchased yesterday were piled on a bench against the far wall. A few items hung over the sides.

Rounding the bed, he gathered up the bags as Ariah, dressed, emerged from the bathroom. Her brows hiked upward.

"My bag is on the bed." Ariah pointed to the simple duffel resting alone on the white comforter. "Planning on returning the purchases?"

"Thought you'd like choices."

Ariah laughed, brushing her side bang from her eye. She had pulled her hair half up. "Trying to get me to settle in with you so soon, I see."

"Trying to alleviate the stress of returning back here, under the circumstances. I'd rather set you up at a bed-and-breakfast in town than experience the anxiety you suffer stepping foot in this house." Alazar winked. "However, why break our streak now? You spent last night at my house."

Ariah tilted her head, thrusting her sweet lower lip out in a thoughtful motion as she came closer.

"In the guest room."

"That can be rectified."

She stood before him, pressed to her toes, and laid a soft kiss on his lips that burned him up from toes to head. "Mmm. I think that would be a good idea."

"Oh, so do I."

Alazar focused on keeping his breaths steady as she lowered to her heels, her palm trailing down his chest until it dropped to her side. She sat on the edge of the bed and tugged on her boots, then slung her duffel over her shoulder.

"Ready?"

"After you, Ace."

Alazar adjusted the bags to get through the door and followed Ariah to the stairs. The witch's energy that had hummed through the mansion since they arrived erupted, instantly placing him on guard.

He found Mark waiting at the bottom of the stairs.

A woman, brunette and willowy, drew her slender fingers over Mark's shoulder as she began to climb the stairs. Her viperish gaze on Ariah, a cold smirk crossed red-painted lips. Alazar held the dragon in tight restraints.

"Farewell, dear step-niece. Our time, sadly, was so short."

Then, Miriam lifted her gaze to Alazar.

Her smile dropped at the same time the world closed in on him. He stared at her, his feet moving of their own accord down the stairs, but his attention focused on the witch. Dark eyes flecked with silver. A strange, static-like shift around her brunette hair revealed streaks of black.

Glamour. Very strong glamour.

Alazar followed the witch with his eyes, their passing like a slow motion video. Their gazes stayed locked. Alazar shut down his expression to nothing more than stoic. He leashed his dragon as the beast raged to get free. His lungs burned with a mixture of fire and smoke he refused to exhale.

More static. More short-circuited magic that revealed the truth beneath the seductive witch.

A hint of a black tattoo along her neck.

"Mark, get my jewel. And don't make it obvious."

"Why?"

"Just do it!"

His brain tried to process what was happening as his body continued to move on autopilot. Only when he couldn't watch Miriam any longer did he finally tear his gaze from her and finish his descent.

"Alazar?"

Ariah's concerned voice filtered into his mind. What should have calmed him ignited a fierce explosion of urgency. He had to work triple-hard to keep his calm and laid-back manner as he stepped off the last stair and casually pressed a kiss to Ariah's temple. As he did, he cut his heavy-lidded gaze to the loft over the foyer. Miriam watched him with narrowed eyes, her expression anything but seductive. A moment later, she turned on her heel and disappeared down another hallway.

"Everything is okay, sweetheart." He herded her in the most gentle of manners into Mark's office. Alazar was thankful Mark had closed his office doors, otherwise Miriam would have seen his Keeper retrieving the box with his jewel and its key from a hidden shelf in the bookcase.

Mark turned, his expression full of unspoken questions. He crossed the room and held out the box. Alazar grabbed his wrist, burning his gaze into his Keeper's.

"Do not question me, Mark. Get your keys. You are coming with us."

"I shouldn't—"

Alazar's upper lip peeled away from partially formed dragon fangs. Smoke filtered through his teeth. Ariah stepped up beside them, a hand coming down on Alazar's.

"Now." Alazar hissed the word as low as he could. "Right. Now."

Alazar grabbed the box and stuffed it into a pocket on the inside of his jacket.

"Al—"

Alazar pressed a finger to Ariah's lips, silencing her with the motion and a hard glance. Her eyes widened. He pursed his lips in a silent "shh" and snapped his attention back to Mark. He gave a sharp jerk of his head toward the door and ushered both Mark and Ariah from the office.

"How about I whip up dinner tomorrow? Maybe it'll help with the tensions, hmm?" Alazar asked, slapping a relaxed smile on his mouth while he simmered under his skin. Mark's creased brows and displeasure at being forced from his home without explanation shadowed his face. "I think it's only proper."

Mark played along. "Sounds good. Do you still make a mean cordon bleu?"

Alazar kept a hand on Ariah's hip, his fingers tense. He sensed her confusion as thick as fog, but to his relief, she kept quiet and watched the spectacle between him and Mark as his Keeper suggested, "Or how about that steak saltimbocca?"

"Whichever you'd like. Ace? Do you prefer chicken or steak?"

"Uhh…chicken?" Her brows furrowed, glancing up at him as they moved closer to the door to the front porch. *"What the heck is going on here? I think I just stepped into an alternate reality."*

Alazar's eyes flashed. He caught the flames' obscuring slashes in his vision. Ariah's hard swallow confirmed it.

"Chicken it is. I'll make the saltimbocca next time."

"Mark, darling. Where are you going?"

Mark paused, keys in hand, and turned to the stairs. Ariah stiffened against Alazar. Alazar dared to cast the witch a look. She was all coy, sensual appeal standing at the head of the stairs.

"I forgot some paperwork in the car. I'd like to see my niece out as well. I'll be back shortly."

Miriam tilted her chin skyward, her eyes narrowing. She stared down the fine, sharp slant of her nose.

At Alazar.

Alazar flashed her a smile, waved, and pushed Ariah out the door, pretending to trip over the threshold as he went.

Mark closed the door behind them. Alazar handed off half the bags to Mark, forcing him down the sidewalk and to the driveway. He dug out his car keys and slapped them into Ariah's hand.

"Open the trunk and then get in the car. Now."

"What is—"

"Hurry," Alazar snapped. Ariah began to protest. She must have seen something in Alazar's face because she nodded, turned, and jogged the rest of the way to the Mustang. The trunk popped open and Alazar headed that way. To Mark, he said, "You. Follow me and don't you dare, under any circumstances, answer your phone."

"Alazar, would you like to tell me—"

Alazar flashed him a smile that was anything but happy. "Sure."

Ariah dropped into the passenger seat and pulled the door closed. Alazar shoved the bags in the trunk, closed it, and rounded to the driver's side as Mark jammed his share of bags into his Jaguar. He paused when he opened the driver's side door and looked at Alazar over the roof.

"You've been duped, my dear friend. And now our enemies know exactly where we are."

Chapter 18

Ariah couldn't shake the persistent waves of cold from her skin. They came from someplace deep inside her body, leaving her arms and legs covered in goose bumps. Even with the heat that rolled off Alazar, the chill seemed impenetrable.

She dared a glance at the speedometer as Alazar opened up down the low-traffic back roads. They were five minutes from her uncle's house, her uncle's Jaguar riding their back bumper, and Alazar had said nothing about his strange behavior and sudden onset of caution. She figured he didn't care for Miriam either. Her gut instinct about the woman had warned her that beneath the pretty, made-up, fashionable woman facade lay nothing but pure black evil. Her dragon man's intuition was probably ten times better than hers and his unease began the moment they started down the stairs.

A sharp cuss fled Alazar's mouth, catching her completely off guard, the foul word fleeing his lips so sharp it made her gasp.

"Alazar, what is it? Tell me."

"I think I just figured out how the Baroqueth found Kaylae a few months ago. Miriam works at the credit union, right?"

Dread began to pour down her spine. "Yes."

"Kaylae was never taught in her powers. She had no clue how to scramble her aura and Miriam picked up on it." Fire burned in Alazar's eyes when he chanced a split-second glance at her. He was going way too fast not to have his full attention on the road. Not even his speed could match the sickening churn of her stomach over the puzzle pieces dropping into place. "Mark taught you how to protect yourself and conceal the truth of who you are. That's the only reason she wasn't able to figure out who and what you are. She probably didn't realize precisely why she was drawn to you. Mark as well. Your father's powers are dormant. Her draw was to you, not him. As with Mark. Her focus has been on you."

The cold turned to ice. She shivered.

"You're not making sense."

"Miriam is Baroqueth. She's a witch, too. Her sorceress blood is diluted, but her magic is still powerful. Her glamour is impressive, but it couldn't stay in place against my sight." He wrung the steering wheel, his nails tapering to talon points. Ariah tried to swallow, but her throat had gone dry. "Have you always seen her eyes? Dark with silver flecks?"

"Yes."

"That is a key characteristic of the Baroqueth. Dark,

almost black, eyes. Flecks of silver, circulating power. They usually have tattoos on their neck, sometimes their faces. Runic, power binding tattoos to harness their powers and make them stronger. Their hair is black."

Ariah squeezed her eyes shut and shook her head, trying to digest this information. "Miriam has brown hair. And just because her eyes are dark with silver flecks doesn't mean she's an enemy. She's evil, but she's not our enemy." Her voice trailed off as she looked at Alazar again. His expression was fierce and dangerous, so unlike him and yet perfectly him. "She can't be. Can she?"

"Trust your intuition, Ace. Take the gamble. What do you think?"

Her heart and her stomach plummeted to her feet. "For ten years?"

"You're stronger than you think. She couldn't break your shield, if I were to guess. It pissed her off because she couldn't get a read on you or Mark. She bided her time and it paid off." He scowled, releasing a sound that vibrated in her marrow. Smoke created a thin haze inside the car. "Because of me. She recognized me."

"How?"

"It's not hard to remember eight faces. I'm sure the Baroqueth have figured out a way to share our likenesses with their descendants."

"But...but why wouldn't she have tried to go after Zareh again? Why wait?"

Alazar ground his teeth, but remained silent. Ariah ached to crawl over to him and curl up on his lap. She wanted to feel the security, the promise of safety in his arms.

The formidable man beside her reached for the touchscreen on the dash and pulled up his phone directory. He commanded the system to call Zareh and Cade on a conference call.

Cade answered first, a gruff greeting that sounded more like grinding rocks than a voice. Zareh answered a ring later.

"Three way?" Zareh asked. In the background, Ariah could hear laughing and music. "Are you on your way home? We've got Nick and Willa here with Ivan and Monalisa. Pandora and Cole are on their way and I have the grill fired up."

"We've got a problem," Alazar said shortly. "Mark's wife is Baroqueth."

Silence. Dead, devoid of life, silence. Stifling silence that nearly drowned out the masculine roar of the Mustang's engine. Every hair on Ariah's body tingled with fear.

"Are you certain?" Cade asked.

"For once, Cade, I'm not screwing around. She's been hiding behind some strong magic. She's not full-blooded, but she's in league. I saw the tattoos. She works at the credit union."

"Kaylae had mentioned—"

"Exactly. She recognized Kaylae and probably tipped off her buddies. I have Mark tailing me back home, Zar. We're going to need to come up with something, and fast. She knows where we live, and she knows we're on to her. Cade, we need to get Ariah's father out of jail before the Baroqueth get to him."

"I'll be there within the next few hours," Cade said. His line disconnected. The background noise from Zareh's line had faded, as though he'd gone into another room and closed the door. Ariah looked at her uncle's headlights in the side-view mirror.

"What do you want to do, Zareh? I'm willing to return to The Hollow, but I know you've got your feet pretty well planted in Nocturne Falls."

"We'll get through this together," Zareh said. "I'll put a call out to Sheriff Merrow. I think our barbeque is going to have to be a strategy planning session. Careful, brother."

"You, too." Alazar ended the call, but his shoulders, his entire body, remained stiff. Ariah slipped her fingers over his forearm, cautious not to rile the dragon treading so close to the surface. "You'll be fine, Ace."

"Will you?" She grabbed the dashboard when he took a steep curve. The tires squealed, but he maneuvered the vehicle with envious precision. Her uncle never came off their bumper.

"Humor me, sweetheart. Would you choose forever with a dragon or a life of freedom and luxury?"

Ariah gaped. "What kind of question is that?"

"A brutally honest question."

It was a no-brainer for her. "Forever with a dragon. With *my* dragon. I don't need luxury. I've done without it for years. And freedom? I would be free with you. Where is this coming from?"

"My heart."

Ariah's brows creased, the shameless truth of his answer stealing her own heart from her chest and delivering it to Alazar on a golden platter. His sincerity filled the dark void inside her soul until she was bursting with warmth and completion.

Could it be love? So soon?

As quickly as her joy blossomed, another anchor of dread pulled it back down. "Why does that sound like you're expecting something really bad to happen?"

Alazar released one hand from the wheel and clasped her hand, bringing her knuckles to his lips. "As long as there is breath in my lungs, nothing bad will happen."

"If you no longer have breath, bad already happened."

He nodded, her point made.

"Is my father going to be okay?"

"I hope we didn't delay too long. Your father isn't who they're after, but he'd be good leverage."

Alazar took another sharp curve, laying off the accelerator until the road straightened out again. He gunned the engine, bulleting down the dark straightaway. Ariah decided to sit back in her seat and grab hold of the handle along her door. Otherwise she'd have her wish of curling up in Alazar's lap, at a most inopportune time.

"They're after you," Ariah surmised. Wasn't that what the Baroqueth wanted? The dragons' powers?

"Oh, sweetheart. She saw our hand. You're no more safe than Mark or I. If Miriam had not seen me, you'd still be safe. Well, safer. You are my lifemate and in line to be a Keeper, but your Keeper blood will allow you to bear another dragon's child if I die. Our enemies spare no one. The target is emblazoned on your back as bright as it is on mine."

Damn dread. The least it could do was leave her lungs alone so she could breathe a little easier. Wasn't it bad enough they were going to come face-to-face with really powerful sorcerers in the near future?

"I swear to you, Ariah. I swear with every fiber of my being that I will die before I let anyone or anything harm you."

The weight of Alazar's words settled heavy on her shoulders. His promise came with a breath of power, a force of reckoning. She had no doubt in her mind, in her heart, that she would witness her beautiful dragon's death before she suffered her own.

Ariah caught the shadowy sign announcing their arrival in Nocturne Falls. Alazar slowed a notch, but treaded a death-defying speed along the windy, two-lane road.

"Alazar, no one will die. I'm not going to lose you. That would be really, really cruel to finally know true happiness only to have it taken away."

"Reality, Ace."

Ariah couldn't help but smile. The irony. "Yesterday, I was the one stuck in reality, refusing to believe in fairytales. Guess what, you sexy beast."

That got his attention. He even slowed to a normal speed to look at her with a new glow in his eyes.

Ariah leaned over the console and brushed her lips over his ear. "You delivered a fairytale, dragon included, and I'll fight like a madwoman to keep what is mine."

Small, fragile, delicate, emotionally scarred.

Everything a person might deduce looking at Ariah Callahan from a distance. He knew better.

Fierce, stubborn, warrior, spitfire.

Yep. That was his sweet Ace to the core of her being.

Alazar had to keep from puffing out his chest with pride when they stormed into his house on Crossbones Drive. He was vaguely surprised to see the size of the gathering in the living room. Sheriff Hank Merrow with Hugh, one of the Ellingham vampires who ran Nocturne Falls. Delaney, Hugh's vampire wife, Willa, and Monalisa chatted it up with Kaylae and nibbled treats from a platter of fudge, truffles, and a few other creations from Delaney's Delectables.

Nick and Zareh came in from the back patio. Alazar lifted his chin at the sight of Ivan, another Nocturne Falls dragon, following behind them and a smile touched his lips. The guy was not a Firestorm, but he was pretty damn big and his fighting skills would definitely come in handy. It was also nice to have another set of wings and an extra dose of fire at their disposal.

Zareh's steps hastened as he crossed the room. "We've started talking about the problem." He angled his body to Alazar's left as Mark came around him. "Mark."

"Zareh." Mark clapped Zareh's shoulder and received the same greeting from the dragon. "It's nice to see you again."

"Circumstances could be better." Zareh motioned to the living room, where the men gathered. "Head on in. There are beers and sodas in the tub. Steaks and burgers are coming off the grill in a few minutes."

Mark broke off toward the living room. Ariah's fingers tightened, drawing Alazar's attention to her.

"Why don't you go see Kaylae, sweetheart? I'm going to help Zar get the food off the grill."

He placed a kiss on the top of her head before she could muster a scalding glance in his direction. One thing he learned real fast was that Ariah did not like to be thought of as "weak." Suggesting she sit around a chocolate display with women could be taken as the equivalent of telling her not to worry her pretty little head, when in reality Alazar needed the distance in order to think straight. This lifemate business had a way of flaring at the worst possible time.

To his relief, Ariah nodded and joined the group without an argument. Alazar followed Zareh out to the patio, where Nick and Ivan had returned to flip the meat. Nick tipped his beer toward Alazar in greeting. Ivan gave a solemn nod.

"Hear we've got some more roaches coming out of the woodwork," Nick said, moving a few large steaks around the grill. The flames below flared and the juices sizzled. The delicious aromas of marinade and spices made Alazar's stomach growl. "Never a dull moment in the land of paranormals."

"Do you know how many are here?" Ivan asked, his voice thick with his Russian accent.

"Haven't a clue, putting us at a pretty huge disadvantage. For all we know, there are none in the immediate area at this time, but they'll be coming now that there are targets," Alazar said.

He quickly filled the guys in on what had transpired at Mark's house, what his assumptions were regarding Miriam's role as a spy, and reminded their friends of the dangers the Baroqueth would present. The last thing he wanted was a friend hurt and he would understand any of the non-Firestorms walking away from this twisted party. Each man here, each woman present, had something great to risk. Love, happiness, the lives of their partners. A huge gamble even Alazar was hesitant to take.

One thing Alazar and Zareh had learned from the last attack was that the residents of Nocturne Falls did not abandon their friends, regardless of the threat. They came together in times of need and did not back down in the face of danger.

"You guys know how to pick some mean friends," Ivan said, and chuckled. He flipped a line of burgers. "But I think I have faced worse in the ring."

"I'm willing to bet the things you've seen in the ring would probably fall to the Baroqueth." Alazar stuck out his hand. The bet was nothing more than an attempt at levity in a life or death situation. He needed the lightness. Ivan eyed his hand. "Fifty gold coins."

Ivan shook. "Deal, Firestorm. My hoard can use a few more pieces. I am sure an ancient such as you has a few to spare."

"I can't believe you," Zareh grumbled. He grabbed a large platter and held it for Nick to place the finished steaks on. "Making bets during a time like this."

"That's what I do best."

"*Losing* those bets is what you do best."

Alazar shrugged. "Maybe my luck has changed."

Zareh scowled, tossing the living room a pointed look. "Or maybe you're *whipped*."

"I won't deny that." Alazar cinched his brow. "What would that have to do with my gambling?"

"Your head's in the clouds. You're not thinking straight."

Alazar caught the edge in his friend's look, the unspoken implication behind his words. He forced a smile despite the sour effects of Zareh's low jab.

"I'm thinking *perfectly* straight."

The breeze kicked up suddenly. Alazar stepped closer to the edge of the patio, Zareh and Ivan flanking him. The familiar sound of beating wings accompanied the rustling treetops and intensifying waves of air.

A large, looming figure came into view, wings outstretched as the enormous dragon descended from the night-cloaked sky.

"You're kidding me."

Zareh's cuss was nearly drowned out beneath the sound of wings and wind.

Alazar didn't move from the edge of the patio, shock holding him still. The dragon landed and transformed. The man who stood in the backyard flicked a wave of black hair from his forehead, found Alazar and Zareh, and strode toward them.

"Syn," Alazar murmured. His lips curled until he couldn't hold back the smile. "Damn it, man!"

Syn Terravon, one of their lost brothers, flung his arms around Alazar in a tight bro hug worthy of their thirty-year separation. The hard clap of his hand on Alazar's back assured him that their numbers had increased during their time of need.

A similar greeting was shared between Syn and Zareh, then handshakes between the newly arrived Firestorm dragon, Ivan, and Nick.

"Cade asked me to check in on Mark's brother a few hours ago. I went over to the jail, but he wasn't there," Syn said soberly.

The relief that came with the reunion shattered. Hammer-to-glass shattered. Alazar narrowed his eyes.

"What do you mean?"

Syn shrugged. "I scoped out the jail before I went in and asked about Mike. According to the guard, there was no Mike Callahan booked. Checked another jail. Same thing. Went to the police department that made the arrest, according to the news reports, and the officers never heard of him. Said there was no arrest. The guy escaped."

Coldness settled heavy in Alazar's gut. He shook his head. "No. He was arrested. Ariah saw him surrender. He was practically tackled."

"Doesn't surprise me." Syn's calm did little to ease the rising tension spreading like fire along Alazar's muscles. "If the Baroqueth did have him in their sight, then they most likely intervened before Mike had a chance to be booked. Which means—"

"Not good things," Alazar bit out. He cast a shadowed glance over his shoulder. From the patio, he caught movement in the living room, but couldn't see Ariah. The news Syn came bearing would unleash chaos. "I'll have to break this to her."

"Why don't we wait and see what we can discover before that happens? Maybe he did escape. He managed that once before and we all thought he was dead."

Alazar turned the idea over in his head for a brief second before he discarded Syn's suggestion. This was his woman's father. She had a right to know.

Her scent hit him first, followed by a faint electrical zing along his arms. "Alazar? What's going on?"

Syn and Zareh burned their gazes into his head. At least he was spared the hard looks from Nick and Ivan as he turned to face his next biggest hurdle. Ariah stood in the doorway, a hand resting on the glass slider, a subtle crease across her forehead. Worry etched the golden veins of her eyes. Her lips drew taut. Hesitation spoke in the way she rocked the toe of her boot against the floor.

Her attention shifted to Syn for a moment before turning back to Alazar.

Alazar snuffed out the sigh before it made it to his lips. He motioned to Syn. "Ace, this is Syn Terravon. Another one of us."

Ariah regarded Syn with a hint of caution behind a mask of reserve. Alazar was surprised when he received a wave of unease from Ariah, a chill that touched his mind. He was beginning to suspect she had a good idea of what was happening.

"Nice to meet you, Ariah." Syn smiled, lending a subtle calm to the dense air, and held out his hand. Ariah stared at it for a few seconds before she accepted it in a tentative shake. "Cade contacted me for extra backup."

The crease in her forehead deepened. She lifted her chin, her eyes narrowing slightly. "Where did you come from?"

Syn exchanged a shaded glance with Zareh. Alazar separated from the guys and moved toward Ariah, who stiffened at his approach. He paused.

"Ariah?" he murmured.

"What's going on, Alazar? The weight of the world crashed down on you a minute ago. I felt it."

Well, damn.

"Excuse us," Alazar said, slipping his arm around Ariah's waist and pulling her into the house. He didn't stop, ignoring the curious glances from the women in the living room as he guided Ariah up the stairs to his room. The silence was unbearable, unspoken questions churning the air. He urged Ariah into his room and closed the door behind him, bracing himself for the unknown. "There's something you need to know."

"I'm gathering that. And I'm thinking it's not good."

Alazar turned to find Ariah standing in the middle of his room, arms crossed, defiant as ever. Her strength continued to amaze him.

"Syn got here real fast for having been contacted less than half an hour ago. I'm assuming Cade contacted him earlier today about something."

Snagged by her smarts, too. Alazar was on the fast plunge to love, and the timing couldn't have been worse.

"Cade asked Syn to check on your father, but your father's nowhere to be found," Alazar said. Ariah stared at him, that same defiance burning bright. He tilted his head and moved toward her. "He was never arrested per records and he was never booked."

"That's nonsense. I saw the cops arrest him."

He gave a single nod. "I never doubted that you did. What I'm saying is that Syn couldn't find a trail. At all. He went to the arresting department and was told he never made it there."

A blink. The hardness in her expression began to fracture. A crack here, another there, the inevitable webbing between each of those fractures until the mask fell away. Stark realization drew her face sallow.

"You don't think…"

Alazar sighed. "I don't know, sweetheart. I really don't, but this breathes Baroqueth. Your father was familiar with the Baroqueth and what they look like. He would have been able to tell an enemy from a human. I fear they may have intercepted the arrest and captured him."

The moment her chin quivered Alazar gathered her in his arms and drew her into his body. She didn't sob, as he half expected, but he smelled the salt of tears. Her fingers fisted at the back of his jacket.

"We will do everything to get him back safely. I promise you, Ariah. You have my word."

"I know you will." She nodded against his shoulder. "I know."

CHAPTER 19

Three days had passed since Ariah learned the devastating news about her father. Three days and no word, no trace, no idea of his whereabouts. Three days of being a prisoner in Alazar's house. She was going stir-crazy.

Whether her incessant pacing clued her dragon man in or her declining spirits, Alazar finally whisked her into town for lunch at Howler's, as well as a game of pool. His skills continued to impress her, never missing a shot until the entire table was cleared.

"You're his lucky girl," Bridget said close to Ariah's ear as she brought over another round of drinks. They had opted for sodas and a basket of out-of-this-world fries, which they polished off in a matter of minutes. Bridget cleaned up their high-top table, basket included, and jutted her chin toward Alazar as he lined up for a final shot. "Don't know what you've done to him, but he was a cringe-worthy shot before you came along. Zareh would have to win his losses back all the time."

"That's hard to believe." Ariah sipped her soda as Alazar hit the cue ball and sank the eight ball into the corner pocket. "Really hard."

"Aww, Bridge. You can't tell her something nice about my gaming habits?" Alazar asked, his smile wide and triumphant. "I've been waiting for the right time to bring out my skills."

Bridget arched a brow beneath her wild auburn hair, her golden eyes glittering with humor. "A full year is quite a while, especially when you lost a car in a game gone bad."

Ariah gasped. "You *what*?"

"It was only a car." Alazar shrugged like it was no big deal. "Not a leg."

"A car. A *car*?" Ariah rolled her eyes to the ceiling.

"Now look what you've gone and done, Bridge." Alazar rounded the table and smoothed his knuckles over Ariah's cheek. She scowled. "Got her all upset over something that happened a long time ago. But you're right about my Ace being my lucky lady."

Bridget's knowing smirk didn't disappear. She nudged Ariah's arm with her elbow. "He wasn't always this good."

"Thank you, darling Bridget. Now, before you cause irreparable damage to my impeccable reputation—"

"Far from impeccable," Ariah interrupted.

Alazar nuzzled his cheek against hers, his lips brushing her ear. A shiver raced down to her feet.

"That's not what you said last night."

"Oooh, you...you..." Her face heated. Alazar

chuckled, straightening up. Ariah stared at his collarbone while she simmered in those potent memories. "That was unfair."

"Well, on that note, I'll leave you two lovebirds to bicker over your *impeccable* skills." Bridget wiped off the high top with her rag before tucking it in her apron. "Ariah, all jokes aside, he's a good one to keep."

"Alas, finally, a compliment," Alazar said.

Bridget snickered and returned to the bar.

"I'm going to pop that head of yours. I sense too much hot air beneath your skin." Ariah gave his temple a playful poke. Alazar leaned back against the edge of the pool table, drawing her close. "So, where did your sudden skills come from?"

Alazar's uplifting demeanor sank. His smile dimmed. "You."

"That's silly."

Alazar shrugged. "Silly or not, Bridget's right. Up until you met me here that first night, I was lucky to get a ball in the pocket at all. I gambled on the tables almost every night." A heavy breath fled his pursed lips. "Guess you can say it was an outlet."

"Losing was an outlet?" That was pretty counterproductive. "How is that?"

"I didn't play to lose. I played to remember what I had lost."

As Ariah watched Alazar's amber eyes expose vulnerability and pain, she realized he was talking about his secret. In that moment, she also realized something more defining.

Alazar—funny, laid-back, easygoing, sexy dragon man—hid his agony beneath his relaxed, humorous exterior. He hid it well.

"You played knowing you'd lose?"

"It was never about winning. It was a punishment." He moistened his lips, his fingers tightening around her waist. She drew a finger down the lapel of his leather jacket, waiting for him to divulge his story. "My punishment."

"Why were you punishing yourself?"

Alazar pressed off the table, easing her a couple of steps back, and slipped away from her. He replaced his pool stick in the rack and started retrieving the balls from the pockets. Ariah helped him, placing hers in the rack Alazar dropped on the table. She watched him from beneath the locks of hair that had fallen over her eyes, recognizing new shadows stirring over his handsome face. His eyes adopted a haunting haze, one that left her chilled.

"Pool. A game of calculation, precision, and measurement. There is a formula for each shot." Alazar lifted his hand, pinching his thumb and forefinger close. "An exact configuration to sink each ball into a pocket."

He dropped his hand to the felted table, dragging his fingers along the green. "For humans, clearing a table in one turn is almost impossible. For Firestorm dragons, it's a piece of cake. This is how we live, Ace. Our survival depends on our ability to analyze angles, moves, obstacles, and what-have-you at high rates of speed and often at the last second."

He pulled out the last ball from a corner pocket, tossed it in the air, and caught it. Ariah couldn't take her eyes off him as he came up to her, still tossing the ball, catching it each time without so much as a glance.

"Precision." He tossed the ball again. This time, when he lifted his hand to catch it, the ball hit the heel of his palm, rolling to the side and falling toward the floor. She grappled to catch it, but his hand came up beneath hers, securing the ball before it hit the floor. Bent over, eyes levels with each other, faces close and foreheads brushing, Alazar whispered, "Just like that, an accident can happen. *Did* happen. A miscalculation by a fraction because I was too concerned about escaping with my Keeper, protecting him while under fire from the Baroqueth, I went in one direction to escape a power bolt."

His face tightened. His nostrils flared briefly. Anger and anguish saturated Ariah's mind and filled the emotional pool in her chest.

"I went in the *wrong* direction. Hit the side of the cliff I thought I could avoid. Threw my Keeper off my back." His eyes sparked. Ariah stifled a gasp as she received flashes of a scene that made no sense until he spoke again. "I went after him, covered him from the attack until I could get beneath him. I took three hits from the Baroqueth."

Ariah jolted, a shockwave of electricity flooding her body through the streamlining vision Alazar shared with her. She grabbed his arms and held on for dear life, unable to see him clearly in front of her. The horrific scene unfolding in her head stole Alazar and Howler's from her sight.

"That last hit tore my wing. I lost control of my flight for precious moments until I leveled out with my injured wing. My Keeper had plummeted far in the time it took me to regain control. I spiraled down toward him. I reached him, grabbed him, held him close to my belly as I struggled to stop our descent."

Ariah squeezed her eyes shut, but the images continued to play through her mind. An invisible wind hit her face. Fear pulsed through her veins. Adrenaline conquered her and the only sensation she could decipher was the need to save the Keeper. But when she looked down at him through a strange, orb-like vision, something was wrong. Soul-sickening wrong.

"He was dead," Alazar whispered.

A knot formed in her throat. She tried to swallow, tried to breathe, but couldn't get anything past the knot.

"I realized after I got us to safety that when my wing was hit, I knocked him into the side of the mountain. My position, how I cocooned him to protect him, caused his death. Essentially, I killed my Keeper when I was supposed to protect him because I *miscalculated*."

As the scene of the dragon holding the man in their rapid descent to the ground faded and Alazar returned to her vision, she managed to suck in a strained breath.

"Who...who was he?"

"Micah Callahan. Your grandfather."

Alazar straightened up and rolled out his shoulders. He couldn't bear the horrific expression on his Ace's face, opting to place the last ball in the rack in hopes of breaking the intensity of his revelation. He lived with his mistake for decades. Mark stepped into his father's shoes when he was eighteen. He had not been fully prepared, and their relationship had started rocky.

There was a lack of trust. Alazar understood why. Keepers put their lives in their dragon's talons. Mark's father had, and ended up a casualty of poor judgment. Mark had harbored his reluctance for years before finally realizing Alazar had done everything he could to rectify his mistake and save his father.

Alazar asked Ariah to trust him. Promised her that her trust would not be misplaced with him. But could she really put her trust in him after this?

"Alazar, can we go?"

She deserved the truth. You delivered. Now reap the consequences.

He glanced down at her and nodded. She would not look him in the eyes.

"Come on."

He cashed out their tab and followed Ariah out of one crowd in Howler's into a new crowd on the sidewalk. The storefronts on Main Street were bustling with activity. Costumed tourists snapped pictures in front of rickety buildings deliberately fashioned to look like they would collapse any minute. A small group of teenage girls walked by, skin sparkling with gold glitter and their smiles showing off vampire fangs.

On any other day at any other time, Alazar would have gotten a kick out of them. He couldn't be bothered to enjoy the scene, the costumes, the unabashed glee on the faces of the children and the awe in the adults. He hadn't talked about "the accident" in decades, to the point it was all but forgotten by Zareh and most likely the other Firestorms. No one blamed him, except for one person.

Alazar was his own judge and jury, and he knew if he had done one thing different, Micah would have survived. He should have banked right instead of left. Away from the mountainside, not toward. Stupid, simple mistake.

"Where is Delaney's?" Ariah asked. Alazar paused, forcing a small family to split up to walk around him. Ariah came up short a few steps later and turned to him. "Is it close by?"

"Pretty close."

Ariah stretched out her arm, her fingers beckoning him closer. Her brows lifted at his hesitation. He brushed aside a lock of hair that had fallen free of his band and accepted her generous offer.

"Show me," she said, her voice soft, entrancing. He stared at her for a long moment, entirely taken with his lifemate. Only a few minutes ago, he feared he'd lose her to his past. Now, as she held his gaze with nothing but pure affection glowing through those beautiful gold veins amidst the dark brown backdrop, he realized he worried for naught.

In that moment, he knew his heart no longer belonged to him. Ariah Callahan, his strong-willed Ace, stole it from his chest and cradled it in her tender hands.

Hand in hand, Alazar and Ariah meandered down Main Street. A comforting silence settled between them, one that allowed Alazar to replay that fateful event in his mind without self-pity and immense guilt. The warmth of Ariah's fingers between his, the shift of the air around their bodies assured him she was real, a gift.

"No one is perfect. Not even you, Alazar."

He pressed his lips together. Ariah squeezed his hand.

"Everyone makes mistakes. If a person came up to me and told me that he or she never made a mistake, never judged a situation wrong, I'd laugh. It's impossible. Human or not, we are not perfect."

Ariah curled her arm around Alazar's and rested her cheek against his biceps. "What made you go closer to the mountain instead of away? In that moment, why did you make that decision?"

"You're psychoanalyzing."

"I've had some practice with my father. Don't try to change the subject."

"If you must know, I believed the mountainside would provide more protection. Had I gone right, I would have exposed us both in the open until I reached the next peak." It didn't take a genius to see where Ariah was going. "However, being in the open does not mean we would have been vulnerable."

"Are you trying to justify your guilt?"

"Keep in mind my age. I've had plenty of practice with flight. Plenty of practice escaping our enemies, unfortunately. What happened should never have happened."

"Maybe it shouldn't have, but it did. That doesn't mean it was your fault."

He wasn't coming out of this session unscathed. Her understanding alone was breaking him down, peeling away the casing of guilt he'd wallowed inside for far too long.

"You protected him. It was the shot that sent you into that uncontrolled wobble that caused the outcome, not you." Her hand tightened around his arm. "You said that each shot has a formula. An exact calculation to land the ball in the pocket. But you have to take into consideration the variables, and the effects they can have on your calculation. If you don't have control over them, how can you possibly make an exact calculation without some degree of doubt?

"Sometimes, Alazar, the outcome is not what we hope for. What matters is what you did to get to that point. If you tried everything you could, if you did what you thought was right at that exact moment, how can you honestly believe the outcome was your fault? You made your calculations, but you had another force involved. Even the best could have failed because it's impossible to anticipate an opponent's exact intervention. You were missing a crucial piece of the equation, and you could only do the best you could with what you had."

Alazar led her down Black Cat Boulevard, toward Delaney's Delectables.

"I trust you, Alazar. I trust you more than I have allowed myself to trust a person in a very long time. I know that you'll do everything you can to keep me safe, but I've been well seasoned by reality and I know that the best intentions may not pan out the way we hope." Ariah lifted her head from his arm. He hated the separation. "How did I miss this when we were at the Hallowed Bean?"

"You weren't looking for it?"

Ariah laughed, elbowing his ribs. Her mood helped reel him in from the dark corners of his memories.

"Guess not."

Alazar pulled the door open as Ariah rounded him and entered. The succulent aroma of sweet chocolate made his jaw ache. Ariah had already maneuvered halfway to the display case where Delaney helped a few customers by the time he spotted her. The woman could slink like a cat.

Delaney smiled at Ariah and raised her gaze, finding Alazar. She gave a small wave before returning to her customers.

Alazar's large frame didn't allow him the same ease Ariah had weaving through the volume of customers mulling over the numerous stands displaying pre-wrapped confections. By the time he finally reached Ariah, Delaney was placing double dark chocolate truffles in a box.

"Delaney says those are your favorite," Ariah said, straightening up from the display case and turning to face him. Alazar couldn't hold back his smile. "And since I still owe you Delaney-made truffles, I'm delivering."

"I forgot about that bet." Alazar pulled his wallet from the inside pocket of his jacket and removed two twenties. "Delaney, would you mind adding a pound of the fudge that Zareh orders?"

"Certainly. How are things going?" Delaney held her smile steady, but Alazar caught the flicker of concern in her eyes as she handed the truffles to Ariah. "Hugh filled me in."

"On guard, as always."

"I heard from Pandora that Alice Bishop is trying to enlist some extra hands," Delaney said, referring to the local coven leader who'd helped contain the Baroqueth when Kaylae was targeted. She moved toward a section of the case with the fudge. "It'll all blow over like the last time."

It's a bit more complicated than that.

"One can hope." Alazar reached for the truffle box. Ariah smacked his hand away and tsked. "What?"

"Not right now."

"Here you go." Delaney handed over another box with the fudge and rang up the order. Alazar slipped her the money and gathered his change. "Tell Zareh and Kaylae I send my regards. Enjoy the treats."

"You know that's a given," Alazar promised, dropping his hand to Ariah's back. "Have a good one."

Once they hit the sidewalk again, Alazar stopped Ariah and turned her to face him. There was no doubt in his mind that she knew exactly what he was thinking and feeling. Her expression spoke volumes, called to his dragon, and left him putty in her presence.

"You never lost your abilities," she said. "They're who you are. You locked them away with that memory because, subconsciously, you wanted a reminder of your perceived failure. I don't know how I changed that, what I did to unlock it, but it never left you."

"Woman." He cupped her face, pulling her closer. "You are…you are…"

"I am?"

Alazar groaned. "You are a thief."

He closed his mouth over hers before she could respond, sweeping his tongue through her pliant lips, possessing her in a kiss that bordered on inappropriate in public as emotions swelled and burst from the deepest part of his soul.

When he broke away, leaving them panting and flushed, Ariah quirked a brow. "A *thief*. Uh, thank you?"

"You've stolen my heart, Ace. I don't know what I'd do if I didn't have you with me."

255

"You'd still be gambling away your gold and putting on a funny front to ease others while you wallow inside." She pushed up on her toes and nuzzled her nose against his. "I'll protect your heart, dragon man."

"I hope one day you'll trust me with yours."

Ariah pursed her lips, a short breath of a laugh caressing his moist lips. "One day?"

Alazar chuckled, stealing one last kiss before embracing her, craving the feel of her in his arms, real, here, and *his*. "Yes, Ace. One day. When you're ready."

Before he dropped to his knees in a desperate plea for that day to be today, right now, he brought them across the street to the Hallowed Bean. Those truffles would have to do for the time being, and a hot coffee was the key to washing them down.

CHAPTER 20

"Ariah, my girl. Can you hear me? Ariah!"

The panic, terror-filled thoughts pierced through her lazy dreams, shredding the subconscious calm to smithereens. Ariah jerked upright in bed, weakness flooding her as a faint shiver struck her spine.

"Sweet girl, please, please hear me. Please."

Ariah's eyes widened. *"Dad?"*

She hadn't a clue whether her father could hear projected thoughts like she could, but the clarity of her reception of this thoughts assured her that her father was close by.

Throwing the blankets aside, tearing off her pajamas and switching them out for a sweatshirt and jeans, she caught the time as she grabbed her lucky coin from the nightstand—she didn't go anywhere without it—and bolted from Alazar's room. She recalled her uncle's insistence of retrieving important Keeper belongings earlier in the day after he confirmed Miriam was at work. He had stopped back at Alazar's house for a few minutes before leaving again without disclosing a destination to Ariah or Alazar. When night fell and he hadn't returned, Alazar and Syn decided to search for him. Zareh and Kaylae had invited her to Howler's for a drink, but she opted for an early night.

She felt safe in the house alone. Apparently some of the witches in Nocturne Falls set wards around the property to keep ancient evil sorcerers from trespassing.

It was ten o'clock and her lifemate hadn't returned. She checked their mental bond. There was no indication he was in trouble, putting her at ease.

The sound of her father's pleas, however, had her scrambling down the stairs and into the dark living room. She peered through the curtains onto the quiet, dimly lit Crossbones Drive, searching for the man who somehow eluded police.

"Ariah? Mark gave me this address. He's in trouble. I tried to warn him, to get him to leave, but he wouldn't listen to me."

"Uncle Mark's in trouble? Where are you?"

Silence.

Ariah scanned the front yard, shoulders stiff, fingers digging into the sofa. The hard pound of her heart drowned out the quiet hum of the fridge in the kitchen, leaving her lightheaded.

At first, she wasn't sure she heard the scratch toward the back of the house. Her breaths came in short gasps. Adrenaline thrummed through her veins, making her skin hypersensitive to the slightest shift in the air. She crept through the living room, back to the foyer, and listened at the bottom of the stairs.

Another scratch, followed by the sound of metal scraping metal. Keeping to the shadows of the darkened house, she hurried toward the noise until she came to the sliding doors that led to the patio.

A figure moved in the dim moonlight, staying close to the wall as he fiddled with the lock. She glanced around, searching for a weapon, finding nothing. Dragons didn't need baseball bats or guns. They had a gut-load of fire to spew as needed. She, on the other hand, had nothing.

Giving the coin a hard rub, she tiptoed up to the slider and tapped a finger against the glass.

The figure startled, jumping back. When the hood fell away from his head, Ariah's knees threatened to buckle.

"Dad!" Ariah fumbled with the lock on the slider. To her utter confusion, her father grabbed the handle and held it closed, shook his head once, his eyes wide and filled with fear. He mouthed the word "no" over and over. Ariah stared at him, making sure the lock was still engaged, trying to figure out what the heck he meant. "You can't stay out there."

"My girl, open the door for me. I need to get you away from here. They know where you are. They'll be hunting you."

The entire time her father projected his desperate thoughts, his head shook harder and harder, the "no" becoming a fervent, albeit silent, chant. Her father's eyes sparkled, and not from moonlight.

"What is going on?"

"You're in danger. They caught your uncle. Miriam. She's one of them. She's one of their spies. Come on. We've got to go."

Ariah's gaze lowered to her father's hands. One gripped his wrist in an attempt to tug away the hand picking the lock. When she turned her attention back to his face, he clenched his teeth behind peeled back lips. Tears streamed down his face.

His desperate eyes snapped up to her. Pinned her with terror. He mouthed the word *"Run!"* as if he wanted to scream it. The veins in his neck bulged. His face turned a shade darker in the night's shadows. He mouthed it again. The hand fidgeting with the lock worked faster.

In that moment, her entire body whipped into action. She didn't bother with shoes or her purse. There was no time. She snatched the keys to the beat-up Toyota—thankfully, she was able to convince Alazar to bring it to the house—and bolted out the front door. The air chilled her skin, but the essence of dark, pulsing energy closing around her injected another dose of adrenaline into her escape.

She reached the car, climbed behind the wheel, turned the engine, and burned rubber down the driveway. The tires squealed as she jammed the brakes, shifted to drive, and peeled down the road. It wasn't until she was heading down the winding road leading out of Nocturne Falls that she cussed herself for not grabbing her cell phone.

"Alazar? Where are you? Please, I hope you can hear me."

As foolish as it was, she reached into her pocket and rubbed the circular coin tucked safely in her jeans.

"Get me out of here, coin. Get me far enough away from them. Get me to Alazar."

She pressed the accelerator as hard as she could.

"Ariah, what's going on? Are you okay?"

"No. I'm not." A rush of relief flooded her. Alazar's sharp tone, mixed with his barely hidden concern, did wonders to her shaking muscles. *"I don't know what's going on, but my father is at your house. I think they're controlling him. He tried to get me to leave with him, but he kept mouthing for me to run. He couldn't speak, and his thoughts didn't match his panic."*

"Where are you now?"

"Heading out of Nocturne Falls."

"We're coming back now. Don't stop—"

Static exploded in her head, drowning out Alazar's voice. She shrieked, her ears ringing. A flash of dark blue light shot across the street, creating a fog-like net. She jammed on her brakes, but the car plowed straight through the fog.

The static died out. A sizzle went throughout the car a split second before the engine, and everything else, died. The Toyota rolled to a stop.

Ariah sat stone still in the car, her hands gripping the steering wheel until her knuckles ached. The eerie silence that followed was cut only by her racing heartbeat and her short, gasping breaths.

Staring at the dark street ahead, flanked by thick, dense forest, there was no doubt she was not escaping.

Not when magic was involved and she possessed nothing but the ability to talk to her dragon through her mind.

She didn't even have shoes.

"You have to try. You're as good as dead staying here."

Swallowing against the parched texture of her mouth, she lowered a hand to the door handle, her eyes scanning every inch of her surroundings. Slowly, she opened the door, holding her breath as it creaked on its old hinges. The noise could have been a foghorn for how loud it echoed in the dense silence. Cautiously, she climbed out of the car, casting a glance down the road behind her, where the net had been and was no longer.

"Alazar?"

Ariah left the door open and broke into a sprint in the direction she had been headed. She stumbled when she ran over a sharp rock, flailing her arms to stay vertical. As she started to veer closer to the side of the road in hopes of blending into the shadows, she made a last-minute decision to keep to the center. The forest was dark. Danger lurked. Her gut screamed the warning. Her head throbbed from rushing blood and adrenaline.

And fear.

"Alazar!"

A large, black-cloaked figure appeared out of thin air in front of her. A fabric-draped arm lifted, fingertips stretching out from beneath the cuff.

Her toes and heel took a beating when she jammed a foot down, twisted, and hung a left, barely escaping the figure. Another cloaked figure materialized in her new path. She ducked beneath the arms that swung for her.

A *whoosh* sounded from behind her. A fierce rush of air knocked into her back, pitching her forward. She shrieked, tucking into herself as she hit the pavement and rolled. A sharp pain jolted down her arm from her shoulder. Dull throbs erupted from her hip and knees as she rolled out of her fall and scurried to get up.

An invisible weight crashed down and flattened her, belly down, to the ground. She growled, thrashing against unseen iron cords, unable to lift her legs from the pavement. Her hands lay splayed over the cool ground, her fingertips barely able to pull away from the road. She could lift her head without a problem and twisted her neck enough to see a herd of dark, shadowy figures surrounding her.

"Alazar! Help me!"

Ariah had no idea what Alazar would do, what he *could* do. He had no power in the human realm. Apparently, those rules didn't apply to the Baroqueth.

"Get her up."

Ariah scowled as her body levitated off the ground, tilted until she was upright, floating at least a foot off the road. She still had no control over her limbs, but the wild rage that erupted when she located Miriam standing at the front of the group left her grinding her teeth.

The woman she'd despised for the last ten years smiled up at her. That smile was anything but warm, reminding her of a snake.

"My years of patience have finally paid off."

Miriam snapped her fingers. Ariah's attention shifted from the witch to the figures of two men forced through the sea of black cloaks. She hid her shock, her panic from her expression as she recognized her father and Uncle Mark. Deep down, she'd known her father's words rang true when he said her uncle had been captured. These malicious sorcerers had turned her father into a puppet. They took her uncle. Now, they had her.

Miriam closed the distance between them. Ariah prepared to spit in her face, but the blasted witch sealed her lips closed.

"Manners, Ariah. A young lady does not behave so poorly." Miriam laughed. She stretched out her hand and wiggled her fingers. "Let me have the dragonstone."

Ariah twisted her face into the best angry glower she could muster. Miriam's smile took a quick southward dive.

"The stone, little girl."

Ariah snorted. Oh, the colorful words leaving tread marks in her head right now screamed for the chance to manifest on her tongue.

"Alazar, Miriam and about seven other Baroqueth have us. Uncle Mark, my father and I."

If she could stall the group long enough for Alazar to tear into Nocturne Falls along this very road, she might have a chance to escape.

"Mark, did you lie to me?" Miriam asked, turning enough to look at Uncle Mark from over her narrow shoulder. His face was cast in a mask of dark fury, his eyes glowing like lit coals. "Do *you* have the stone?"

"Even if I did, it would never come near you," Uncle Mark spat.

Ariah groaned. Well, damn. It wasn't fair that her uncle could speak, but she couldn't.

Miriam whipped back to her, grabbed her by the chin in a painful grip that made her wince, and yanked her head within inches of her enemy's. "Where is the dragonstone, Ariah?"

Ariah grumbled. Miriam scowled, unleashing the seal on her lips with a flick of her hand. Although Ariah still wanted to spit at the witch, she refrained for the sake of her freedom of speech.

"I don't have it."

"Your father gave it to you."

"Well, I *don't have it*. And if I did, you'd have to pry it from my dead hands."

Miriam's eyes narrowed, her head tilted, and that serpentine smile stretched across her red lips. "My dear, that can definitely be arranged."

Chapter 21

The instant the telepathic connection severed, Alazar roared. Then he was on the phone with Zareh. Syn called Cade when Alazar alerted him Ariah was in trouble. The dragon inside him wanted to take to the sky and get to his woman.

That would be foolish. He couldn't barrel into a situation without knowing what to expect other than finding the Baroqueth holding Ariah, Mark, and Mike hostage. He couldn't risk unleashing his fury. He needed to keep his head to save his lifemate.

He blew through the dark side roads in his Mustang with no heed for the danger of his breakneck speed. He and Syn would survive a wreck. He wasn't sure if he would survive the next ten minutes it would take to reach Nocturne Falls.

"Cade wants us to hold back."

"No."

"Alazar—"

"No!" Alazar flung Syn a poisonous glance. "I'm not holding back."

"We don't know how many there are."

"And Ariah is with that unknown number, helpless to protect herself. If they want to harm her, they can and they will. I won't let it happen."

"Shouldn't we call in your friends? They told us if anything happened—"

"Enough, Syn. There's no time. Zareh's securing Kaylae with Willa and Pandora, and I would like nothing more than to have Ariah with those three right about now."

Alazar pressed the accelerator harder when he caught the reflective siding of a police cruiser lying in wait. The lights came on before he had passed the cop. Syn groaned. Alazar merely glanced at the car fading in his rearview mirror. He cut his headlights and switched to his dragon's sight as he pushed his Mustang faster.

"You should try for the Daytona 500 or something."

"I'm not in the mood for jokes," Alazar growled. The reflection of the cruiser's lights cut through the thickening forest banking either side of the road. He slammed his hand against the steering wheel before wrapping his fingers around the leather again. "I shouldn't have left her alone."

"Al, she was safe until she fled the house."

"If I was there, she wouldn't have had to flee the house."

"Listen, she doesn't have your jewel, so they'll use her as leverage to get it from you. She's alive for the moment. You know that."

"And Mark? Mike? They're pretty much disposable to the Baroqueth. Ariah is the gem. She's the prize." A new sense of urgency surged. "I'm not about to lose another Keeper and I'm certainly not losing my lifemate."

The sign for Nocturne Falls flashed by them. A minute later, Alazar slammed both feet against the brake pedal, the car spinning as he veered to avoid hitting the person standing in the middle of the road. At that same moment, he caught a glint of metal—a car—as he regained control of his car and slowed to a stop, facing the wrong way on the road. The police cruiser's lights drew closer.

Alazar threw his door open and rushed around the hood of the car, his focus on the cloaked Baroqueth standing exactly where he had when Alazar almost hit him. The man threw off his hood, dark eyes flashing with shards of silver. Alazar lunged toward the slayer.

He slammed into an invisible barrier, stumbling back on his feet. He tried again with the same results. This small show of power struck a harsh dose of reality into the situation. Yes, the Firestorm suspected their enemies had gotten stronger, but the ease behind this slayer's ability to cast that spell showed just how power*less* Alazar was in this world.

"If you wish to save your lifemate, you will forfeit your dragonstone. You have one hour, Alazar Brandvold. One hour to deliver the dragonstone to your Keeper's home." The corner of the slayer's mouth quirked. "Zareh and his lifemate are more than welcome to join us tonight. It is only a matter of time before we go after him again."

"If you dare harm Ariah—"

"You will determine her fate."

With a snap, the Baroqueth vanished. Alazar clenched his fists, fire flickering in his vision. Smoke burned his throat and formed a thick haze around his head. His head throbbed, panic and anger swelling.

The rumble of his car's idling engine was muffled by the roaring in his ears. Syn threw open the passenger door and hitched his thumb toward the flashing lights.

"Get in. We've gotta book."

Alazar dropped into the seat and pulled the door closed as Syn opened up the engine on their way into Nocturne Falls.

The clock was ticking. He had one hour. One hour to come up with a plan that would save Ariah's life, as well as Mark and Mike. There was no sense in contacting Sheriff Merrow or Hugh or Alice Bishop. Their friends would not survive against the power and the magic he feared he'd face in one hour.

No. This was his to deal with. One way or another, he would make sure Ariah was safe. If that meant he handed over his dragonstone, and his life, to the Baroqueth, he was prepared to do just that. But not without a fight.

A lick of fire rolled over his tongue. He swallowed it back.

Tonight would be the ultimate gamble.

Tonight, he gambled for Ariah's life.

"I can't sit around and wait for them to decide our fate," Ariah said, pacing the floor in front of the fireplace. Her bare feet throbbed from the abrasions, but it didn't stop her from moving about. She needed to burn off this anger enough to think clearly. She tossed her uncle several glances, receiving his back as he perused the books on his shelves. They were locked in Uncle Mark's office, biding their time until Alazar showed up to make an exchange. Though Miriam refused to tell them what the exchange was, Ariah wasn't an idiot. "Uncle Mark, he can't give up that stone."

"He will."

"He *can't*. He'll forfeit his life if he hands over that stone." She was too angry to be upset by the prospect of losing Alazar. She would *not* believe it was even a possibility. "This is ridiculous. Is there nothing we can do?"

"We have no power in this world, Ari. The Hollow is our source of magic and has no direct connection to this realm. Therefore, we have no direct connection with our motherland."

"What are you looking for over there? Now isn't the time to start reading."

"Ari, I know you're mad, but you need to get yourself under control."

"Trying here." Ariah threw her father a perturbed look. "This all started with that stunt at the auction house." She narrowed her eyes, crossing her arms over her chest, and angled her body to face her father. The man sank deeper into the leather sofa, his frown tugging hard. "Why would you ever do that to me?"

"They were there. It had to look authentic. I had to make you scared enough that you would abandon me. I prayed they didn't realize you were my daughter. It was the only hope I had of getting you and the dragonstone far away from me and the Baroqueth."

"How did you know the jewel would be there? After all these years?" Uncle Mark asked, at last turning away from the bookcase. Her father's shoulders sank.

"Luck, really. I happened to catch wind of a strange box that was being put up for auction by a local museum. A former coworker's client mentioned it. He had a catalog and I saw a picture of the box. Knew instantly it was your lost dragonstone. How it ended up at an auction, your guess is as good as mine. Unfortunately, it was public enough that the Baroqueth must've heard of it as well."

Ariah jammed her hands into the pockets of her jeans. Her fingers wrapped around the coin she'd tucked away. She could definitely use some luck right now.

"What can we do? Alazar is not going to give them

the dragonstone. I won't let him. No one has magic or power, except for them." Ariah jerked her head toward the closed office doors, indicating their Baroqueth captors. She pursed her lips. "How that's even fair is beyond me. Give the evil players the upper hand."

Uncle Mark turned back to his books. Ariah groaned, her attention panning to the curtained windows. She had tried every possible exit to escape, but the evil sorcerers sealed up the room. The curtains might as well have been cement and the doors nothing more than an illusion.

They were trapped.

Ariah met her uncle by the bookcase. "How can you browse your books at a time like this?"

Uncle Mark's lips quirked. He tapped the old leather spine of a thin tome before pulling it off the shelf. Ariah moved closer, curious as her uncle rested the ancient-looking book on a stand. The lettering on the leather front had been worn by time. The edges of the spine and the covers were torn, tattered until the book itself looked like it might fall apart where it lay.

"What is that?"

Uncle Mark opened the book, taking great care as the spine creaked. The pages, yellowed and dried like cornhusks, had hand-written passages and faded colored drawing. The language was a mystery.

"Can you read that?" Ariah asked, her voice just above a whisper.

"Me? No. Alazar, yes. And since I bled into the dragonstone upon stepping into my position as

Keeper, I can translate it through my connection with him."

"What is this book?"

She dared not get her hopes up, especially as the corner of the page broke off when her uncle turned it.

"Is that what I think it is?"

Ariah looked up at her father, who had come to stand behind her. The sparkle in his eyes prodded her hope. Maybe this thing that looked like it would disintegrate into a pile of ash if breathed on was a good omen.

She held her breath.

"Yes," her uncle murmured, turning another page with excruciating care. Ariah caught herself beginning to wince, praying the page didn't flake into a million pieces. "I had forgotten about it."

"Do you think you can find a spell? And would it work?"

Uncle Mark looked up and scanned his bookshelves. He went to the glass cabinets that flanked either side of the bookcase, pulled one door open, and withdrew a rough-looking rock.

The low-resonance rumble of Alazar's car approaching brought Ariah up straight. *"Alazar? Can you hear me?"* One, two, three heartbeats. Silence. This was definitely not good. *"Alazar."*

Her uncle continued to sift through his displays of artifacts, statues, and stones while her father pondered the scripts in the book.

"Damn it." Uncle Mark pulled out a chunk of quartz

that barely fit in his hand and rested it beside the first rock. "I knew I should've stopped back at our old home, Mike. I have the perfect crystal there."

"Want to start filling me in, Uncle Mark?" Ariah asked. She licked her dry lips when the rumbling outside stopped. Time was running out. "What that book is about and why you're pulling out rocks?"

"It's best you don't know. In case they try to control your thoughts."

Ariah gave her father a pointed look. He shrugged.

"Isn't that what they did to you?"

She couldn't believe the barbs on her tongue tonight.

The latch lock on the pocket doors jostled. Instinctively, Ariah shuffled closer to her father, who pulled her into his chest. Uncle Mark closed the glass cabinet door, snatched up the rocks, shoved them in the pocket of his jacket, and closed the book. He tucked the delicate object under his arm and pulled his jacket over his chest as the pocket doors separated and slammed into the walls. Two large men loomed in the doorway.

Ariah's brows furrowed at the sight of the dark-haired, silver-speck-eyed handsome men with jagged black tattoos etched along their necks and the sides of their faces. She wasn't sure what she expected these enemies to look like, but it certain wasn't this rugged, almost normal, appearance. She'd seen worse in her days. These guys didn't give her the heebie-jeebies like some of those others.

The queen of the heebie-jeebies appeared between the men, her brown hair coiffed, make-up impeccable, and designer pantsuit crisp. Her red lips separated in a cold smile, her dark eyes calculating.

She didn't look like a viper. She was *the* viper.

All Ariah needed was a shovel. She'd do away with the snake real fast.

"Your dragon is right on time. Let us see if he brought what was asked of him, shall we?" Miriam taunted, her words leaving ice forming along Ariah's vessels. The witch held out a hand. "Come here, Ariah. I'm certain he will ask to see you first."

Ariah's nostrils flared. "He can come in here."

Miriam's smile melted into a scowl. The woman had that talent down pat.

The two brutes flanking her raised their arms. Ariah shrieked as her body tore away from her father's arms and pitched through the air. She flailed her arms, kicked her legs, trying to slow herself before she fell into the clutches of Miriam's minions. Their steely hands snagged her by the biceps and forearms, keeping her suspended a foot above the ground as they pulled her into the foyer. She thrashed, every brightly colored word she could think of spewing from her mouth.

"Big cloaked bullies! Let me go!" Her bare foot caught one Baroqueth in the hip. The guy grunted but didn't budge. She swung her legs, yanked her arms, and screamed between clenched teeth until an invisible restraint cocooned her, holding her still. "Oh, you cheaters!"

Her fight slowed when the front door opened as though pulled by unseen magic. Her eyes widened and her throat swelled when she spotted Alazar ascending to the stoop, his expression unreadable. His amber eyes pinned her with their piercing gaze. Only his eyes showed her the staunch determination that fueled each step closer to this terribly unfair standoff.

"Alazar," she said, her voice strained, her heart aching with stark understanding. She shook her head as he crossed the threshold into the house and the door slammed shut behind him. "No."

Miriam came to stand in front of Ariah, facing Alazar. Ariah could only imagine the look on the witch's face as she tasted victory a few feet away. Her uncle and her father stood at the opening to the office, the invisible barrier preventing them from leaving the room, but allowing them to behold the devastating exchange about to occur.

"You are far more wise than I took you for, Alazar. You surprise me."

"I'm full of surprises," Alazar said. The smile that curled his lips was far from the warm, heart-melting expression Ariah loved. It ignited flames in his eyes, eyes that slipped from Ariah, to Miriam, and back again. He hooked his thumb on the pocket of his jeans and lightly tapped at that pocket. His gaze hardened on Ariah. Her confusion mounted. "That's my job."

"Actually, your job was to protect your Keeper and your lifemate." Miriam twisted at the waist, her gaze scouring over Ariah before turning back to Alazar.

"Seems you have failed in your duty as dragon." She flicked her fingers. "Again."

"Alazar, don't. Don't let her get under your skin. Please, I hope you can hear me."

If he could, he gave no indication of it. Instead, a dark shadow fell over his eyes, a direct effect of Miriam's crass reminder.

"Alazar, look at me," Ariah demanded aloud. Alazar's storm-churning gaze lifted to her. She hated that she couldn't read his expressions, feel what he was feeling, hear him in her mind. She stared at the man who renewed her hope, showed her magic and tenderness, and promised her a fairytale. She was not going to accept this ending. "Don't. Do you hear me? Don't you dare."

"Shut up," Miriam snapped.

"You want the dragonstone. I have it." Alazar took one step closer to Miriam. From the shadows of the house, Ariah sensed movement, a heaviness closing in on them. Her anxiety skyrocketed when she realized the rest of Miriam's Baroqueth crew was coming to the party. "It's yours."

"Alazar, no!"

Miriam spun around, raised her hand, and brought it down at Ariah's face.

"Touch her, Baroqueth, and you do not get it."

The dark threat in Alazar's voice chilled Ariah to the bone. Miriam stiffened, her hand within inches of Ariah's cheek, her face twisted with resentment. Slowly, she lowered her hand to her side, regained her composure, and faced Alazar.

"I am done playing games, Alazar. I have waited over a decade for that jewel. I played the perfect girlfriend for your Keeper's brother, thinking he had that stone. I played the perfect wife when I realized Mike was worthless to my cause and Mark was the one I needed. I waited over a decade, beginning to doubt that I had a Keeper at all. I dealt with this wretched child and all the fawning and doting by those two brothers. I am owed my due." Miriam held out her hand. "Give. Me. The. Dragonstone."

Ariah's attention lowered to Alazar's tapping finger. It had not stopped tapping away, slow and methodical. When she looked up again, Alazar nodded, a motion so slight she wasn't sure she saw it at all.

"I think that, as my last request, I should be allowed a moment with my lifemate." Alazar shrugged. "I mean, you're planning on using the dragonstone to control me long enough to siphon my powers from my heart. Is it so much for a dying man to ask?"

"Show me the stone and we'll discuss requests."

Alazar dug his hand into his jacket pocket and twisted until the box containing his dragonstone came free. The key was taped to the bottom of the box. "Right here. Can you taste it?"

Miriam started toward Alazar. Alazar pulled the box back, raised a finger, and ticked it back and forth.

"That wasn't the deal. I want a minute with Ariah, no magic attached. Oh, and line up Mark and Mike next." Alazar winked. "You know. A 'nice knowing ya' farewell. Maybe a group hug."

Ariah gaped at Alazar's ability to joke during these grim moments.

Miriam remained silent, her thoughts almost palpable. At last, she snapped her fingers and pointed toward the office. "Bring them out."

"No magic," Alazar demanded.

"You're requesting more than your lot, dragon."

"Hey." He chuckled with a shrug. "Just remind yourself I'll be dead by morning, you'll have stolen all of my powers, and that should make you happy enough to give me these last few moments with those I love."

The binding around Ariah disappeared, as did the hands holding her up. She gasped as her feet hit the floor and her knees almost buckled under the unexpected drop. She stumbled, caught herself before she fell on her butt, and harrumphed.

"And you say I lack manners," she groused under her breath.

Miriam cut her a vile glance as she brushed by, ignoring the scalding gaze glued to her back. The witch could simmer until her skin fell off...in a cauldron...over a big fire created by Alazar. Three additional Baroqueths had joined them, releasing her father and uncle from the office prison. There were two enemies missing, although she sensed them nearby.

Every inch of her wanted to run and jump into Alazar's arms, but she kept her wits about her, slipping her hand into her pocket and wrapping her fingers around the coin. He looked so darn good at the worst possible time.

279

Ariah stepped up to Alazar, lifting her eyes level with his. "Don't do this."

Alazar sighed, drawing his knuckles over her cheek. "Ace, luck is on my side." His hand dropped, his fingers sliding down her arm until they reached her wrist. "But anything more you have would help."

Ariah understood the silent implication. She had seen correctly when he nodded a few minutes ago. Slowly, she withdrew her hand from her pocket and pressed her closed fist, coin inside, to his chest. He covered her hand with his, leaned down, and pressed a tender kiss to her lips.

"I love you, Ariah Callahan."

In a flash, something hard and sharp thrust against her chest and she was flung away from Alazar. She couldn't get her bearings, her body spinning, bouncing, stumbling until she fell to the floor inside the office.

A flood of sounds echoed in the foyer, voices mixing together in a language she had never heard. She jerked her head up from where she lay on her belly, the hard object digging into her chest.

Alazar's dragonstone box.

"What have you done!" Miriam screeched.

"Oh, no, no, no." Ariah scrambled to her hands and knees.

The doors slammed shut. Her heart shattered.

The last thing she saw was Alazar's eyes engulfed in fire.

Alazar hated the look of helplessness he caught on Ariah's face as the doors locked her within the safe confines of Mark's office. Ancient words scrolled through his mind as he whispered protection spells to enhance the barriers around Ariah. He clenched the gold coin she had slipped him, praying for luck and that the connection to The Hollow in this small piece was enough to draw on the magic from his land.

Miriam screeched, losing her grip on her glamour, her brown hair turning black and the tattoos along the side of her face making a show. She lunged into the office doors, bouncing off the wood like a ragdoll.

The rest of the Baroqueth in the foyer began to converge on Alazar and his male charges, magic pulsing, a living entity in the room.

"Alazar, what's the plan?" Mark asked, his voice hitched with anticipation and worry. His Keeper stepped up beside him, arm holding the secreted book under the protection of his jacket. Mike stood a step behind, his eyes wide as their enemies prepared to unleash chaos.

Sweet goddess, he hoped this worked.

He released the reins on his dragon. His body thickened and stretched, growing larger, taller. Scales scraped along his skin. He recited the words in his head, recalling their sound, their pronunciation on the dragon's tongue.

He hissed, the old language weighing heavy with power in his mouth. Fire spewed from his throat, sending the Baroqueth scampering for safety. The incantation rolled fluidly, a natural mixture of speech and sound, a unique magic created for the Firestorm dragons alone.

His half-formed wings spread out from his back. A breeze started, funneling through the adjoining rooms, strengthening with each second, each word he roared. The gold coin in his palm warmed until it glowed from the scorching heat fueled by the magic.

The breeze turned into a small-scale tornado, whipping Mark's precious relics and expensive décor off tables, shelves, and hangers. The chandelier lost pieces of crystal that plunked to the floor amidst the shattered décor.

A pair of Baroqueth bolted toward the back of the house.

They ran straight into Cade's half-transformed bulk.

His leader's eyes burned with fire as he joined in the incantation.

"No!"

Miriam fought the howling wind and stood in the center of the foyer. Squinting against the debris, she raised her hands, bolts of bright blue light flaring between her palms.

Alazar couldn't break his concentration. The spell was coming to a close. Each second that passed drained him of energy. He couldn't stop. If he did, he wouldn't have the strength to perform it again, leaving them all vulnerable.

Mark grabbed at the scales that had formed in splotches over Alazar's belly, pulled himself against the current, and positioned himself in Miriam's line of fire.

No. Not again.

The final sentence of the spell crossed through his mind.

Miriam cast her magic in a sizzling ball of electrical blue.

Alazar twisted, whipping his arm across Mark, ripping his Keeper off his feet. Mark slammed into Mike, and the two men smacked into the corner of the wall.

Alazar howled the last of the spell as the searing ball of magic crashed into the unprotected side of his body. Pain tore through him straight up to his head. His vision went black.

He barely felt his body hit the floor beyond the pain from the bolt.

As the world disappeared from his senses, he gave Ariah's lucky coin a weak squeeze.

The gamble of a lifetime.

A gamble he won, at a very steep price.

Ariah stumbled to her feet and lunged at the door. She tried the lock, yanked at the handles, but couldn't get the door to move.

A bellowing roar started outside the office. A rough, vicious wind howled, rattling the doors. She cringed as she heard items crash and shatter.

"Alazar! Dad! Uncle Mark! Open up!" Ariah banged on the door until the side of her hand hurt. Her heart was about to tear from her chest. She stepped back and lunged at the door again, putting her whole body behind the slam. It did nothing but earn her a dull throb along her shoulder. "Please!"

A double thud against the wall startled her away from the doors. A picture by her uncle's cabinets crashed to the floor.

The noise beyond the door began to subside. The voices silenced. Ariah stilled, prepared to body-slam the doors again. She waited for a long moment, holding her breath, listening for movement.

Nothing.

She shuffled up to the door and pressed her ear to the wood.

Nothing.

Dread hooked her mind and her heart, dragging her down into the thick pit of fear. She bit her tongue in fear of hearing nothing, or hearing Miriam's voice instead of Alazar's. A faint ripple of tremors struck her from head to toe.

"Alazar, tell me you're okay." Ariah tightened her lips before sucking them between her teeth. *"Alazar, don't mess with me."* The first sting of tears touched her eyes. She blinked them away, but they returned a moment later, as did a painful knot in her throat. *"Alazar, please. You have to be okay."*

The lock jostled. Ariah jumped back, clutching the box to her chest. The doors slid open and she found herself staring up into Cade's hard-lined face. His size could not hide the rags of clothing sprawled over the foyer's pristine floor, now littered with shattered ceramic, glass, and porcelain. Slowly, she moved closer to the doors, hyperaware of Cade's intense focus on her with each step. She couldn't find her voice, her thoughts zapped from her mind. Her eyes skimmed the fallen forms of cloaked Baroqueth until she saw two familiar figures braced against the wall, looking like they had just finished a dozen rounds in the ring. The ancient book lay open on the floor, rocks scattered around it.

Her father and her uncle were alive.

Cade shifted his weight, angling his body toward the foyer.

Ariah's gaze landed on a figure sprawled there, unmoving. Zareh and Syn hunched over the figure, their expressions stoic. Panic tore through her. She lunged forward, but Cade's arm whipped out, catching her about the waist and lifting her into the air.

"Alazar!"

She kicked and punched, growled and cried as Cade held her, his arms tightening as her fight intensified until, at last, she caved in to the sobs that wrenched through her chest.

"No!"

The gamble of a lifetime.

Alazar squeezed his eyes shut, the sharp, exploding pain that had knocked him unconscious having dulled to an annoying throb along the side of his body. He remained still, unmoving, assessing the damage until he was certain he'd live.

Well, at least the price wasn't as steep as he originally thought.

Until he heard Ariah's heart-shattering sobs.

He groaned, slowly shifting onto his uninjured side, and peeled his eyelids back in time to catch Ariah dropping to her knees beside him. She grabbed his head in her trembling hands, brushing the strands of hair that had come loose from his hair band away from his cheeks. A drop of moisture splattered over his nose.

"Are you...are you okay?" Ariah asked, her voice shaking as bad as her hands. He reached up and wrapped his hand around her wrist. After another slow moment, he pressed himself off the floor until he was seated upright, an arm draped over one bent knee. Ariah's hands skimmed over him from head to waist, hesitating at the source of his pain along his right side. "What is this? Do you need to see a doctor?"

"No, Ace. Doctors don't like dragons in their offices." He rubbed his forehead with the heel of his palm. "I'll heal. It'll take a couple of hours, but I'll be fine."

"Will he? Be okay?" Ariah asked. Only then did Alazar notice Zareh and Syn. Syn pressed up to his feet.

Zareh nodded once. "His body is dispersing the

magic that slipped past his scales. It'll take a few hours, but he'll be the same old Alazar in no time."

Alazar surveyed the damage in the room as Cade came over to him. "I made a mess."

Cade shrugged. "Nothing a big broom and a dustpan can't sweep up."

"No. The Baroqueth."

"Oh, them." He chuckled. "They'll be out for a while. It'll give us a chance to reinforce a containment spell once I have them back at The Hollow. I'll need to borrow Mark for that, since he's the only accessible Keeper at the moment. Caught all who were here, including the two who were patrolling out back. Seems our little Baroqueth jail is filling up."

"What happened?" Ariah pressed, her sobs coming under control. A fleeting cry fled her lips a split second before she threw her arms around Alazar's neck and clung to him. "You scared me."

Alazar gathered her close. After tonight, he swore he would never let her go.

"It was a little scary, huh?"

He tried to chuckle, but the sound was lost to him. Ariah sat back on her heels, brushing her fingers over his face. He glanced over her shoulder as Mark crawled toward him. His dark eyes were hazy.

"You stubborn idiot." Mark groaned, coming to sit beside Zareh. He clapped Alazar's shoulder. "You are certainly a dragon to be reckoned with."

A small laugh escaped Zareh as he climbed to his feet. "There is more to this guy than even he knows."

He held out a hand for Alazar, which Alazar accepted. With Ariah still tucked against him, Zareh hoisted them to their feet, followed by Mark. Mike shuffled toward them, rubbing the back of his head.

"We need to get to work on these misfits," Syn said. Zareh mussed Alazar's hair before joining Syn and Cade as they dragged unconscious Baroqueth into the center of the foyer.

Ariah tipped her head up and wiped her eyes with the back of her hand. "You, dragon, have a lot of explaining to do. Starting with why you wouldn't answer me when I called to you. The telepathy obviously worked."

Alazar nodded. "It was reestablished, but it was best for you not to know what was going to happen." He sighed. "As it was, I didn't have a plan except to protect you and your family at any cost, including my life. Then Mark told me he found the old *Book of Realms*, an ancient journal with spells and incantations that can connect magic from The Hollow to realms that may strip us of our magic. He couldn't read the old dragon language, but I could with the use of crystals."

Ariah's brows furrowed. She looked toward the crystals and gems scattered on the floor. "And here I thought he wanted to play with rocks."

Alazar snorted. "Not quite. Having that book changed the plan, but only if it worked. It was a huge gamble, one I was willing to take." He lifted his hand between them, producing the gold coin he still held. Ariah's eyes widened. Alazar grinned. "You picked a good coin, Ace. It was a pretty strong conduit between The Hollow and here."

Ariah lifted the coin from his fingers, flipped it over, and glanced back up at him. "I don't understand."

"I needed something from The Hollow with enough residual energy from my homeland to funnel the magic. The coin was enough." He caught her chin as she lowered her head. "You know something? I'm a pretty lucky guy as long as you're by my side. I'd like you to stay. With me."

Ariah's lips formed a cute, shaky smile, her eyes bright and sparkling with adoration and residual tears. "We just defied death together. I don't think I'm going anywhere. Besides…"

Ariah lifted up to her tiptoes and brushed her lips over Alazar's. In that short breath of a caress, the throb in his body disappeared. He had his woman. His lovely, stubborn, spitfire Ace. She was safe. Mark and Mike were alive. He had survived. Luck was on their side tonight. A world of luck.

"I love you," Ariah whispered.

Alazar smiled, slipping his fingers into her hair, and kissed her until he knew in his soul she would never doubt his free-flowing love for his one and only lifemate.

CHAPTER 22

"Are you certain you still want to stay? They'll continue to come here looking for you." Alazar handed the harness to Ariah as he moved to the center of the backyard. Zareh had Kaylae tucked under his arm on the patio as they bid Alazar and Ariah farewell. "First time in forever since you and I will be separated, Zar."

The moonlight caught the bittersweet grin that touched his friend's mouth. "There will come a time when we'll be back together. For now"—Zareh gave Kaylae an adoring glance—"this is where we need to be."

"I expect you two will visit?" Kaylae asked.

"We'd love to," Ariah answered, clasping both her hands around Alazar's. His heart swelled, filled to bursting with love for his woman. A week after the encounter with Miriam and her Baroqueth posse, Ariah's chin remained high, her attitude nothing shy of strong and fierce, and her eagerness to start a life with Alazar back at The Hollow endearing. He and Mark spent the latter half of the week transporting necessities back to their homeland in preparation for the move. "And same for you and Zareh. Come see us until that time you decide to return for good."

"We make a trip every month or so. Next time we're there, we'll make sure to knock on your door." Kaylae snuggled into Zareh's side. "It's going to be strange without you around, Al."

"Oh, I'm sure you'll get over my absence, especially since you won't have to babysit a grown man any longer." Alazar laughed, stepping away from Ariah. "Ready, Ace?"

Alazar didn't need verbal confirmation. Ariah thrummed with excitement that resonated within his own body. He allowed the transformation from man to dragon to come over him, quick, fluid, and natural. He lowered his belly to the ground so Ariah could strap on the harness with Zareh's help, and used the pollex of his wing to lift her onto his back.

Zareh patted Alazar's crest. "Brother, you be well. We'll fly together again soon."

Alazar snorted in response, tipping his head to nudge Zareh. As painful as it was to leave his closest friend, there was no comparison to the promise of his future with Ariah.

He'd been granted one rare and wonderful gift.

His lifemate.

"I'm secured, Alazar."

"Hold on."

Alazar pulled his neck back to bow his large head toward Zareh and Kaylae, then launched straight up into the sky. The sheer thrill of flight encompassed him and bled into Ariah. He sensed her tension, her nervousness, and couldn't blame her. She had flown solo only once before tonight, and it was over the forests of Nocturne Falls.

Alazar followed a clouded path in the sky to hide himself from the human world below, forgoing the frolic of zigging and zagging beneath the dazzling moonlight to get home as fast as he could. Despite an afternoon nap, Ariah was tired, and the concentration and strength it required to hold on took a toll on her thirty minutes into their trip.

"How're you doing, sweetheart?"

"Good. I still can't get over this. It's amazing, and that my body isn't affected by the altitude is a sheer wonder."

"You're not entirely human."

Her muted laughter made him grin.

Alazar broke through the veil to The Hollow and glided over the hills, forests, and valleys doused in a shimmering coat of silver moonlight. Ariah shifted against his back, the tension draining from her muscles as he circled down to the valley closest to his home. He landed and sank to the ground, helping Ariah dismount. He gave her time to unfasten the harness before transforming back to his human form and draping the harness over his shoulder.

"Tired?" Alazar asked, cupping the side of Ariah's wind-flushed face. He stroked her bottom lip with his thumb before giving in to his desire to kiss her. She leaned into him, opening her mouth to each slow, tender sweep of his tongue, soft moans fleeing her lips. He swallowed down the sweet sounds, savoring the flavor of her mouth and the tamed hunger of her kiss. As he drew away, he caught her lower lip between his teeth, licked along her warm skin, and released her after a playful tug. "Mmm."

"To answer your question, yes. I'm tired." Ariah reached to the back of his head and tugged on the band holding his hair up. The gentle breeze that caressed The Hollow ruffled his waves, strands blowing across his face. The tips of her fingers brushed over his brows and tucked the wild strands behind his ears. "But not *that* tired."

"Good, 'cause I have something I'd like to ask of you."

Ariah quirked a brow as Alazar slipped his fingers between hers. "Oh?"

"Oh." He led her down the sloping hill toward the sway of the weeping trees. A soft laugh drew his attention to Ariah. "What?"

"A swim?"

Alazar thought for a moment, pressing his lips together. "That sounds like it might be fun, but no. Or...maybe."

"Isn't the water the only way into your home from this direction?"

"No. There's a hidden entryway that isn't wet."

He held aside the fall of tree branches so Ariah could pass through. She stopped in the calf-high grass beside the rocks around the clear pool. Moonlight dappled the surface like diamonds. The relaxing sound of the water pouring over the rocks and the calm music of the nighttime wildlife wove a perfect backdrop.

Alazar stood directly in front of Ariah and held out his hand. "The dragonstone."

Ariah's eyes flashed before narrowing with curiosity. She dug the box out of an inside pocket in her coat, but didn't say a word. Alazar unfastened the key on the underside of the box and unlocked the lid. He blinked away the disorienting change in his vision as the jewel awoke, lifted it from the velvet bed and placed the empty box on the ground by his foot.

"When a dragon is born, his life essence is connected to a magical jewel. That jewel is a physical part of him until it is shed with the first molt of scales. Over the next century, the jewel grows and changes to fit the dragon's essence until it has matured." Alazar held his dragonstone between them. Ariah traced one of the amber and gold veins. "Dragons guard their jewels with their lives until they are appointed their first Keeper. If it falls into the hands of an enemy who understands its value and can access the essence, the dragon can fall under that enemy's control and ultimately be destroyed. If the dragonstone is destroyed, the dragon dies."

"It's a jewel. It looks delicate."

"It's not as delicate as you think. Created by magic, destroyed by magic. A hammer would shatter the moment it connected with the jewel, not the other way around."

Ariah's gaze lifted to his, her eyes widening. "The Baroqueth can destroy the dragonstones."

Alazar nodded. "And they have. Usually after they have drained the dragon's heart of its power. Guarding the jewel is a job of the dragon's Keeper, once the Keeper bleeds into it." Alazar laid the jewel on his palm and pointed to the red veins throughout the jewel. "Every Keeper I have ever had, including your uncle, is part of this dragonstone. Is part of me."

He extended the tip of his talon from his index finger, fit the sharp point into a hidden hole at the tapered top, and unlatched a small part of the jewel to reveal a reservoir. Wonder came over Ariah that stole his breath.

"You are my lifemate, Ariah Callahan. We don't necessarily do weddings and receptions and all that family and friend torture over who sits where. Our ceremonies are private, between lifemates. Oh, and divorce isn't a possibility."

Ariah spoke, her voice soft, dreamy, and filled with potent understanding. "Bleed into the dragonstone." Her beautiful eyes turned up to him again and a smile crossed her mouth. "You're asking me to make it official. And permanent. Lifemate, wife, partner?"

Alazar moistened his lips. "Yes."

Ariah lifted a hand, but an uneasy furrow touched her brows. "I'm not going to be, you know, part of my uncle or anything, right?"

Alazar stared at her, slack jawed. A burst of laughter exploded from his chest that he fought to control the moment it escaped. Ariah's cheeks darkened, but her smile grew and her eyes sparkled.

"No. Absolutely not. You'll become part of me, and I you." Alazar calmed himself and cradled Ariah's extended hand in his palm. "Dragons are given one lifemate, one final Keeper. Mark will be my Keeper for the remainder of his life, and then you will take his place. Understand that your life expectancy, once you bleed, becomes longer. Quite a bit longer. Possibly a century or two."

"Will you be able to stand me that long?"

"I should ask that question of you."

Ariah slipped her free hand to his chest, splaying her palm flat over his beating heart. "Forever. As long as I'm not laying eggs."

"Sweet goddess." Alazar swallowed another burst of laughter. "No. No egg-laying."

Ariah nodded once. "Good. Then I think we have a very, very long life to look forward to. Together."

In all of his five-plus centuries of living, Alazar could never have imagined the gift that awaited him in the form of a beautiful, witty woman. He would wait another five hundred years to have her, if that was necessary, because he would want no one other than his sweet Ariah.

With her hand in his, he extended the tip of a talon from his thumb, pressed it to her index finger, and pierced the skin. She barely flinched as a single bead of red welled up from the puncture. Alazar guided her finger to the reservoir, milked two drops from her finger, and watched the dark red stream into the jewel. The swirled dragonstone shimmered, accepting the newest essence, binding Ariah to him until the day he died. The compartment lid closed, a spark of light erupting as it sealed permanently.

Ariah would be the last to bleed into his dragonstone. Their binding started a clock on his life, a clock he would cherish as long as his Ace stood by his side.

Alazar lifted her finger to his lips and he licked her wound, closing the puncture.

"Are we supposed to feel something?" Ariah asked.

That single question opened a door Alazar was more than willing to jump through. By the glow of Ariah's eyes, he suspected she was just as willing.

"Want to go for a swim?" Alazar locked the dragonstone in the box and wagged his brows. "Water's warm."

Ariah laughed, scooping up the box and tucking it close to her chest. She slung an arm around his neck. "Remember what happened last time?"

"How could I forget?" Alazar lowered his forehead to Ariah's. "Want to reenact that time?"

"No, my dragon." Ariah pressed her body flush to his, stoking more than playful banter. "I bet we can best that time."

"Mmm." Alazar stole a kiss from her parted lips. "That's definitely a gamble I'll take."

THE END

About Kira Nyte

Born and raised a Jersey girl with easy access to NYC, I was never short on ideas for stories. I started writing when I was 11, and my passion for creating worlds exploded from that point on. Romance writing came later, since kissing gave you cooties at 11, but when it did, I embraced it. Since then, all of my heroes and heroines find their happily ever after, even if it takes a good fight, or ten, to get there.

I currently live in Central Florida with my husband, our four children, and two parakeets. I work part-time as a PCU nurse when I'm not writing or traveling between sports and other activities.

I love to hear from readers!
Contact me at kiranyteauthor@gmail.com

Made in the USA
Middletown, DE
08 November 2017